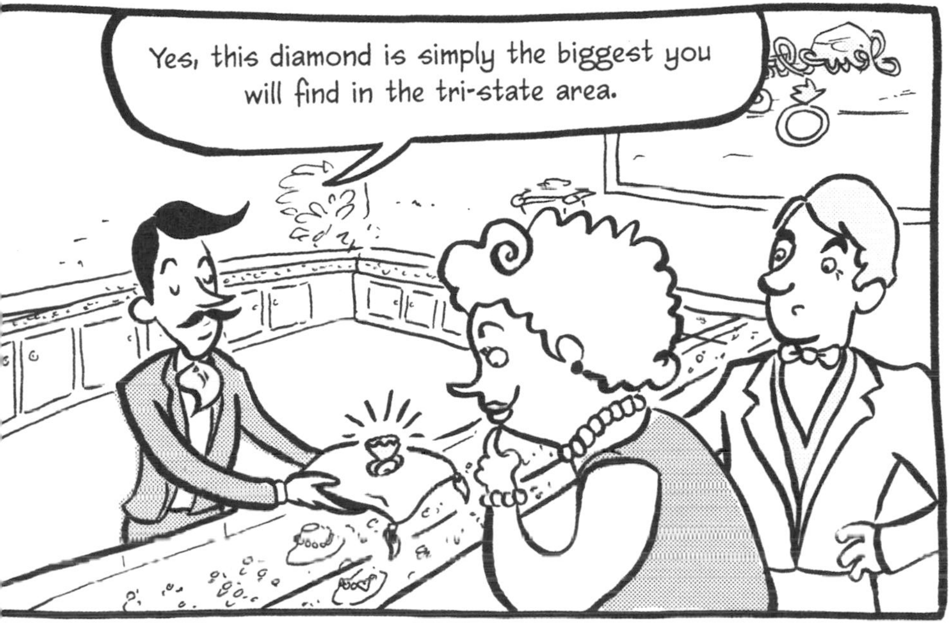
Yes, this diamond is simply the biggest you will find in the tri-state area.

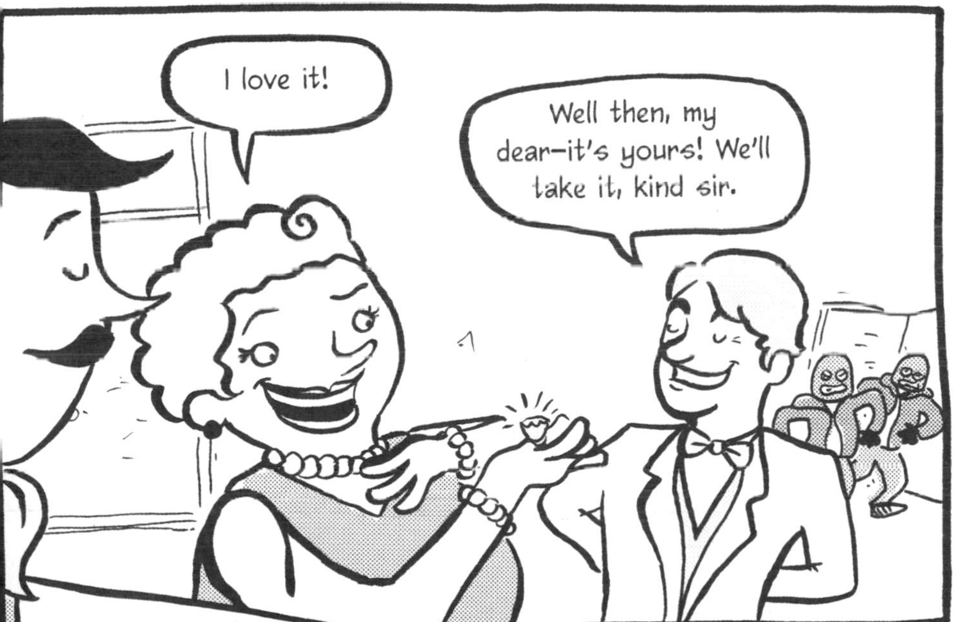
I love it!
Well then, my dear—it's yours! We'll take it, kind sir.

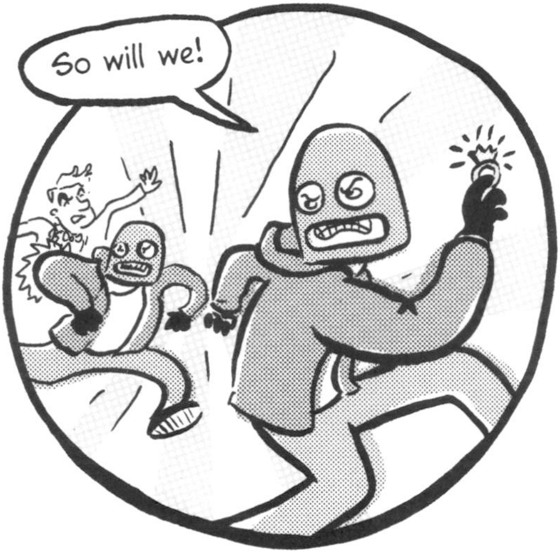
So will we!
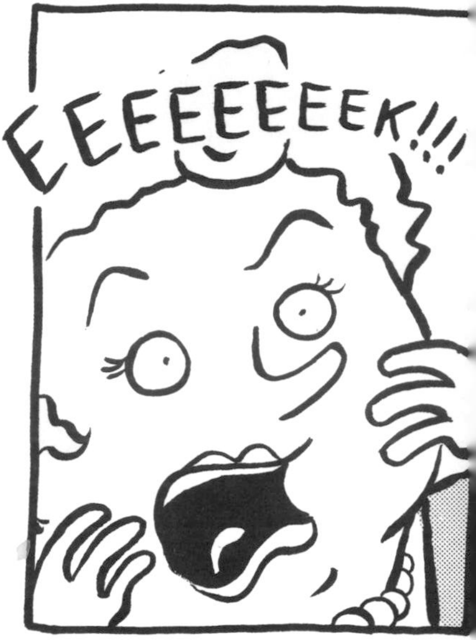
EEEEEEEEK!!!
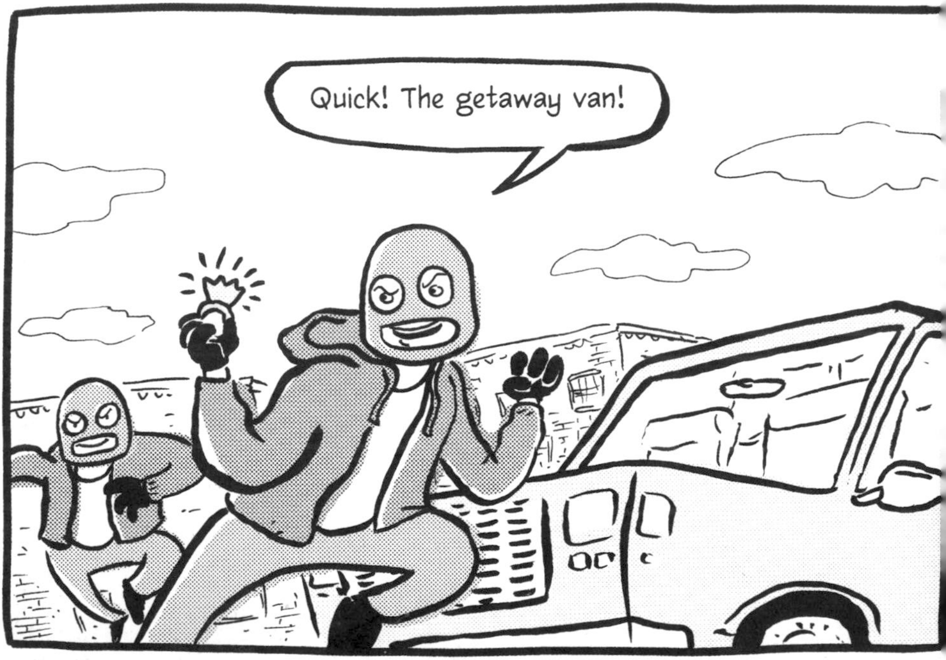
Quick! The getaway van!

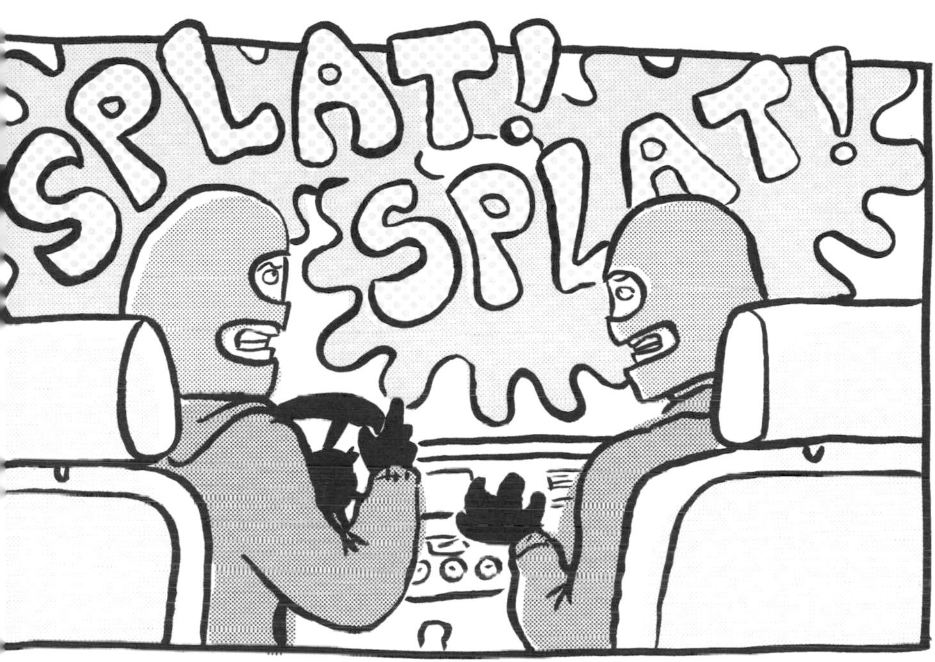
SPLAT! SPLAT!

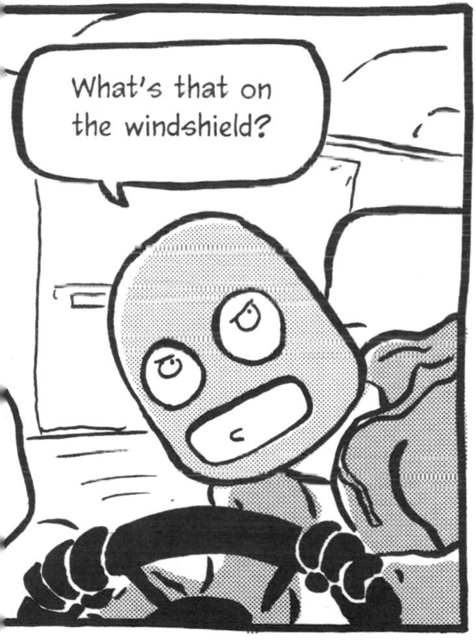
What's that on the windshield?

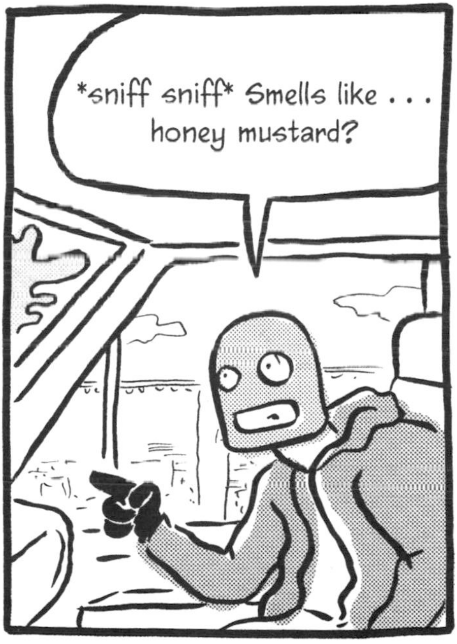
sniff sniff Smells like . . . honey mustard?

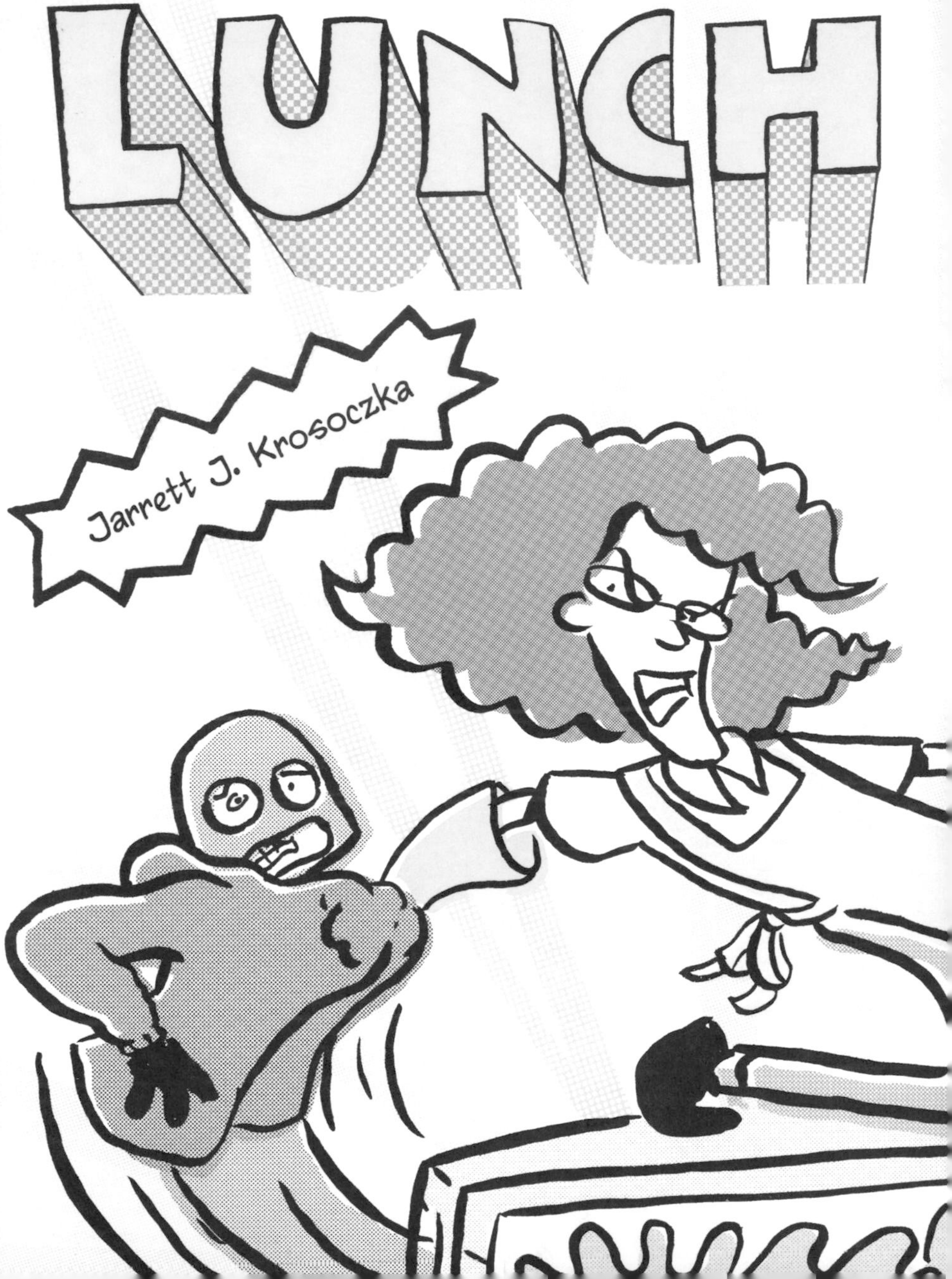
LUNCH
Jarrett J. Krosoczka

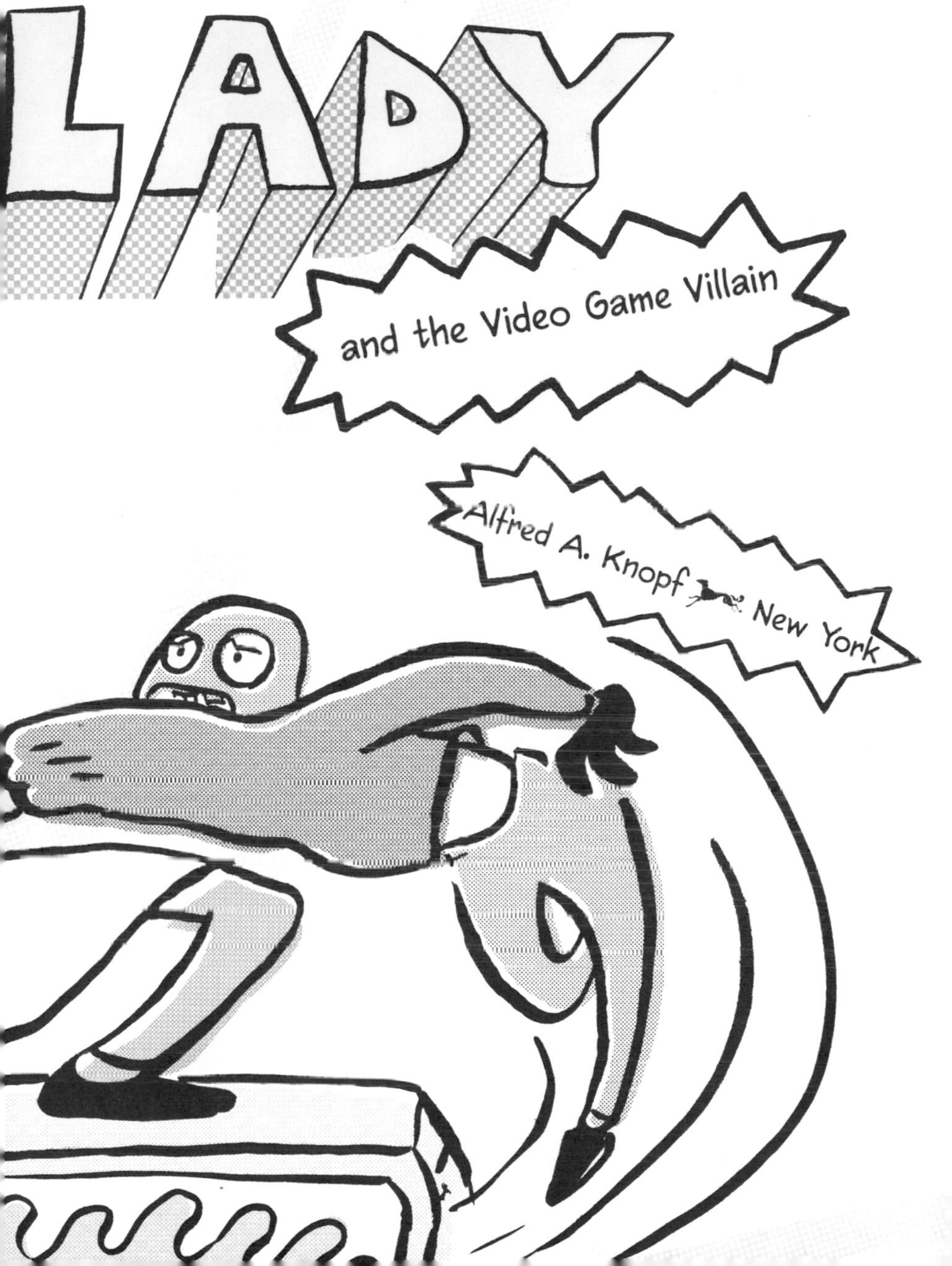
LADY
and the Video Game Villain
Alfred A. Knopf New York

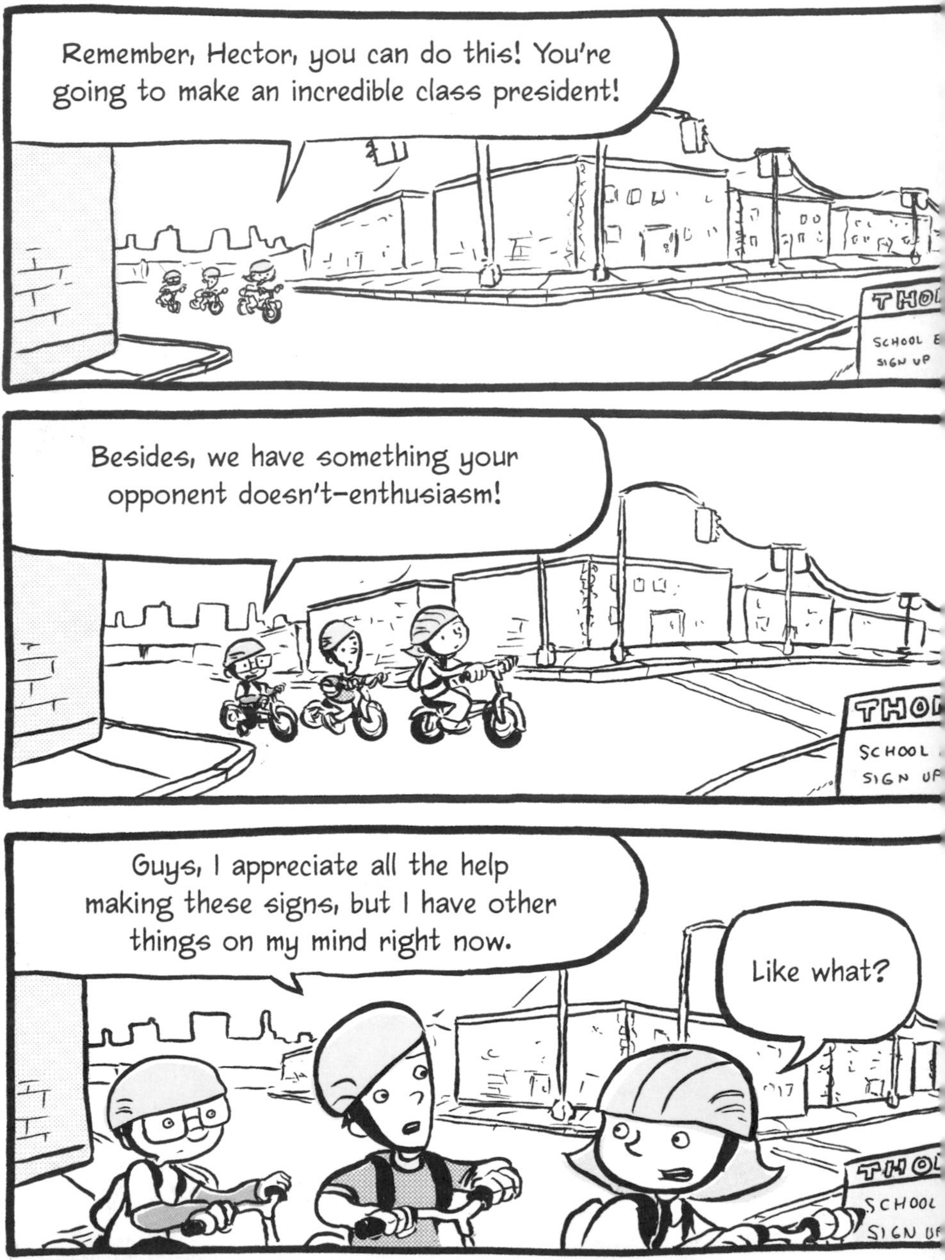
Remember, Hector, you can do this! You're going to make an incredible class president!
THO
SCHOOL E
SIGN UP
Besides, we have something your opponent doesn't—enthusiasm!
THO
SCHOOL
SIGN UP
Guys, I appreciate all the help making these signs, but I have other things on my mind right now.
Like what?
THO
SCHOOL
SIGN UP

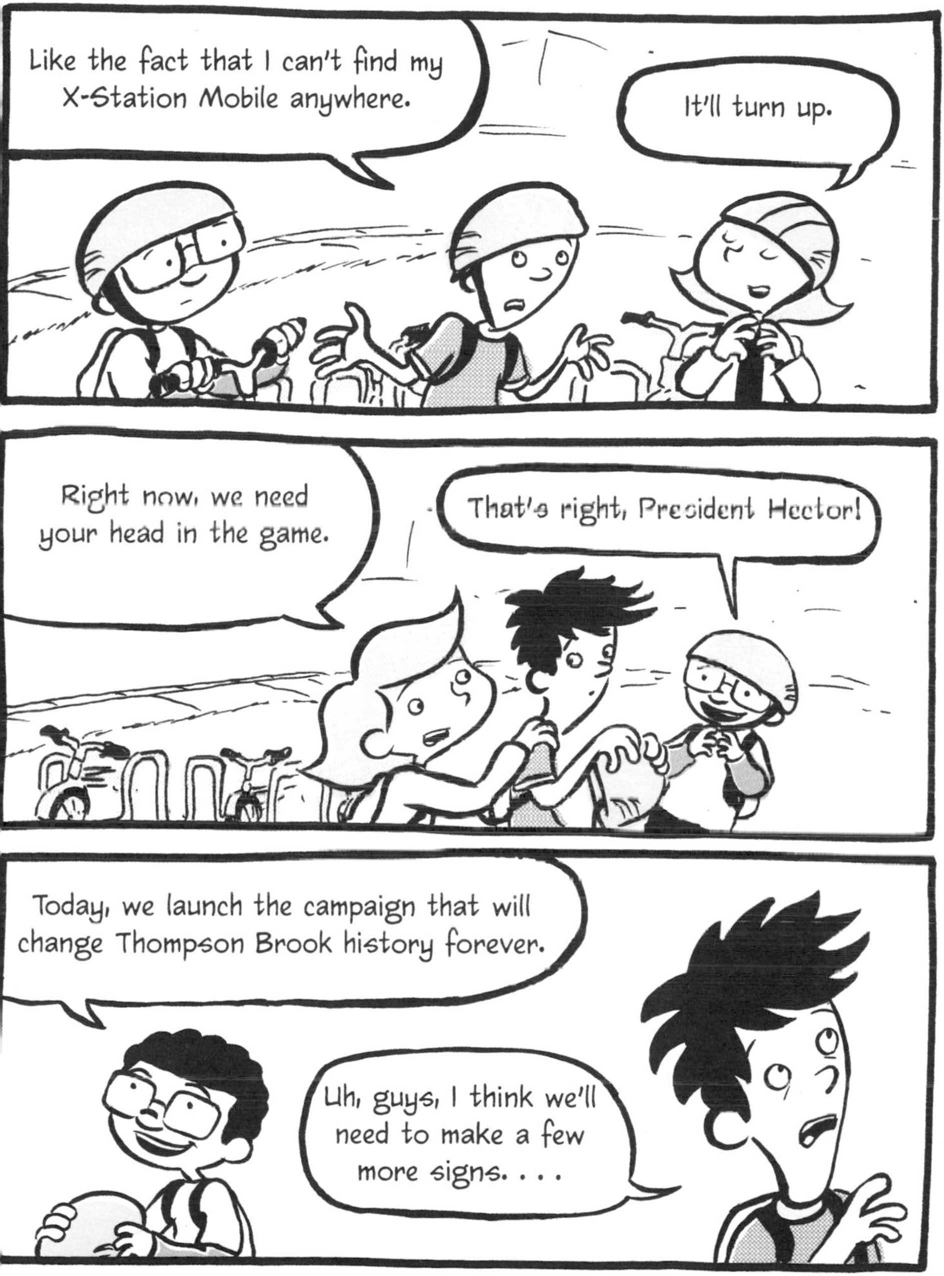
Like the fact that I can't find my X-Station Mobile anywhere.
It'll turn up.
Right now, we need your head in the game.
That's right, President Hector!
Today, we launch the campaign that will change Thompson Brook history forever.
Uh, guys, I think we'll need to make a few more signs. . . .

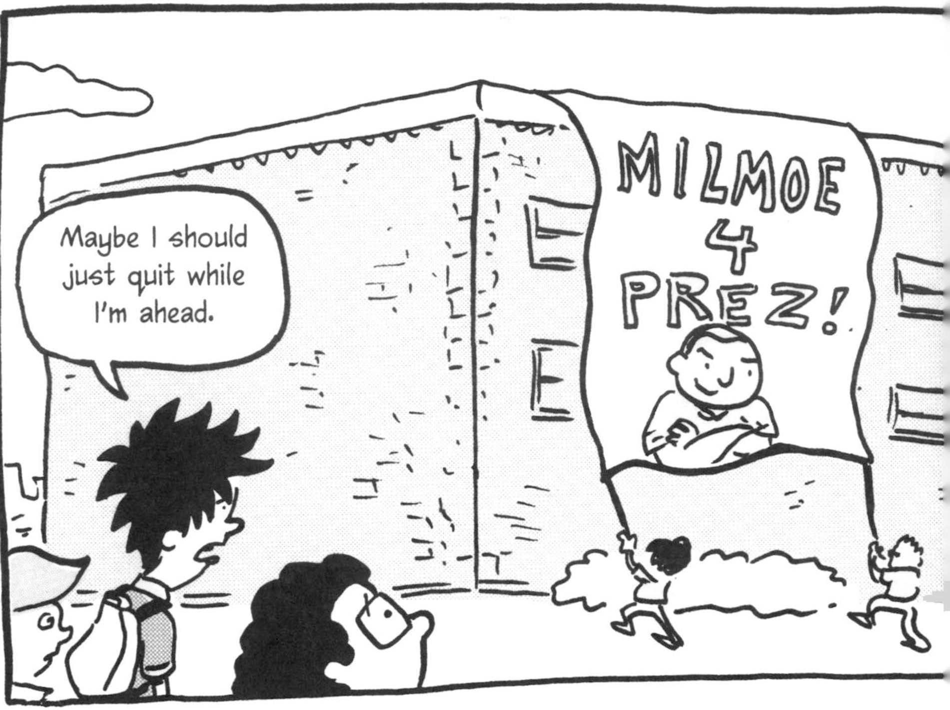
Maybe I should just quit while I'm ahead.
MILMOE 4 PREZ!
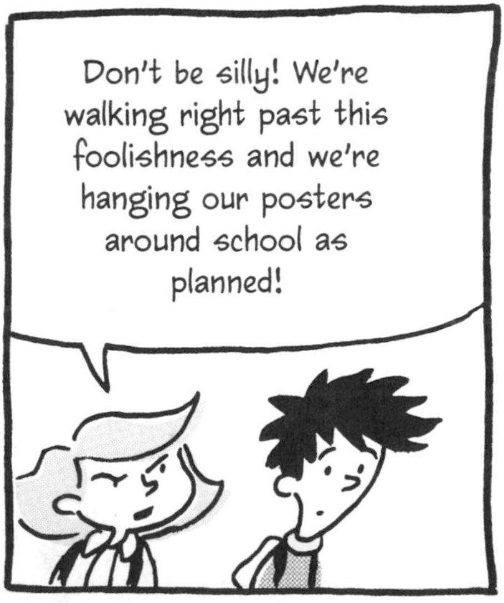
Don't be silly! We're walking right past this foolishness and we're hanging our posters around school as planned!
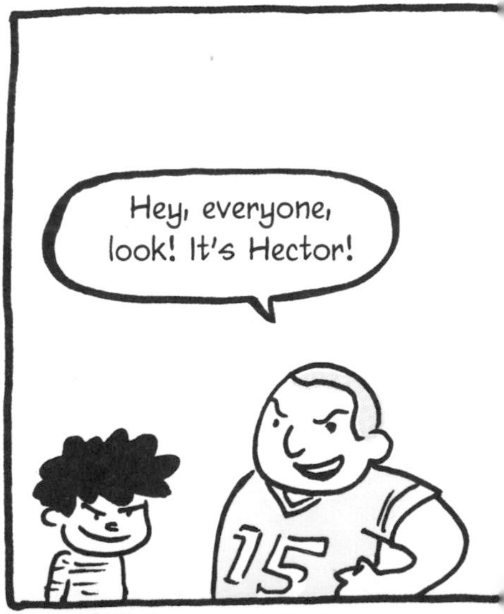
Hey, everyone, look! It's Hector!
15

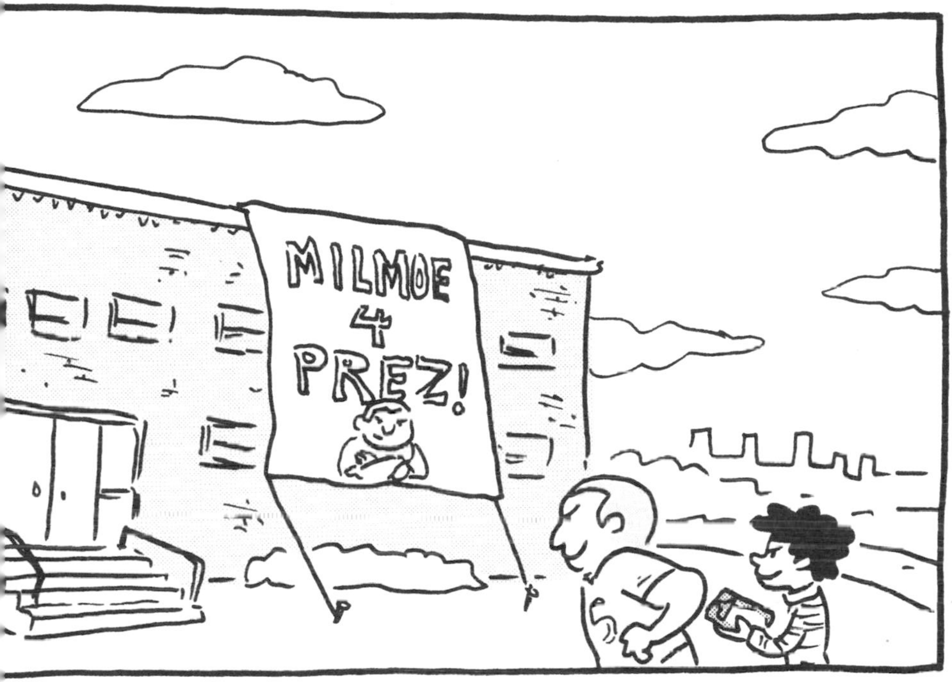
MILMOE 4 PREZ!

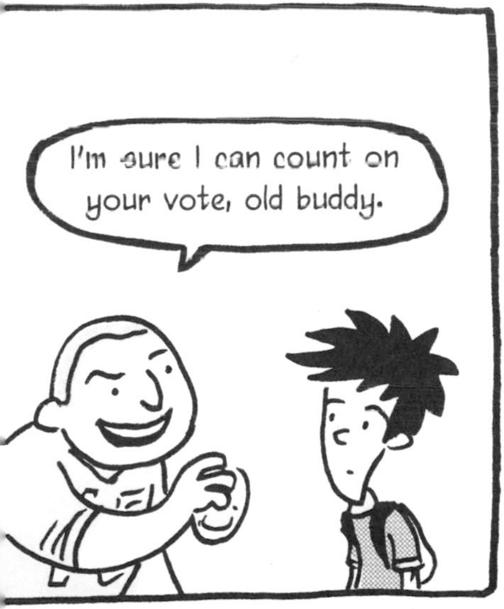
I'm sure I can count on your vote, old buddy.

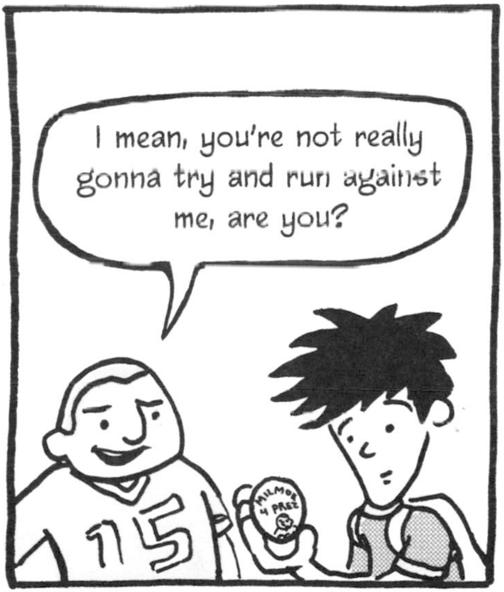
I mean, you're not really gonna try and run against me, are you?
MILMOE 4 PREZ
15

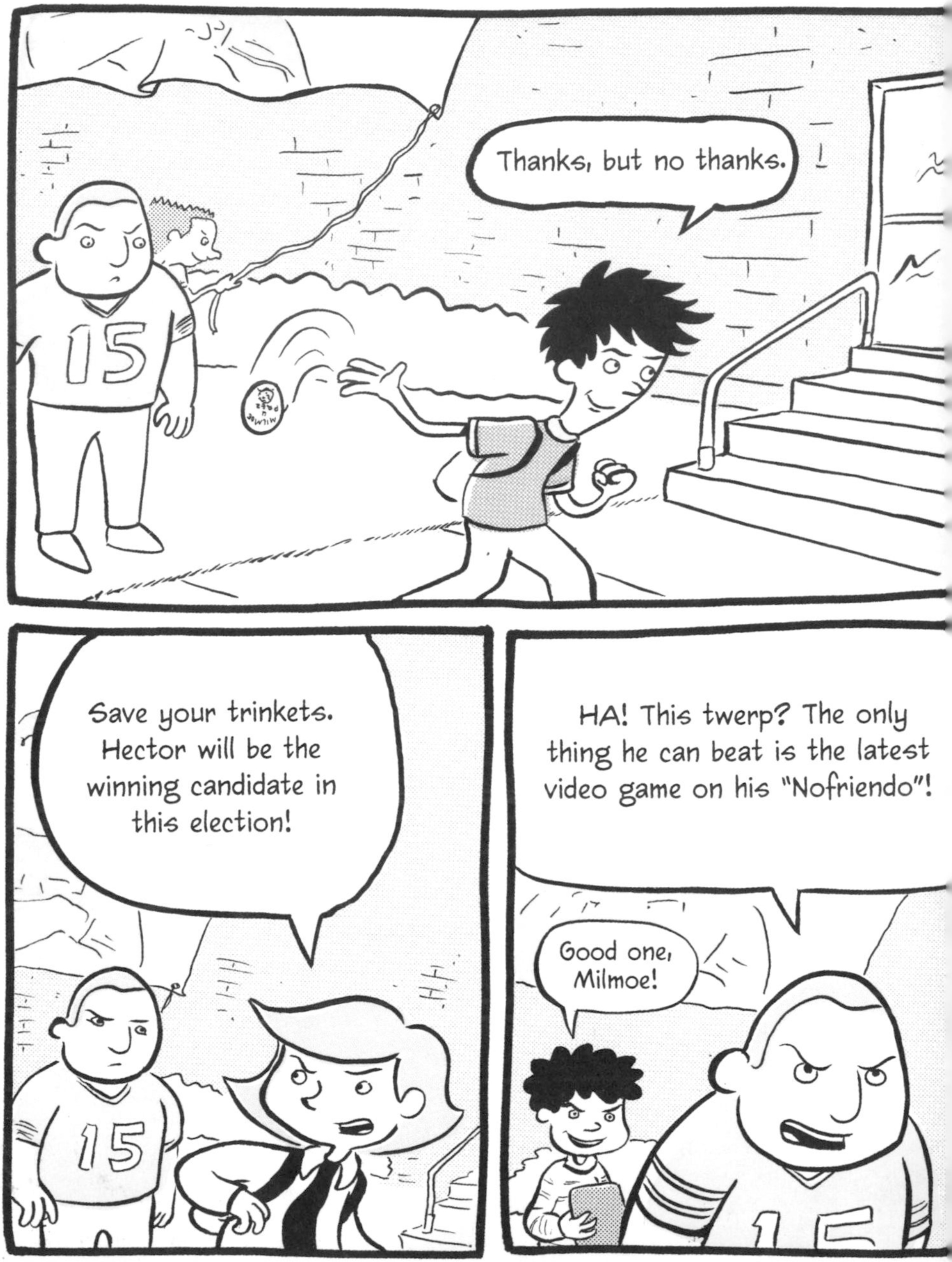
Thanks, but no thanks.
Save your trinkets. Hector will be the winning candidate in this election!
HA! This twerp? The only thing he can beat is the latest video game on his "Nofriendo"!
Good one, Milmoe!

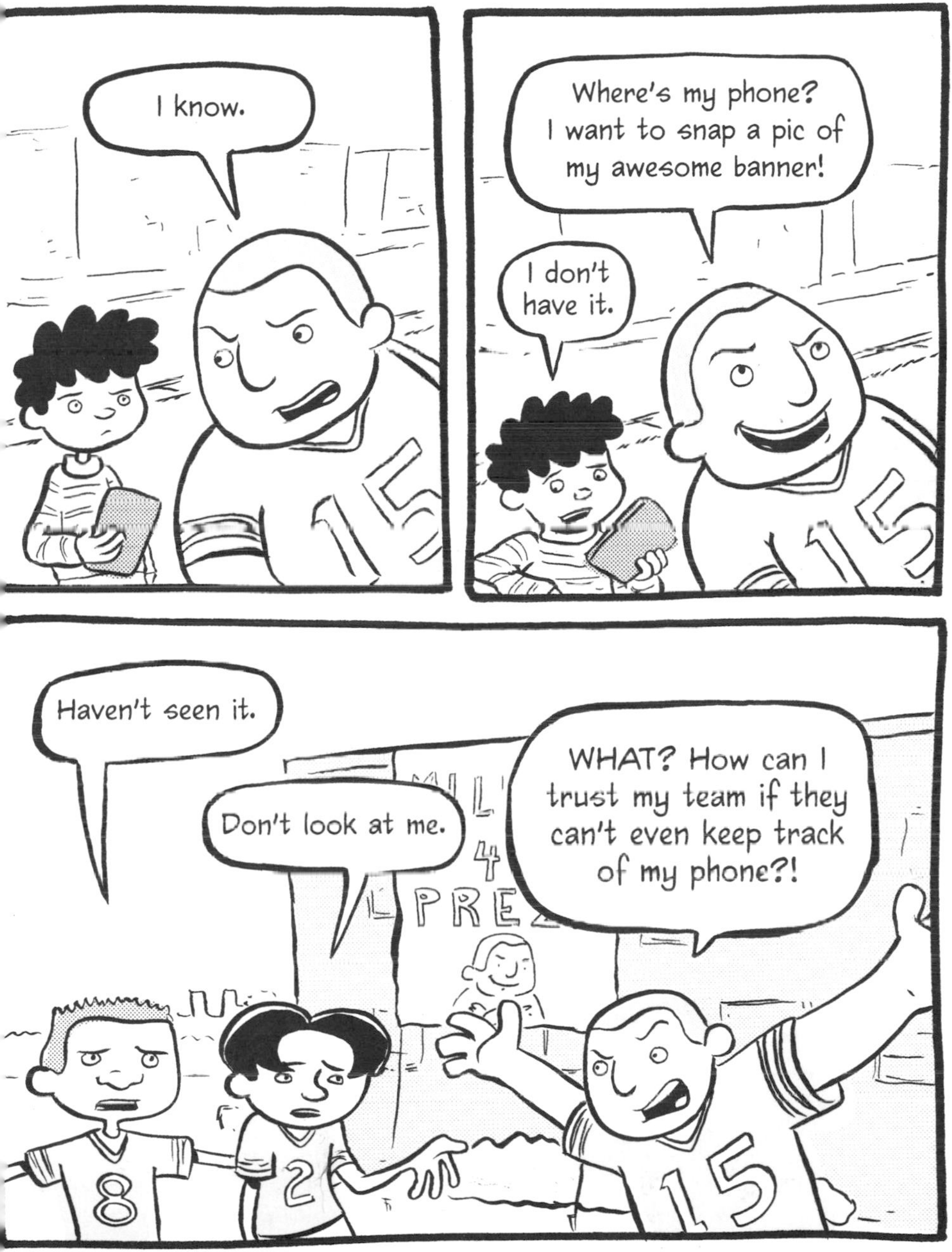
I know.
Where's my phone? I want to snap a pic of my awesome banner!
I don't have it.
Haven't seen it.
Don't look at me.
WHAT? How can I trust my team if they can't even keep track of my phone?!

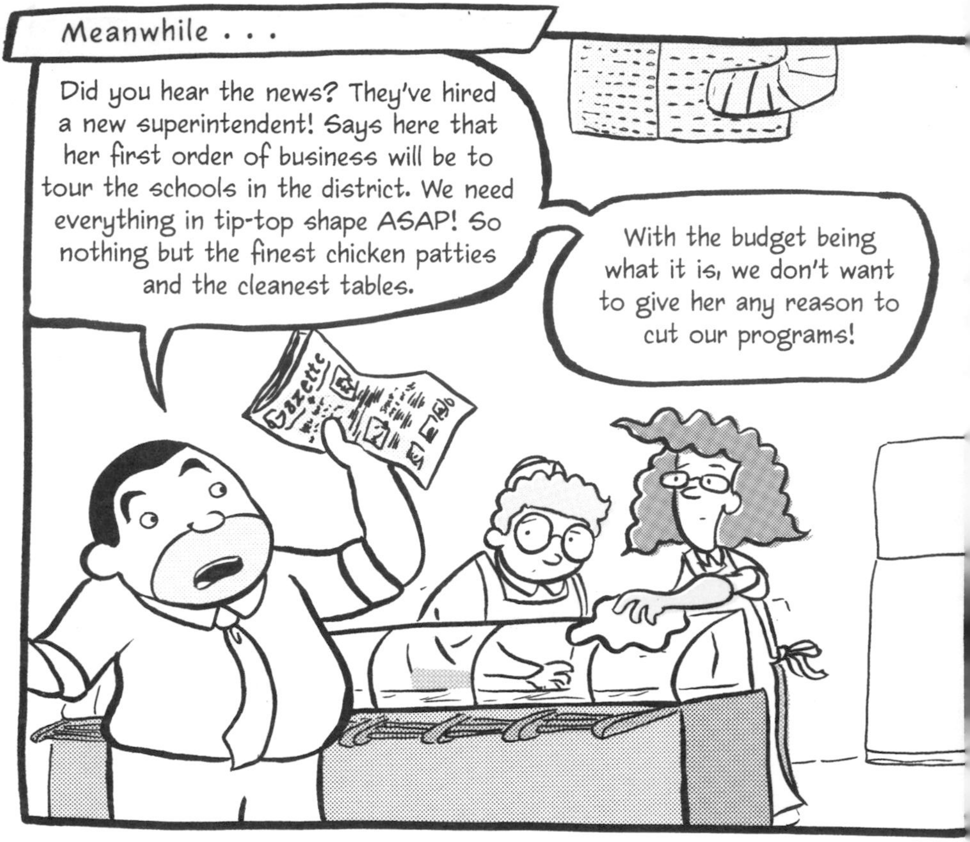
Meanwhile . . .
Did you hear the news? They've hired a new superintendent! Says here that her first order of business will be to tour the schools in the district. We need everything in tip-top shape ASAP! So nothing but the finest chicken patties and the cleanest tables.
With the budget being what it is, we don't want to give her any reason to cut our programs!

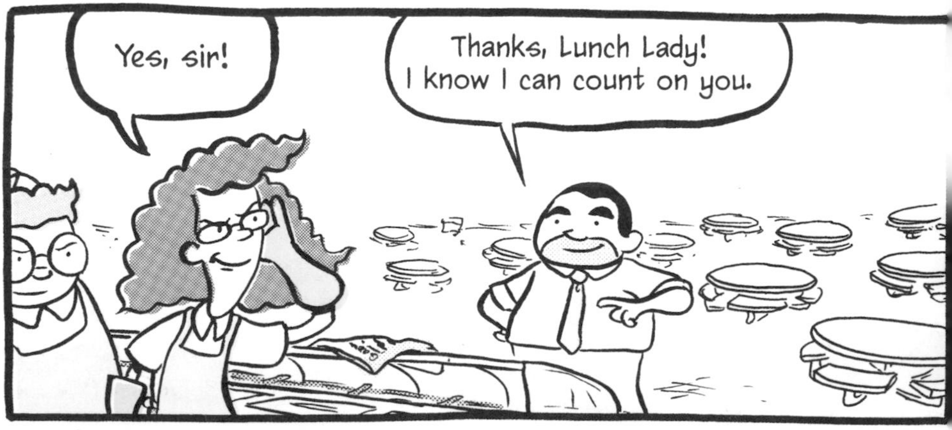
Yes, sir!
Thanks, Lunch Lady! I know I can count on you.

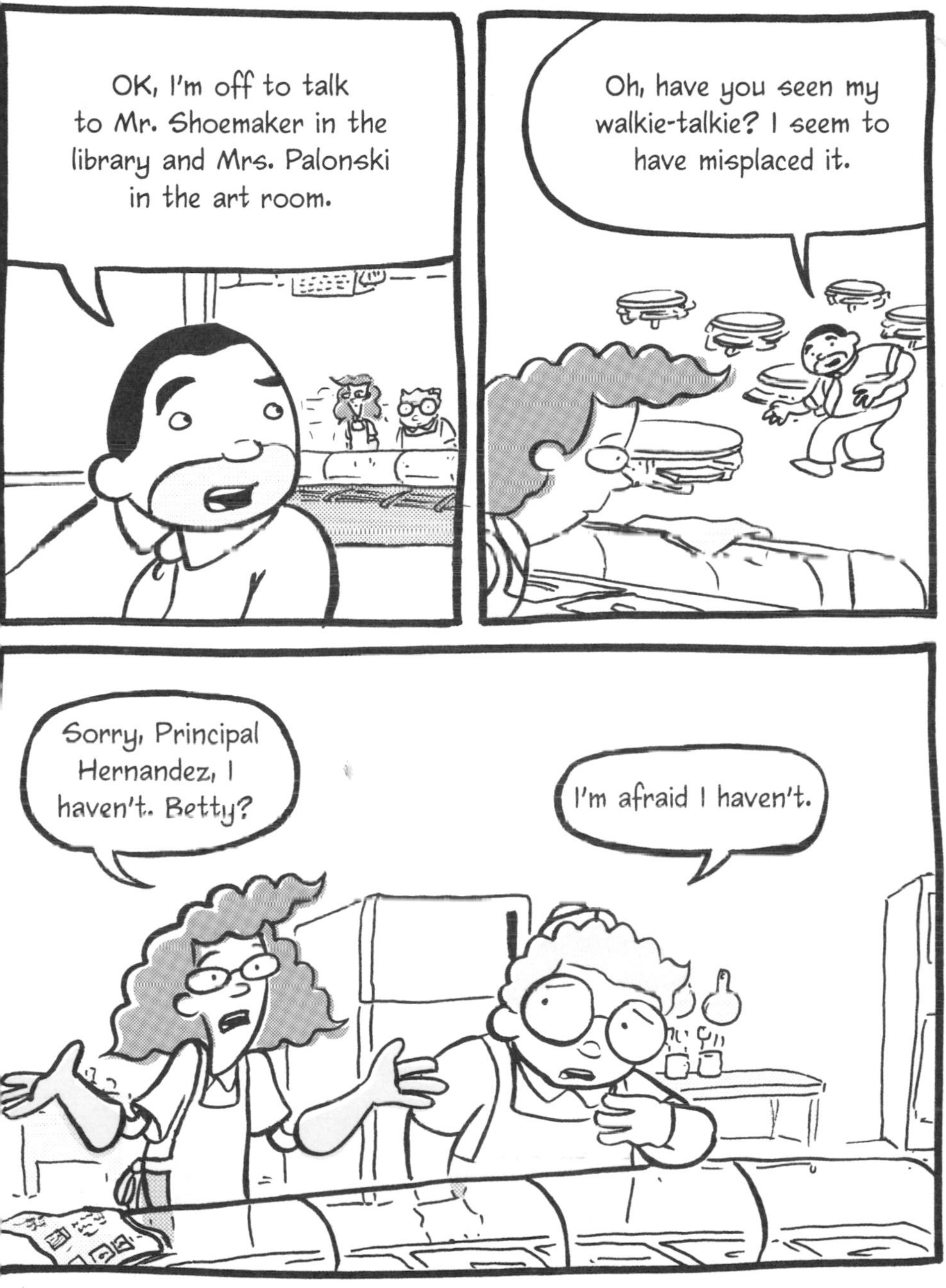
OK, I'm off to talk to Mr. Shoemaker in the library and Mrs. Palonski in the art room.
Oh, have you seen my walkie-talkie? I seem to have misplaced it.
Sorry, Principal Hernandez, I haven't. Betty?
I'm afraid I haven't.

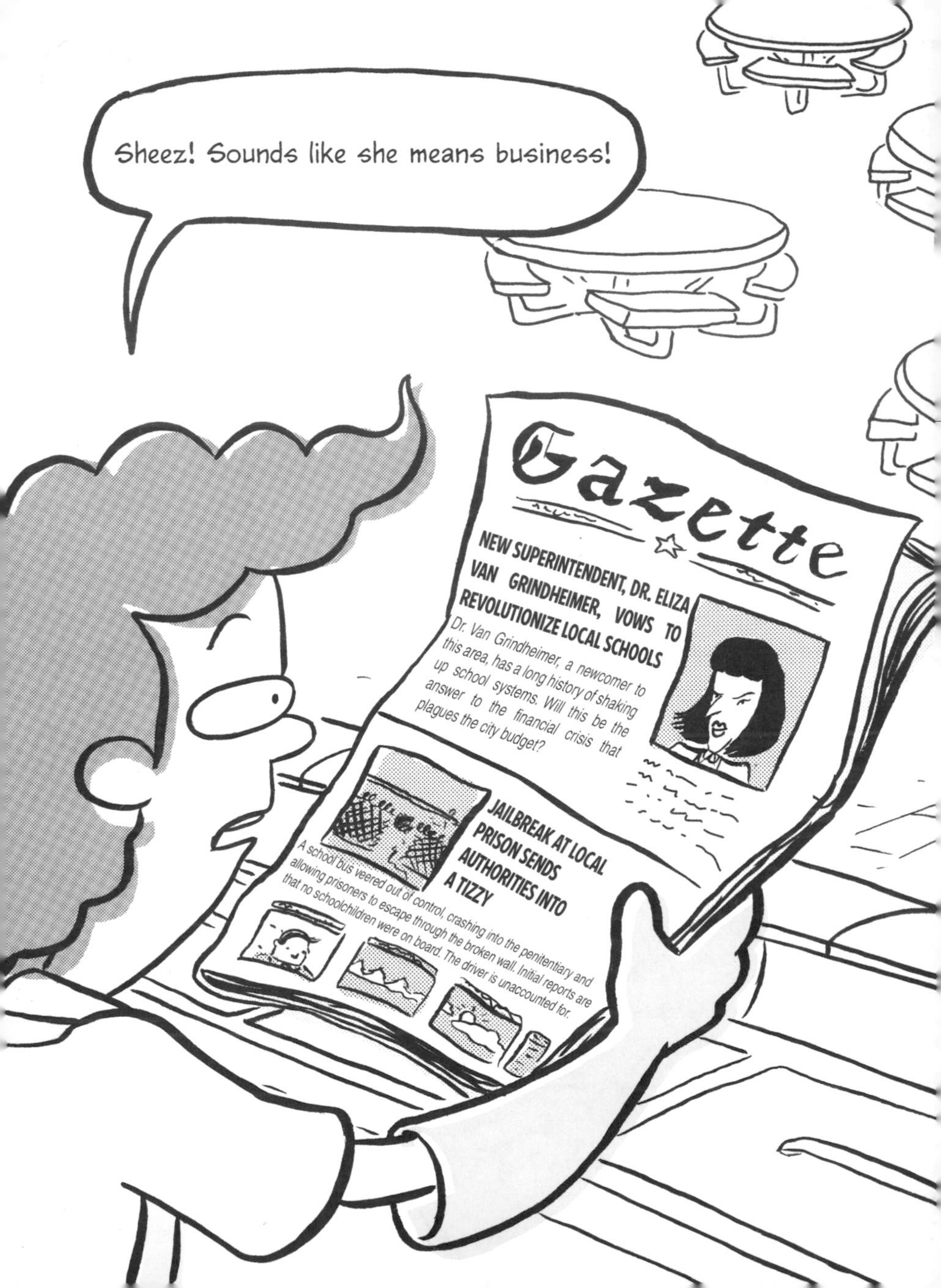
Sheez! Sounds like she means business!
Gazette
NEW SUPERINTENDENT, DR. ELIZA VAN GRINDHEIMER, VOWS TO REVOLUTIONIZE LOCAL SCHOOLS
Dr. Van Grindheimer, a newcomer to this area, has a long history of shaking up school systems. Will this be the answer to the financial crisis that plagues the city budget?
JAILBREAK AT LOCAL PRISON SENDS AUTHORITIES INTO A TIZZY
A school bus veered out of control, crashing into the penitentiary and allowing prisoners to escape through the broken wall. Initial reports are that no schoolchildren were on board. The driver is unaccounted for.

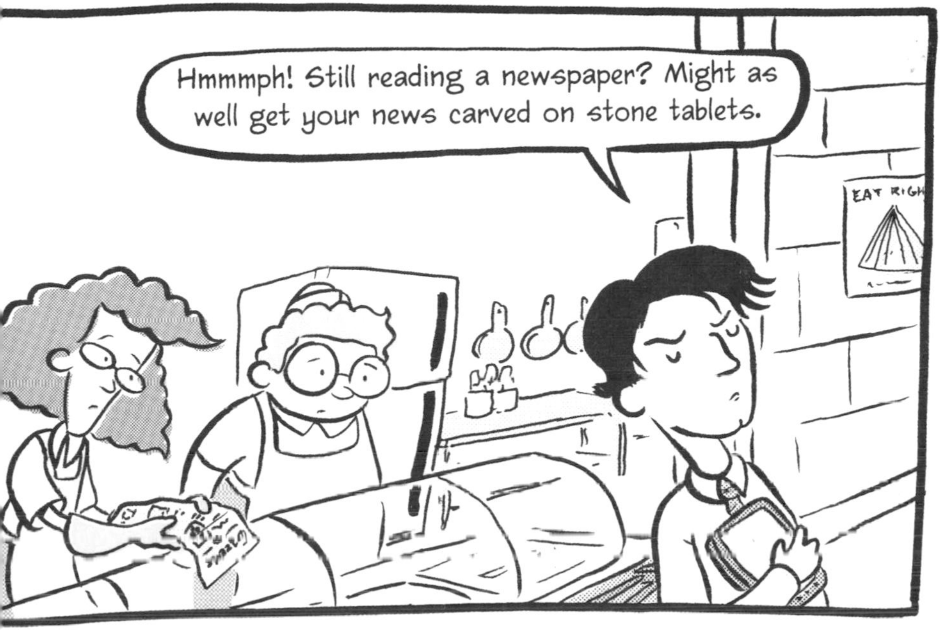
Hmmmph! Still reading a newspaper? Might as well get your news carved on stone tablets.

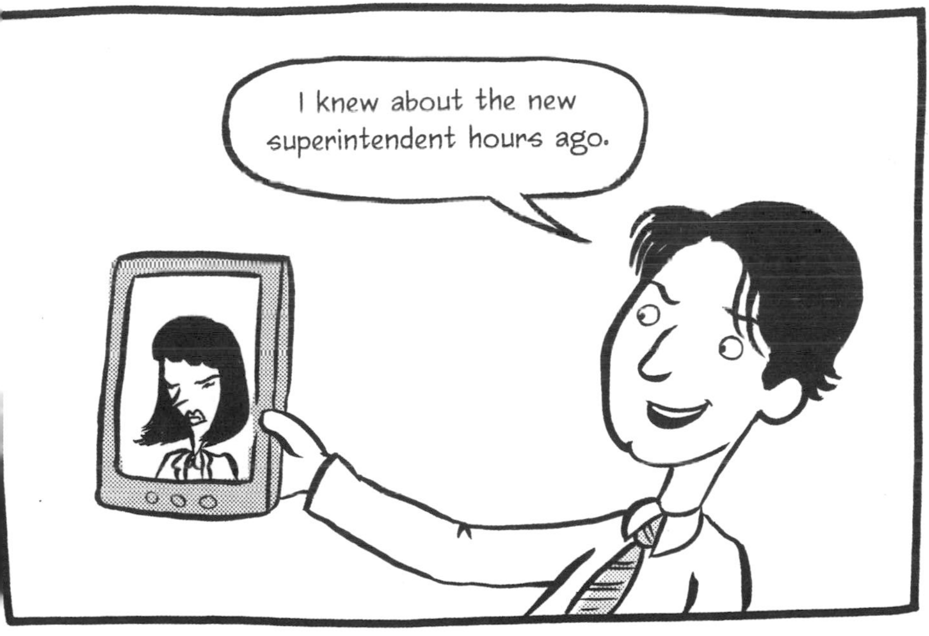
I knew about the new superintendent hours ago.

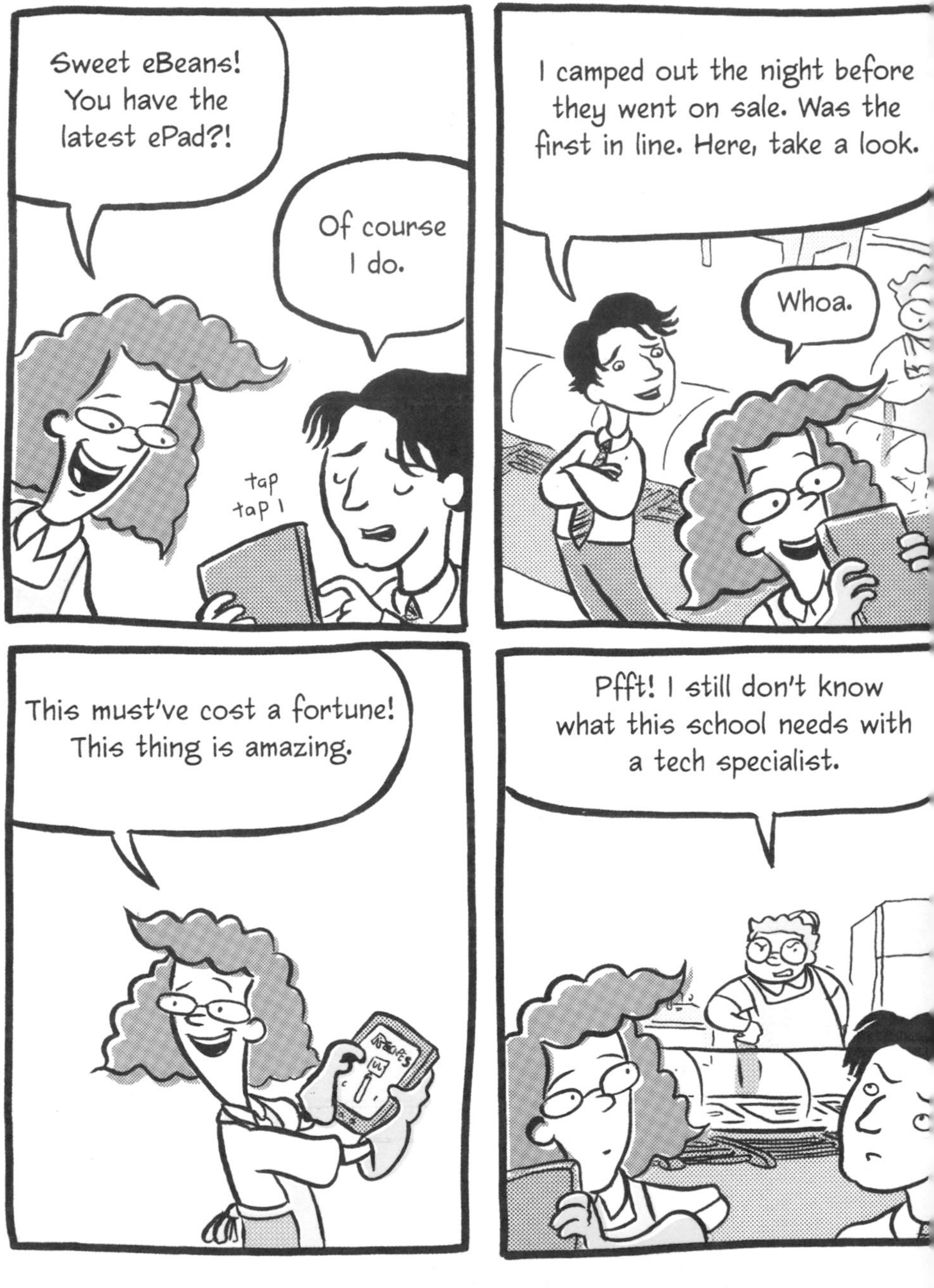
Sweet eBeans! You have the latest ePad?!
Of course I do.
tap tap !
I camped out the night before they went on sale. Was the first in line. Here, take a look.
Whoa.
This must've cost a fortune! This thing is amazing.
Pfft! I still don't know what this school needs with a tech specialist.

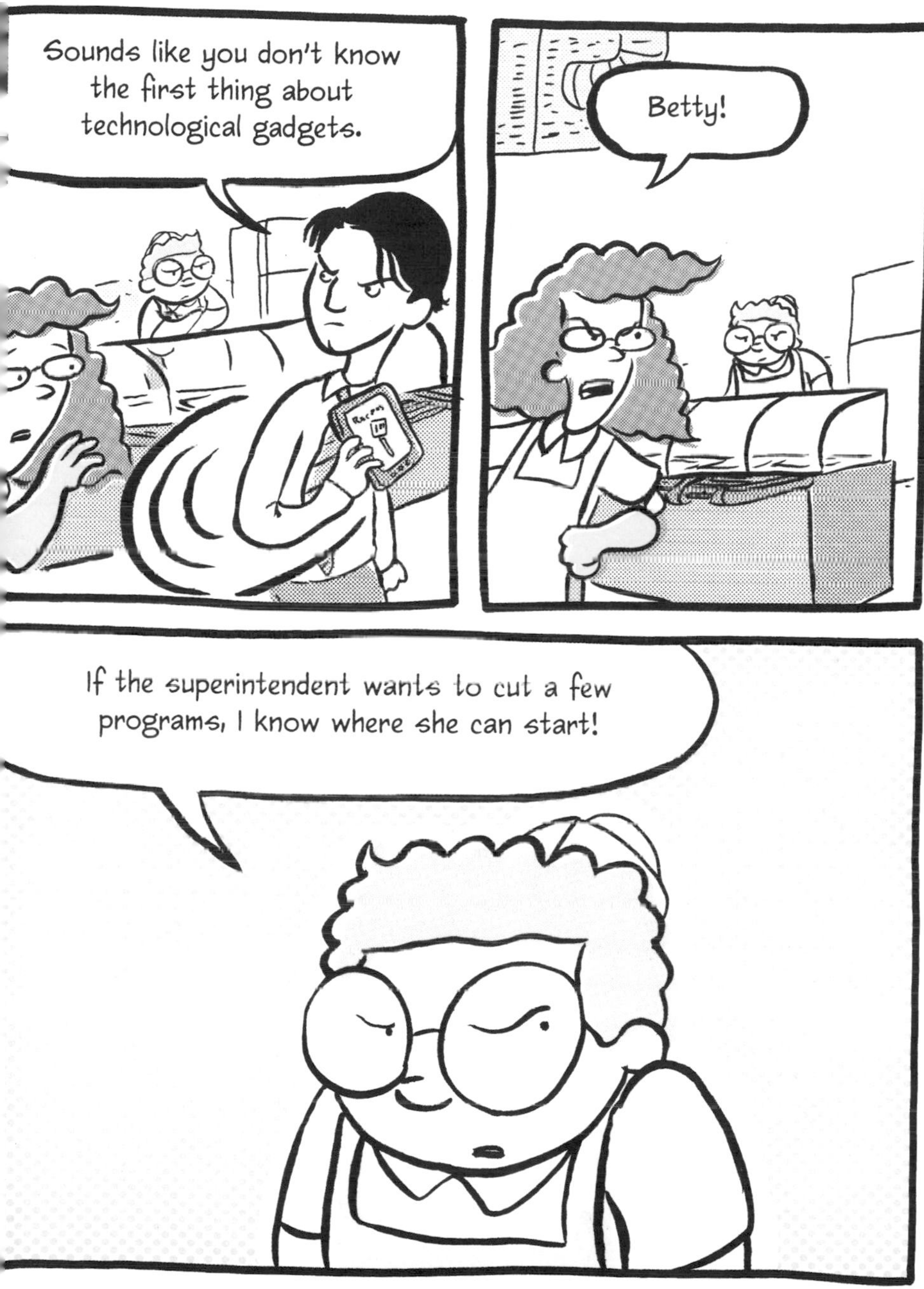
Sounds like you don't know the first thing about technological gadgets.
Recipes
Betty!
If the superintendent wants to cut a few programs, I know where she can start!

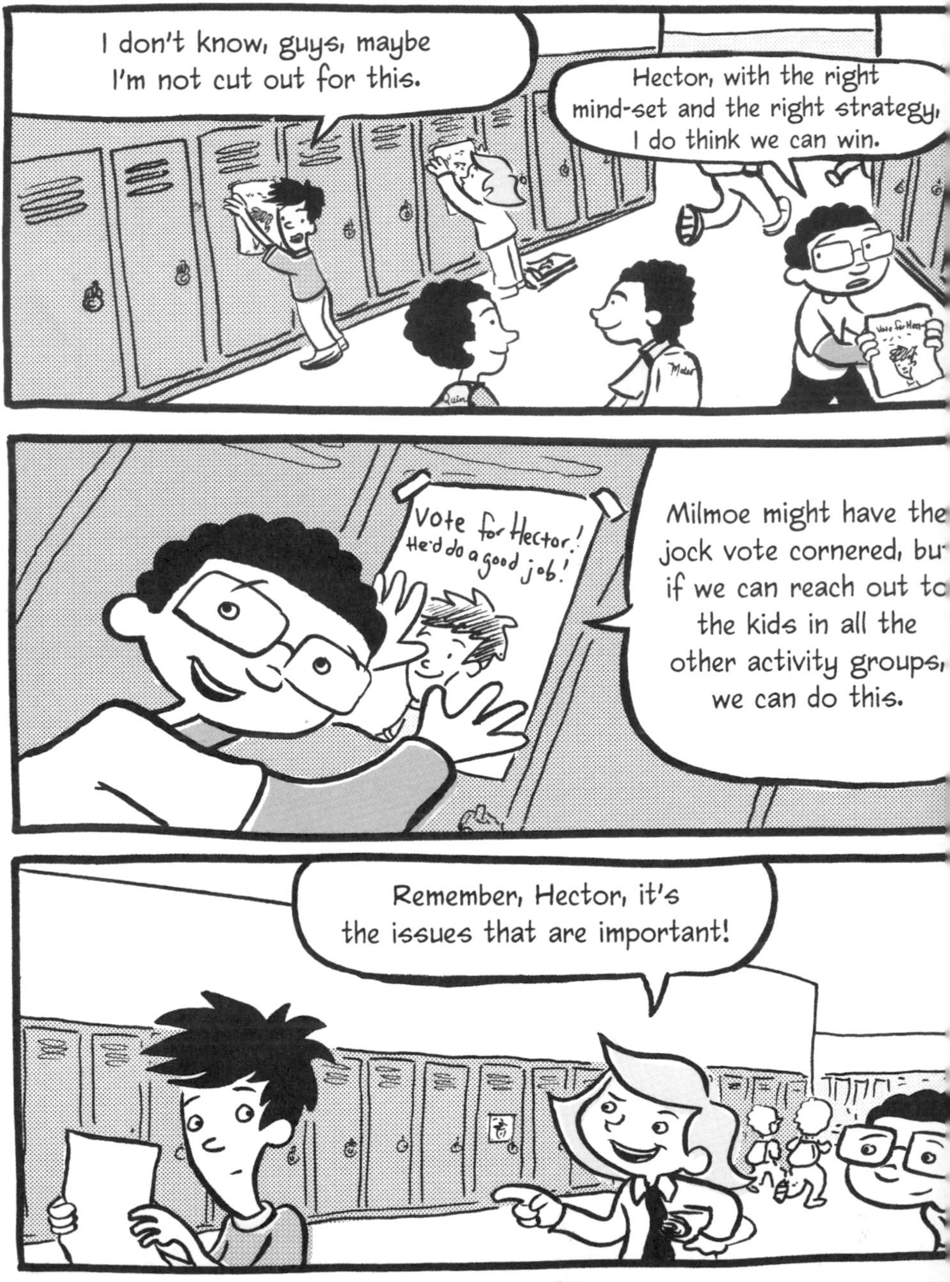
I don't know, guys, maybe I'm not cut out for this.
Hector, with the right mind-set and the right strategy, I do think we can win.
Vote for Hector! He'd do a good job!
Milmoe might have the jock vote cornered, but if we can reach out to the kids in all the other activity groups, we can do this.
Remember, Hector, it's the issues that are important!

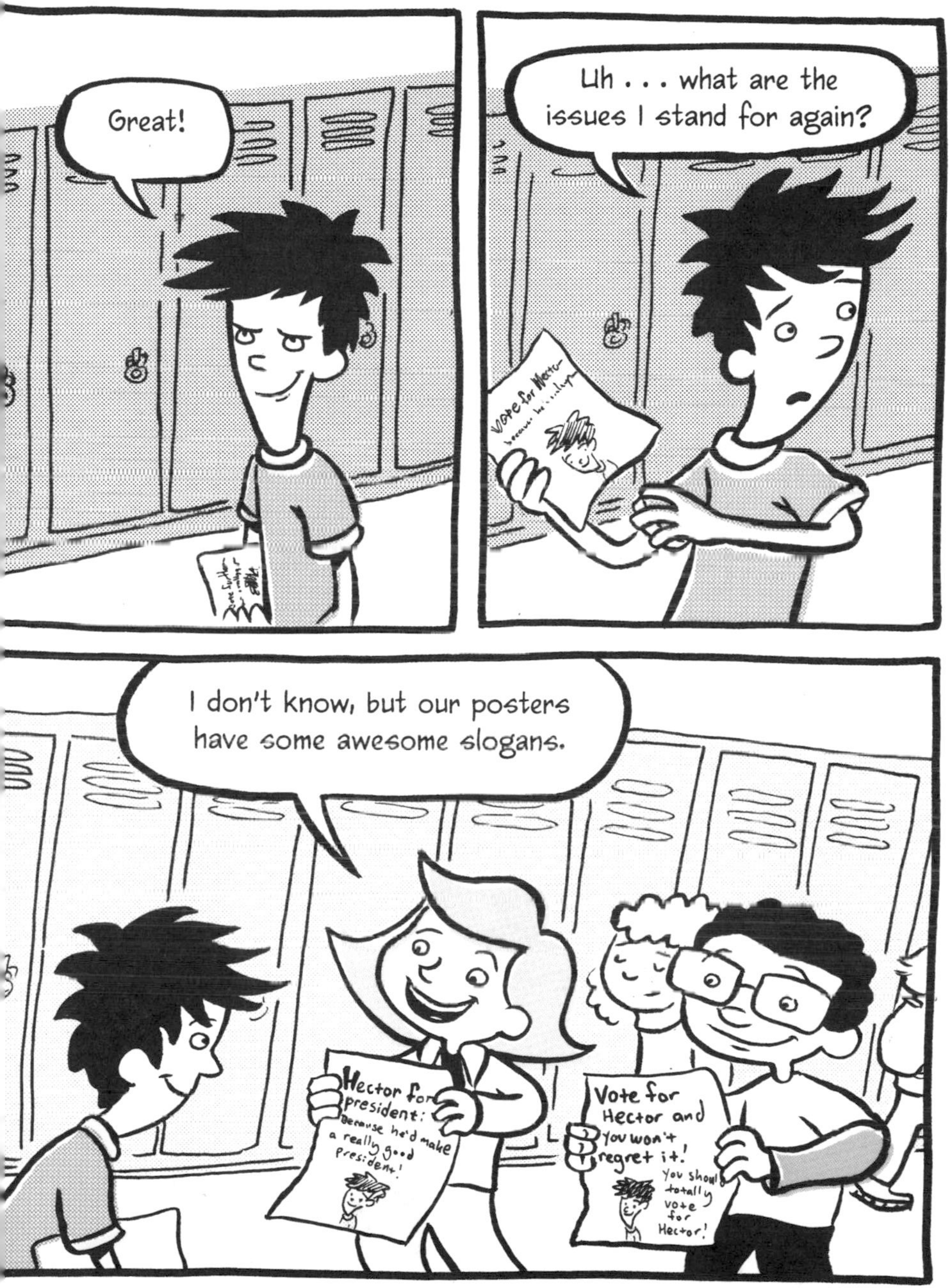
Great!
Uh . . . what are the issues I stand for again?
I don't know, but our posters have some awesome slogans.
Hector for president: Because he'd make a really good president!
Vote for Hector and you won't regret it!
You should totally vote for Hector!

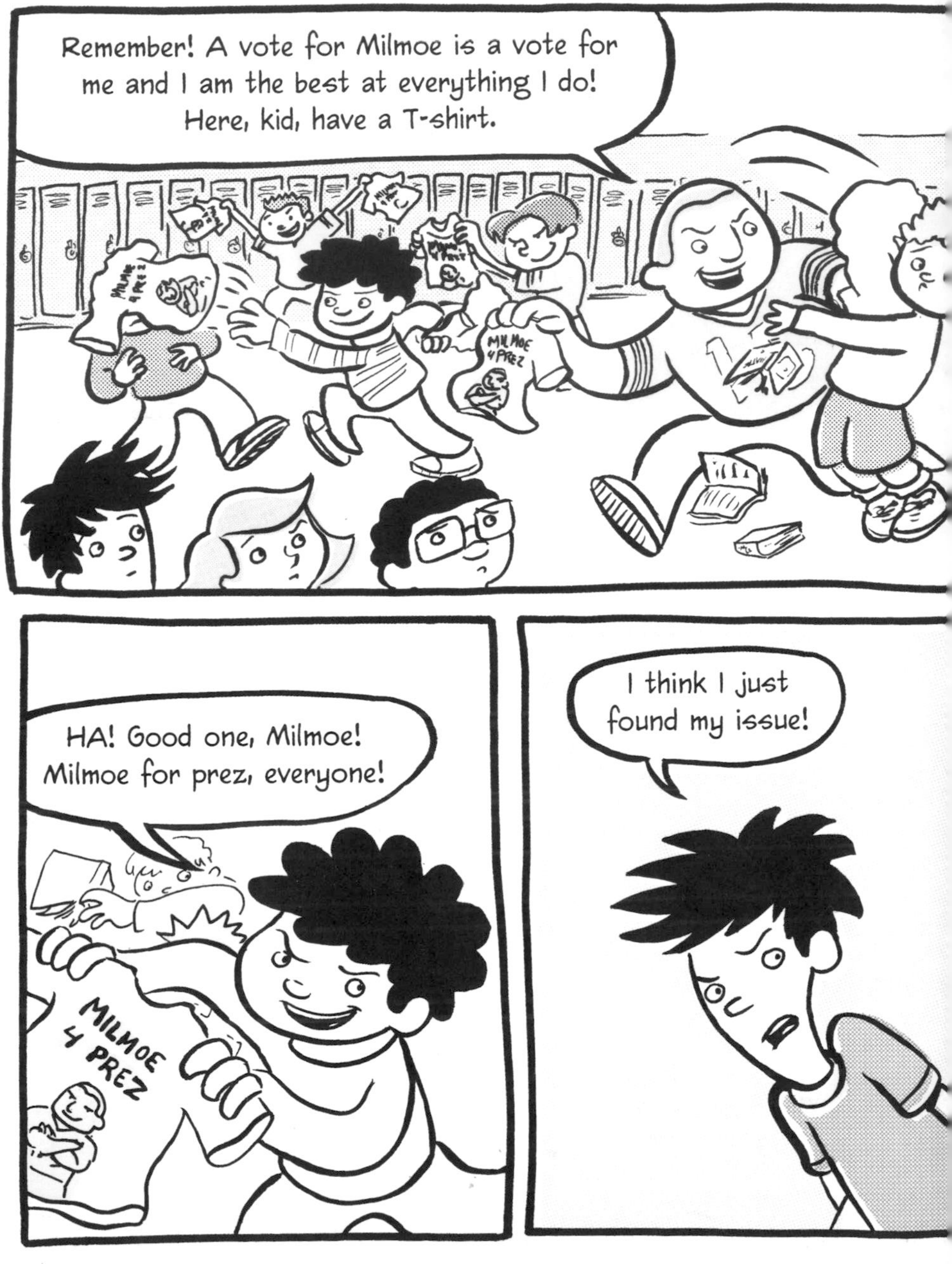

Remember! A vote for Milmoe is a vote for me and I am the best at everything I do! Here, kid, have a T-shirt.
MILMOE 4 PREZ
HA! Good one, Milmoe! Milmoe for prez, everyone!
MILMOE 4 PREZ
I think I just found my issue!

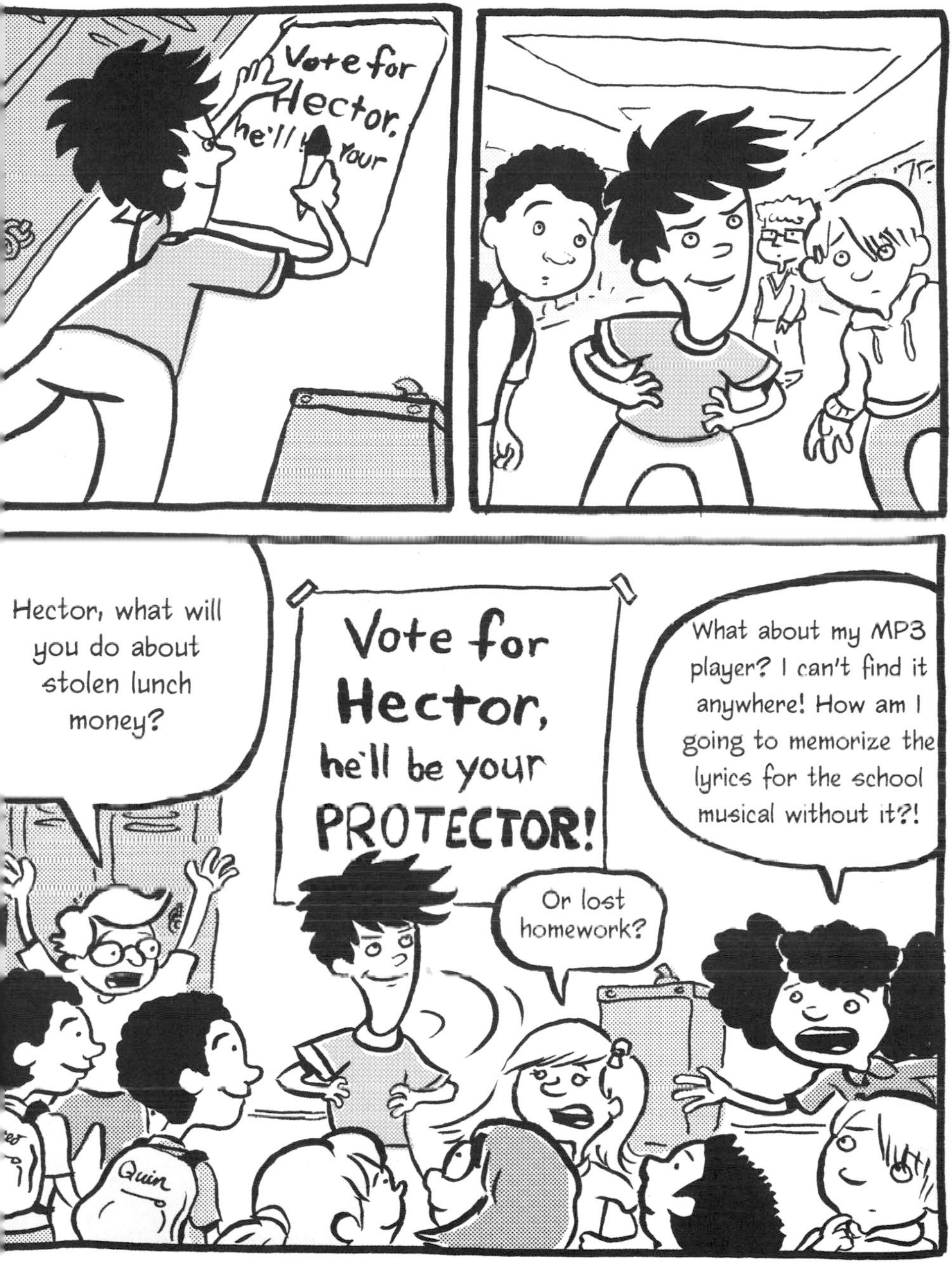
Vote for
Hector,
he'll
your
Hector, what will you do about stolen lunch money?
Vote for Hector, he'll be your PROTECTOR!
What about my MP3 player? I can't find it anywhere! How am I going to memorize the lyrics for the school musical without it?!
Or lost homework?
Quin

I'm sorry, Orson, but no— I haven't seen your graphing-calculator watch.

C'mon, Hector, eat up! Lunch is prime campaigning time. We need to go table to table so you can start shaking hands!

Oh boy. And it's vegetable soufflé day. Can't we wait and campaign on taco day, when people are in far better moods?

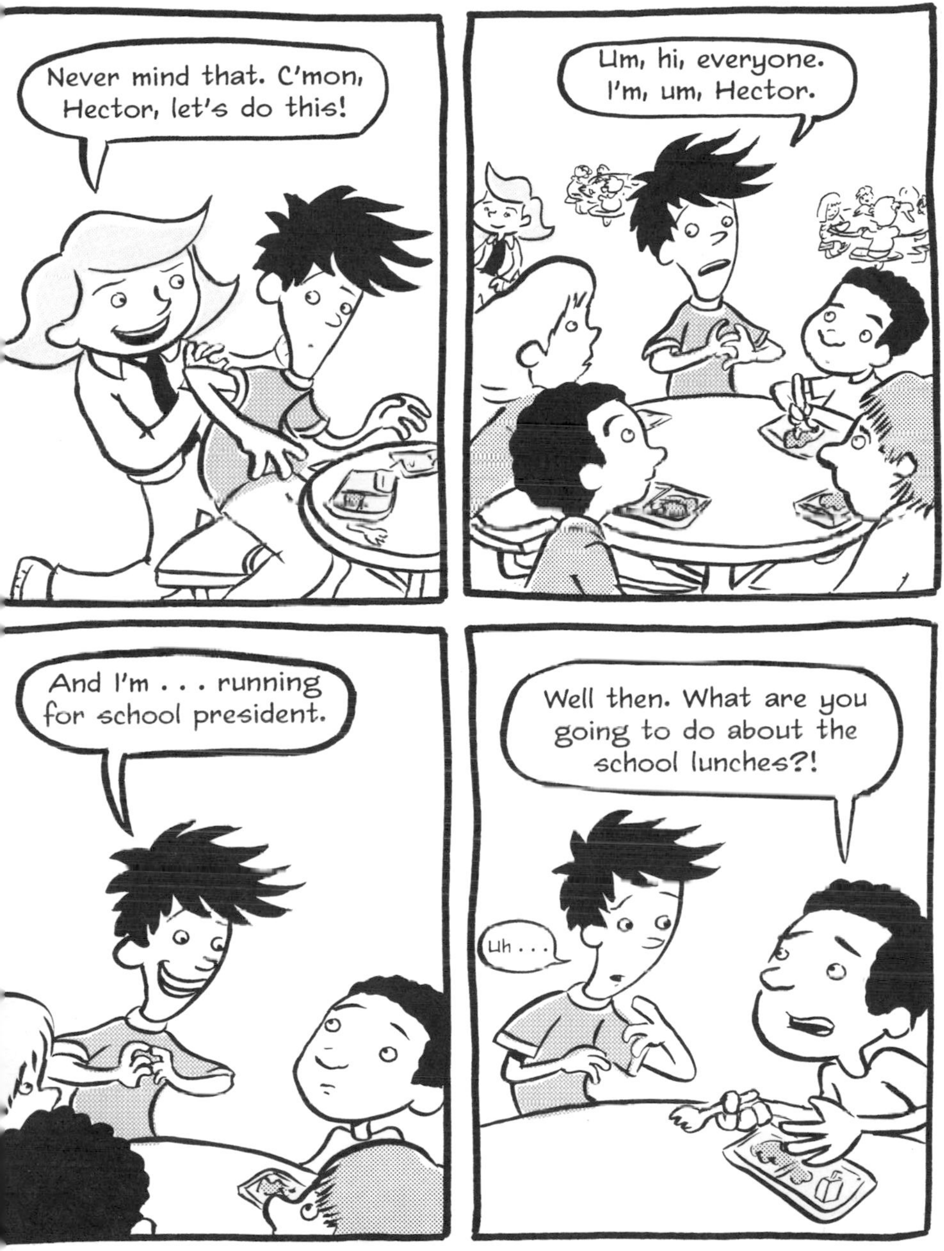
Never mind that. C'mon, Hector, let's do this!
Um, hi, everyone. I'm, um, Hector.
And I'm . . . running for school president.
Well then. What are you going to do about the school lunches?!
Uh . . .

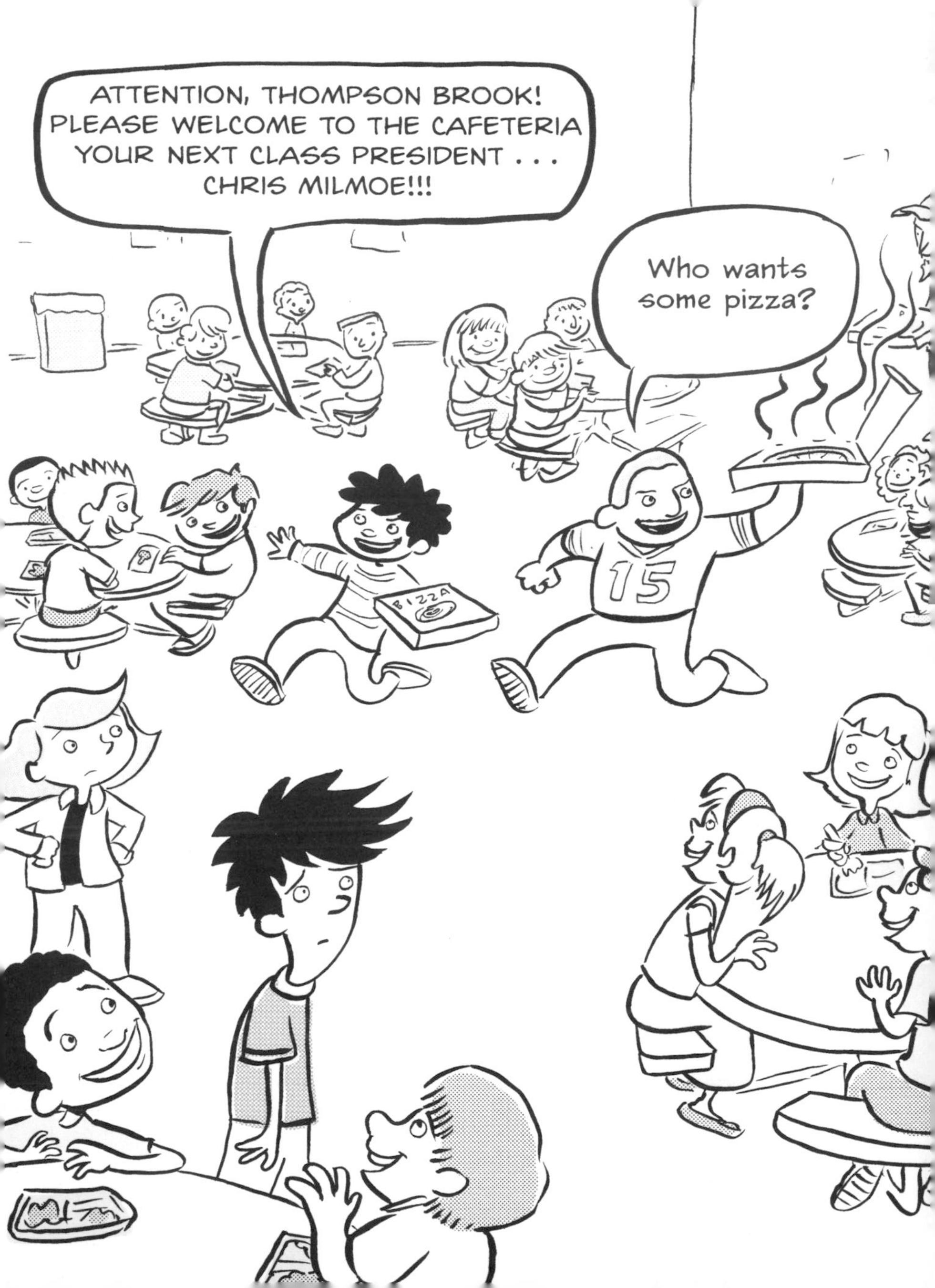
ATTENTION, THOMPSON BROOK! PLEASE WELCOME TO THE CAFETERIA YOUR NEXT CLASS PRESIDENT . . . CHRIS MILMOE!!!
Who wants some pizza?
15
PIZZA

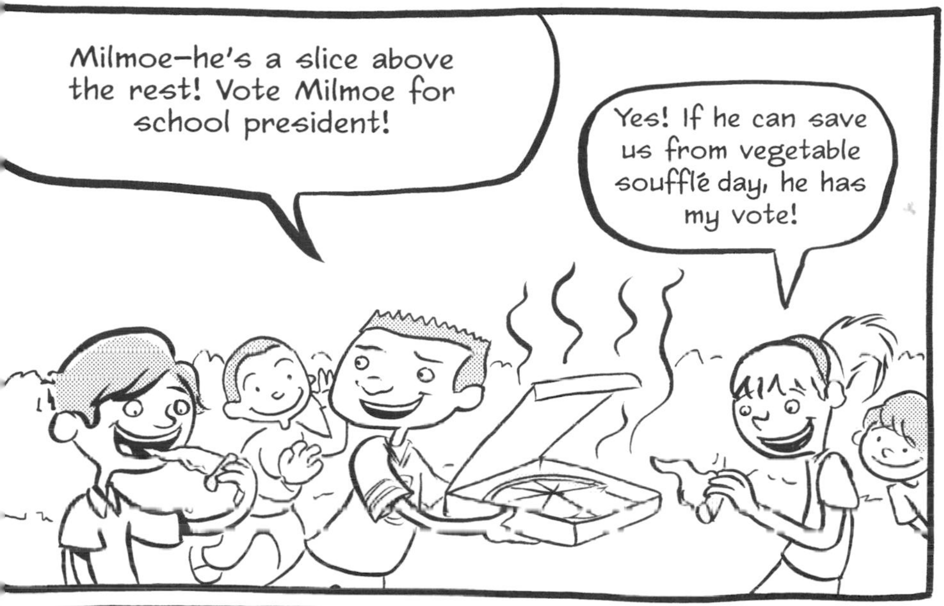
Milmoe—he's a slice above the rest! Vote Milmoe for school president!
Yes! If he can save us from vegetable soufflé day, he has my vote!

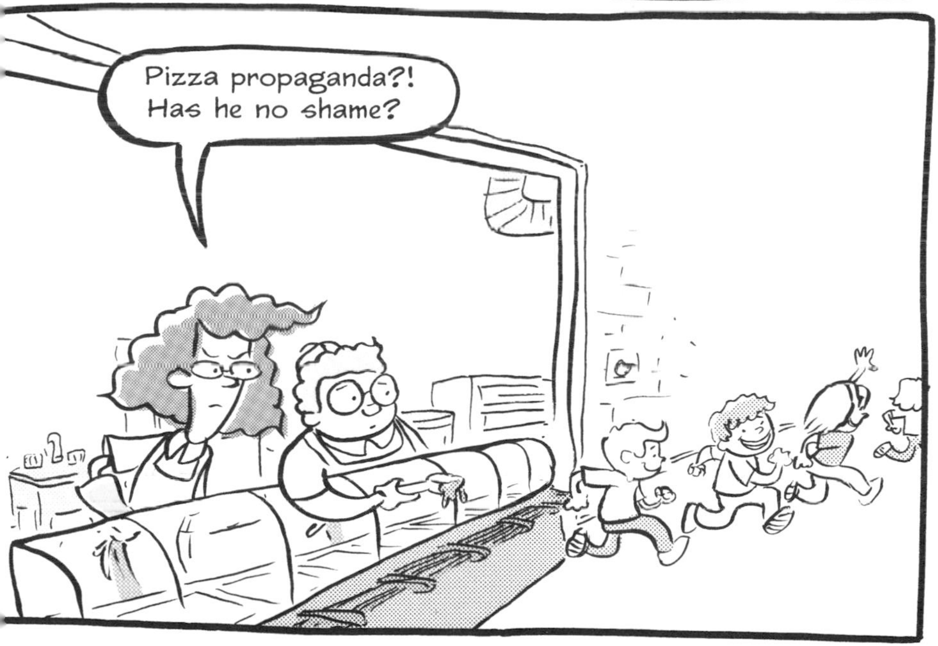
Pizza propaganda?! Has he no shame?

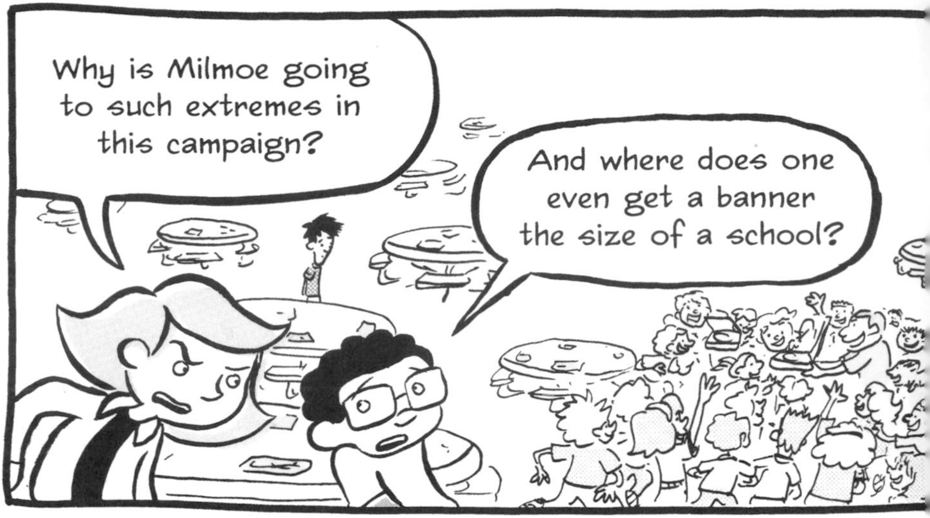
Why is Milmoe going to such extremes in this campaign?
And where does one even get a banner the size of a school?

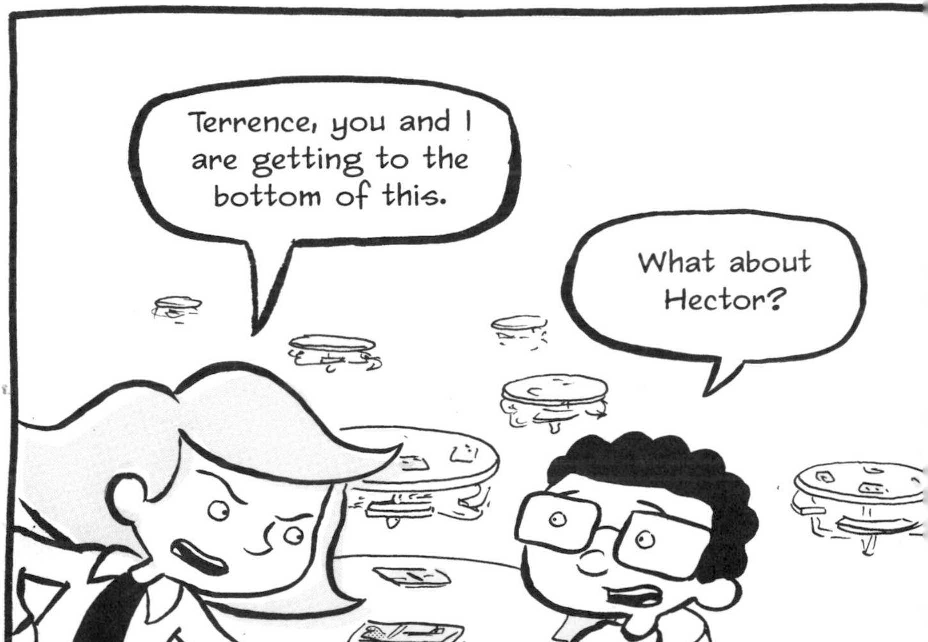
Terrence, you and I are getting to the bottom of this.
What about Hector?

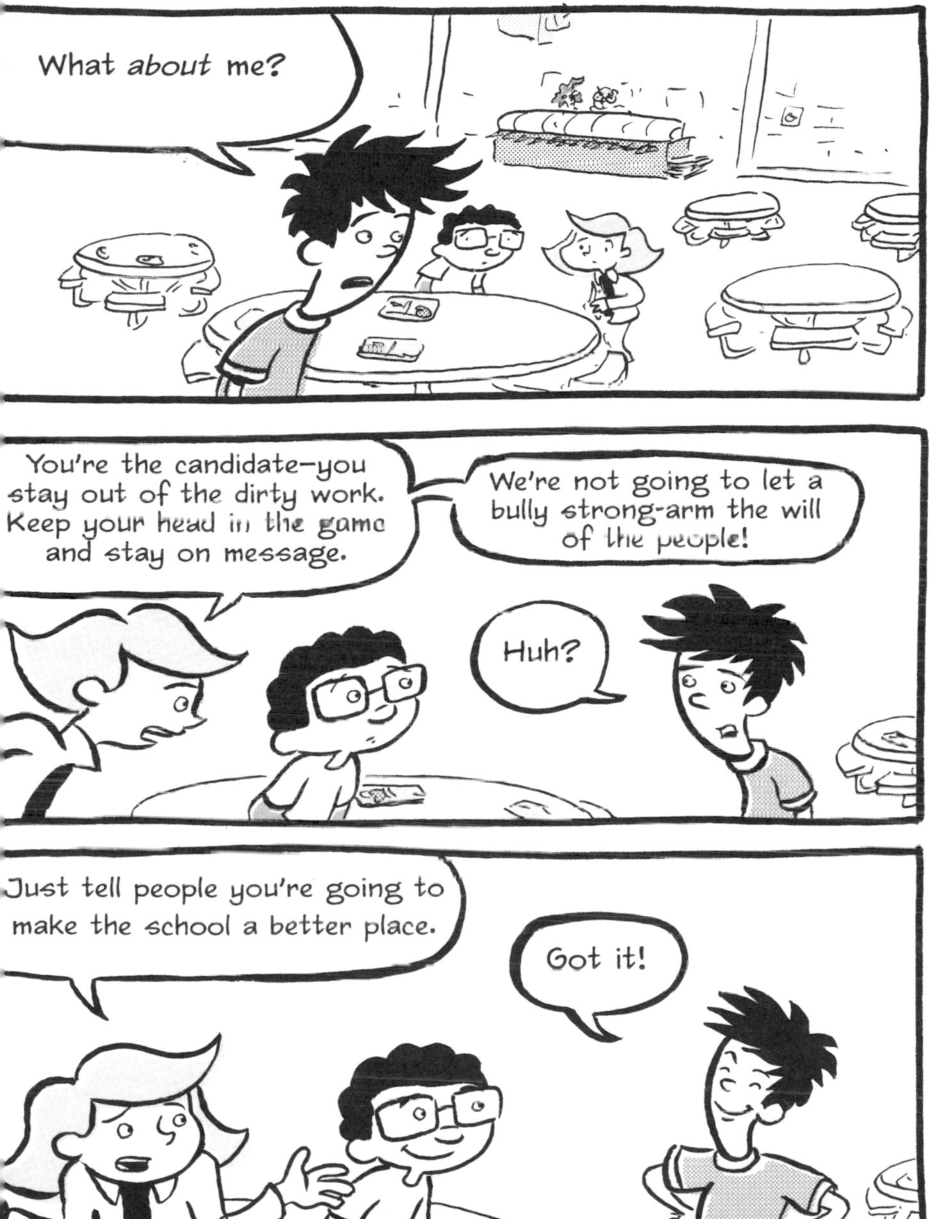
What *about* me?
You're the candidate—you stay out of the dirty work. Keep your head in the game and stay on message.
We're not going to let a bully strong-arm the will of the people!
Huh?
Just tell people you're going to make the school a better place.
Got it!

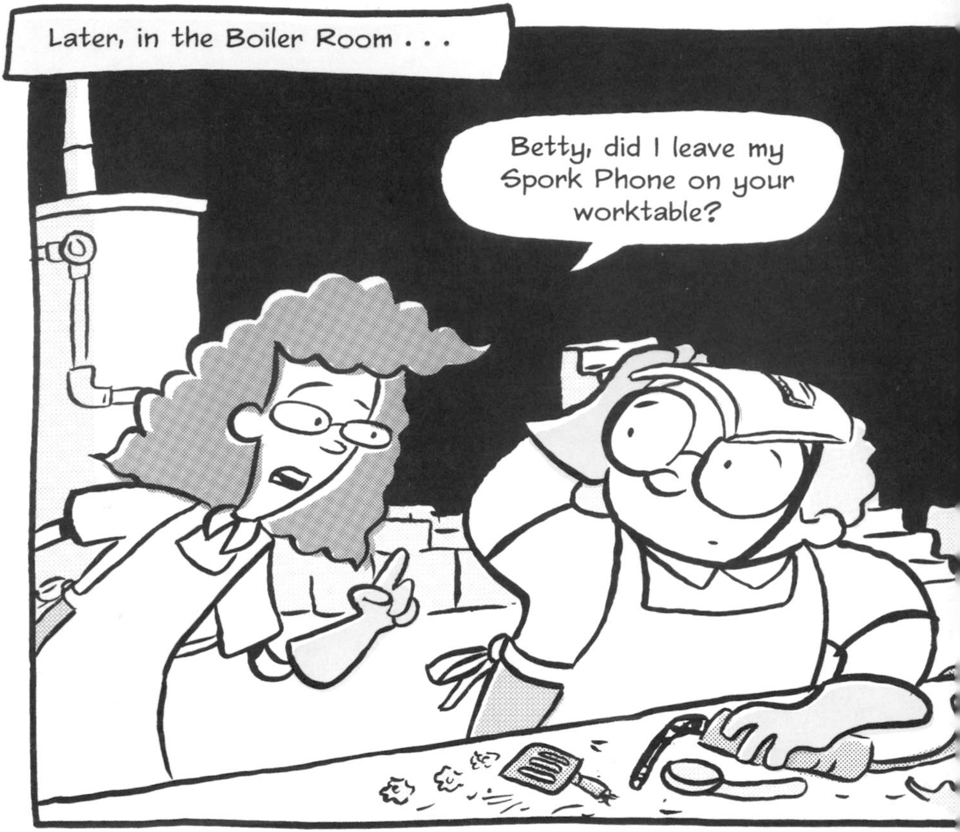
Later, in the Boiler Room . . .
Betty, did I leave my Spork Phone on your worktable?
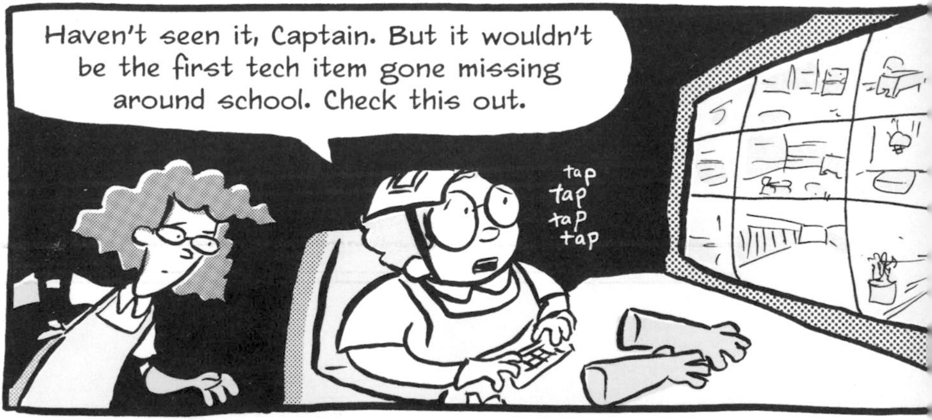
Haven't seen it, Captain. But it wouldn't be the first tech item gone missing around school. Check this out.
tap tap tap tap

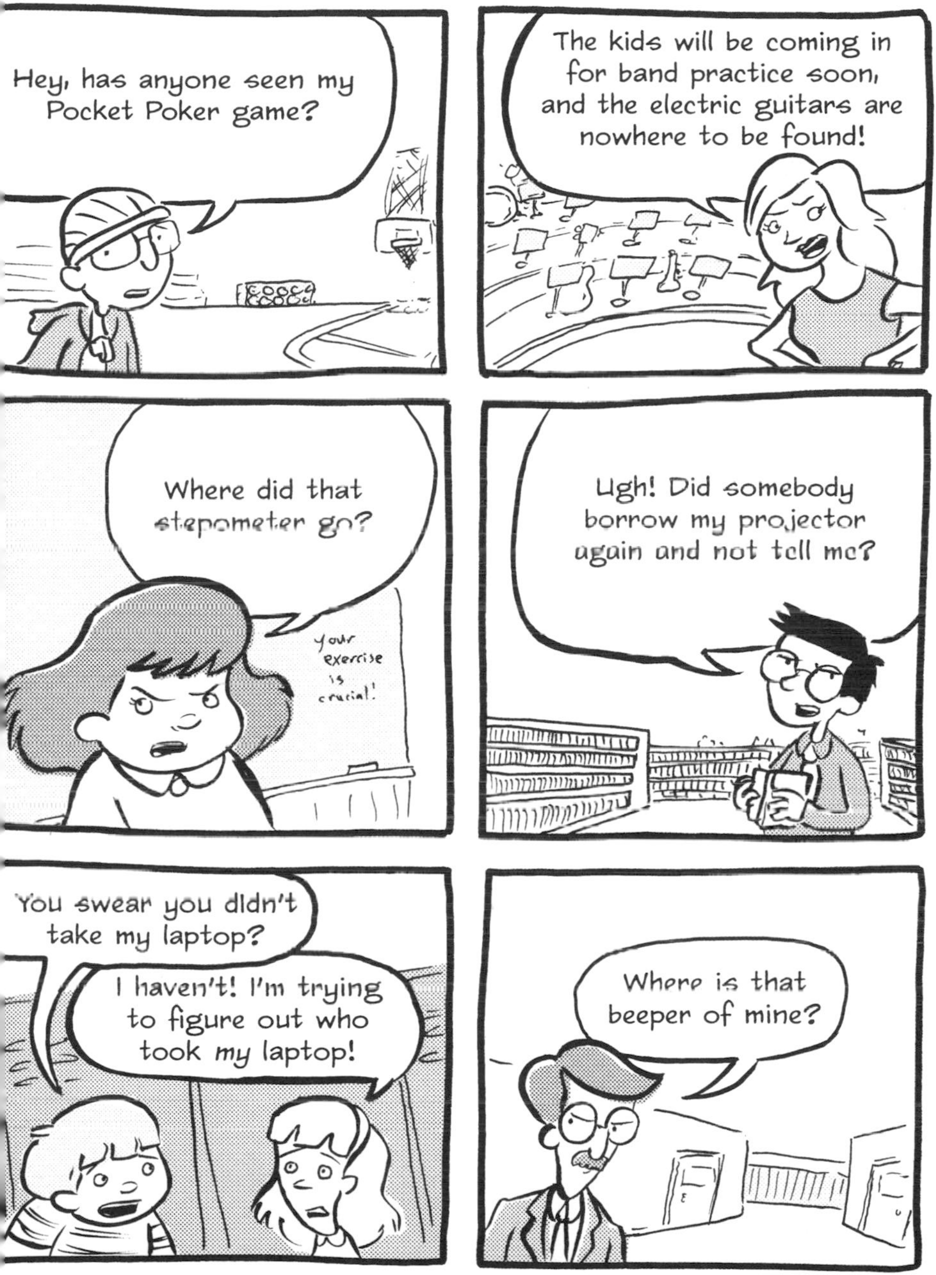

Hey, has anyone seen my Pocket Poker game?
The kids will be coming in for band practice soon, and the electric guitars are nowhere to be found!
Where did that stepometer go?
your exercise is crucial!
Ugh! Did somebody borrow my projector again and not tell me?
You swear you didn't take my laptop?
I haven't! I'm trying to figure out who took *my* laptop!
Where is that beeper of mine?

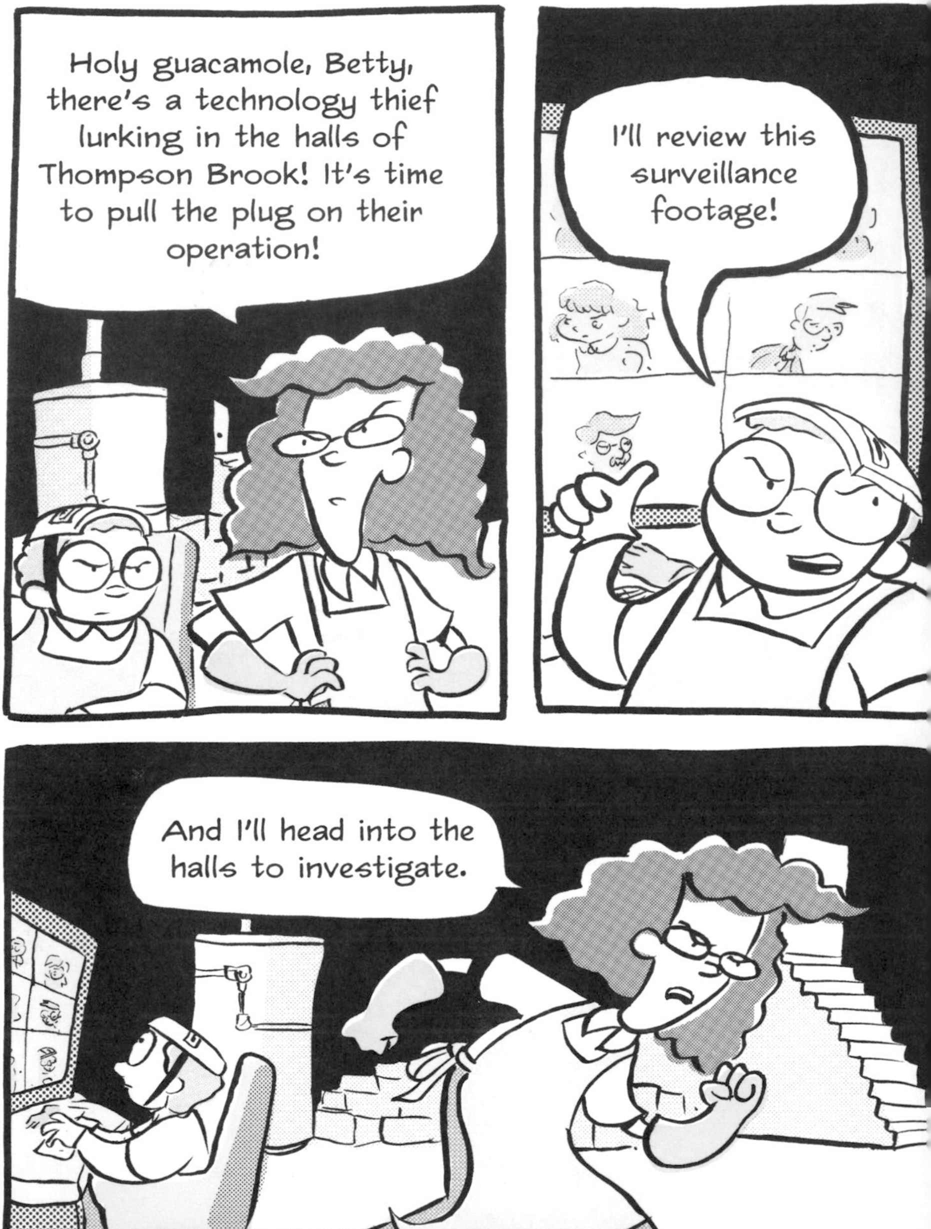
Holy guacamole, Betty, there's a technology thief lurking in the halls of Thompson Brook! It's time to pull the plug on their operation!
I'll review this surveillance footage!
And I'll head into the halls to investigate.

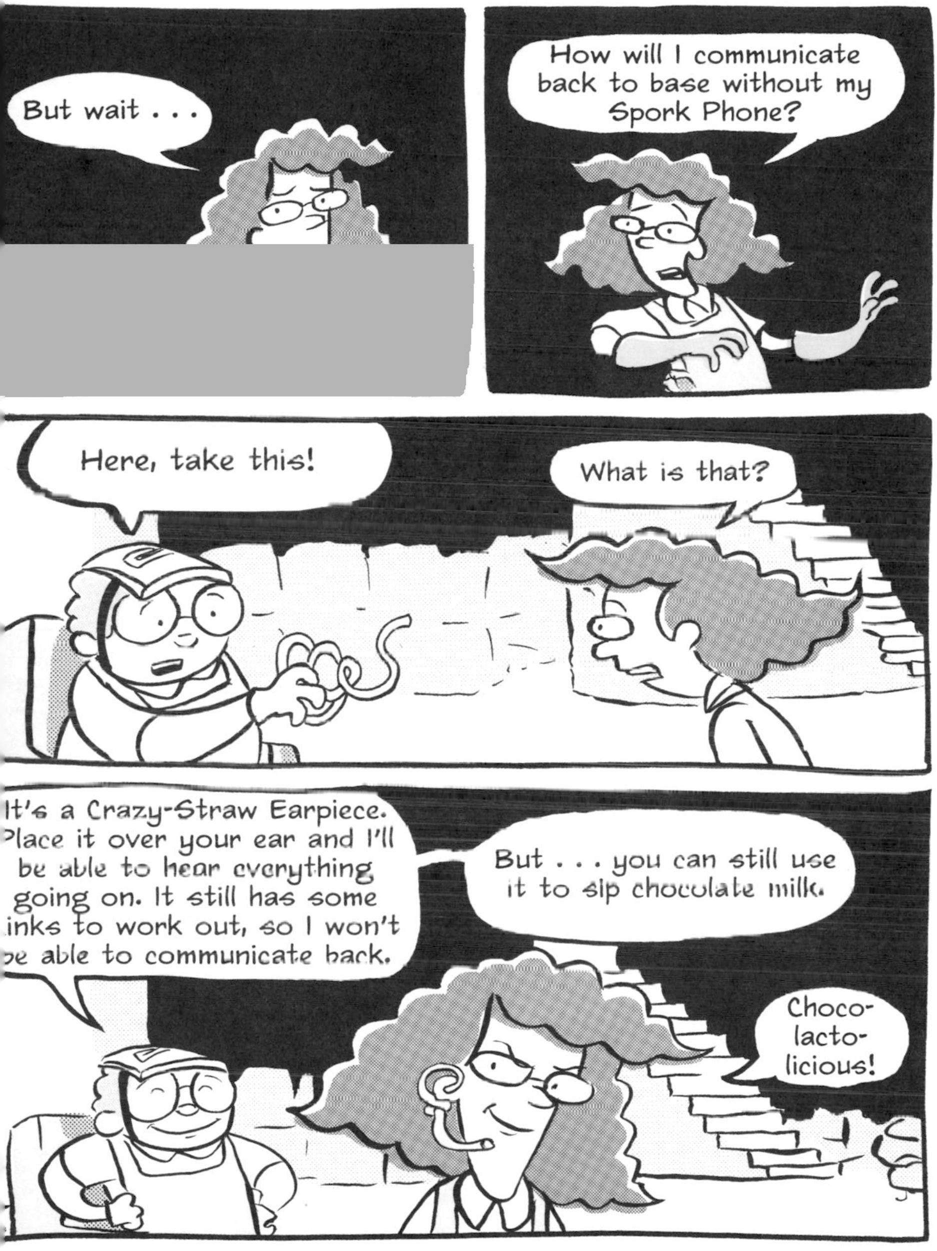

But wait . . .
How will I communicate back to base without my Spork Phone?
Here, take this!
What is that?
It's a Crazy-Straw Earpiece. lace it over your ear and I'll be able to hear everything going on. It still has some inks to work out, so I won't e able to communicate back.
But . . . you can still use it to sip chocolate milk.
Choco-lacto-licious!

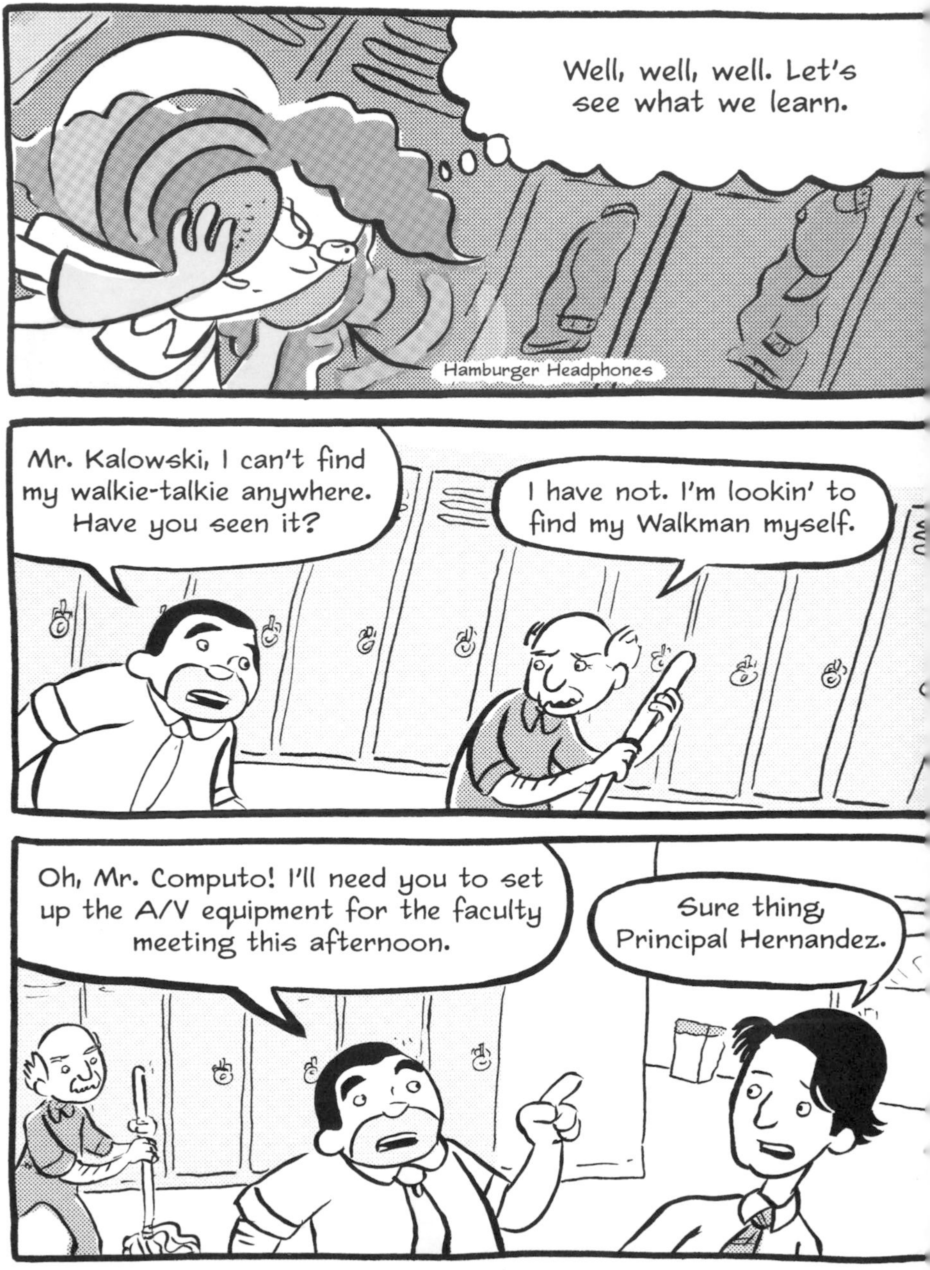
Well, well, well. Let's see what we learn.
Hamburger Headphones
Mr. Kalowski, I can't find my walkie-talkie anywhere. Have you seen it?
I have not. I'm lookin' to find my Walkman myself.
Oh, Mr. Computo! I'll need you to set up the A/V equipment for the faculty meeting this afternoon.
Sure thing, Principal Hernandez.

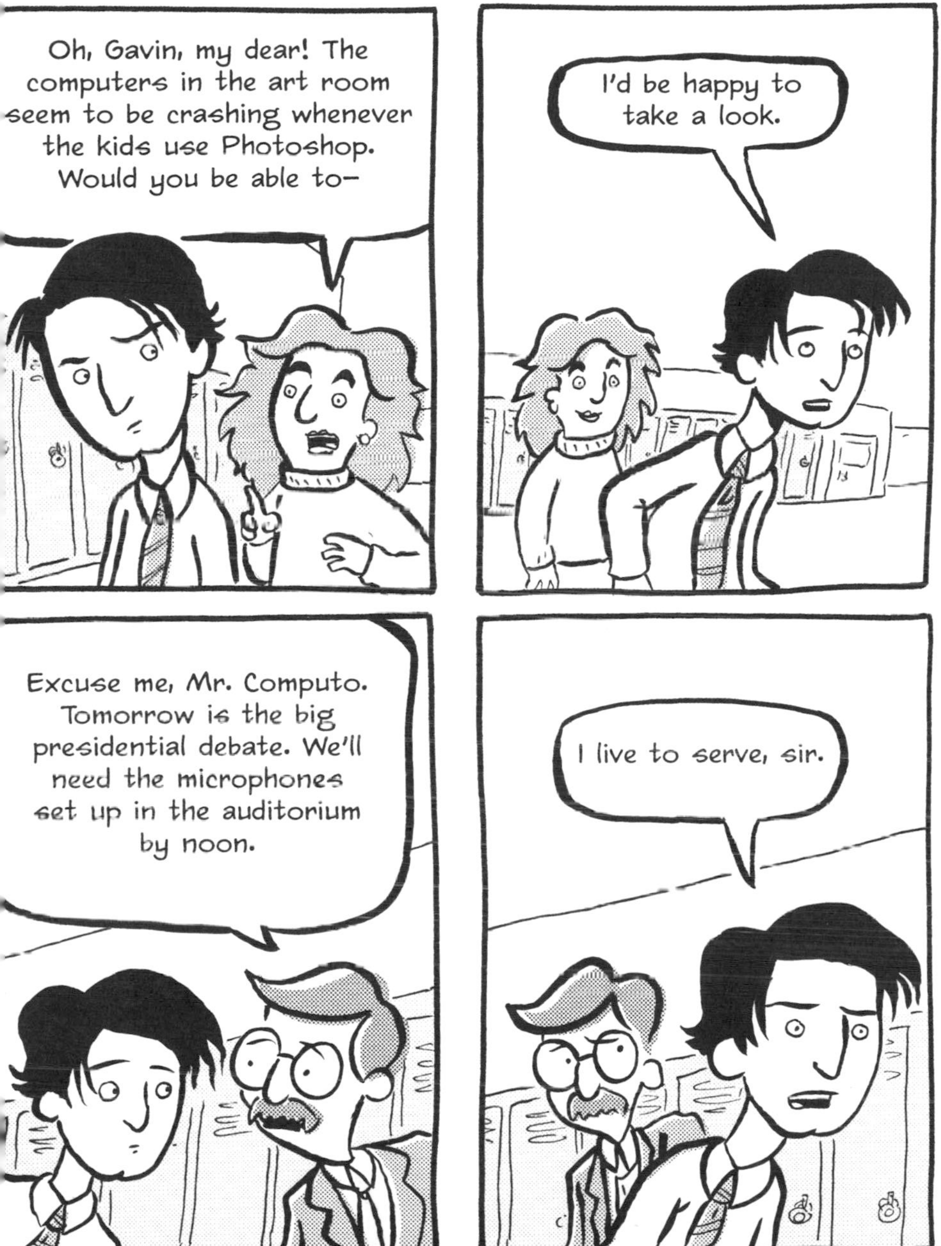
Oh, Gavin, my dear! The computers in the art room seem to be crashing whenever the kids use Photoshop. Would you be able to—
I'd be happy to take a look.
Excuse me, Mr. Computo. Tomorrow is the big presidential debate. We'll need the microphones set up in the auditorium by noon.
I live to serve, sir.

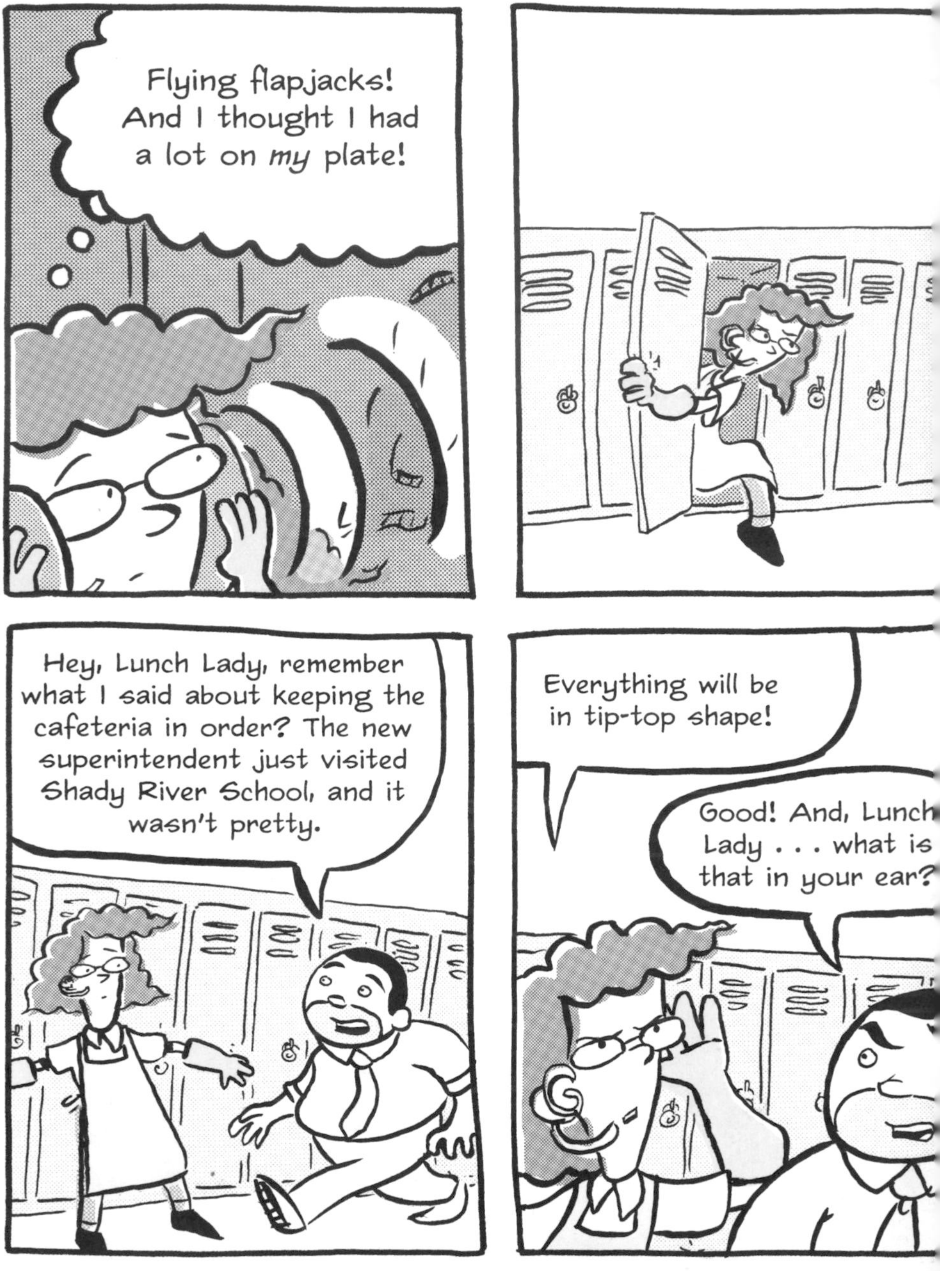
Flying flapjacks! And I thought I had a lot on *my* plate!
Hey, Lunch Lady, remember what I said about keeping the cafeteria in order? The new superintendent just visited Shady River School, and it wasn't pretty.
Everything will be in tip-top shape!
Good! And, Lunch Lady . . . what is that in your ear?

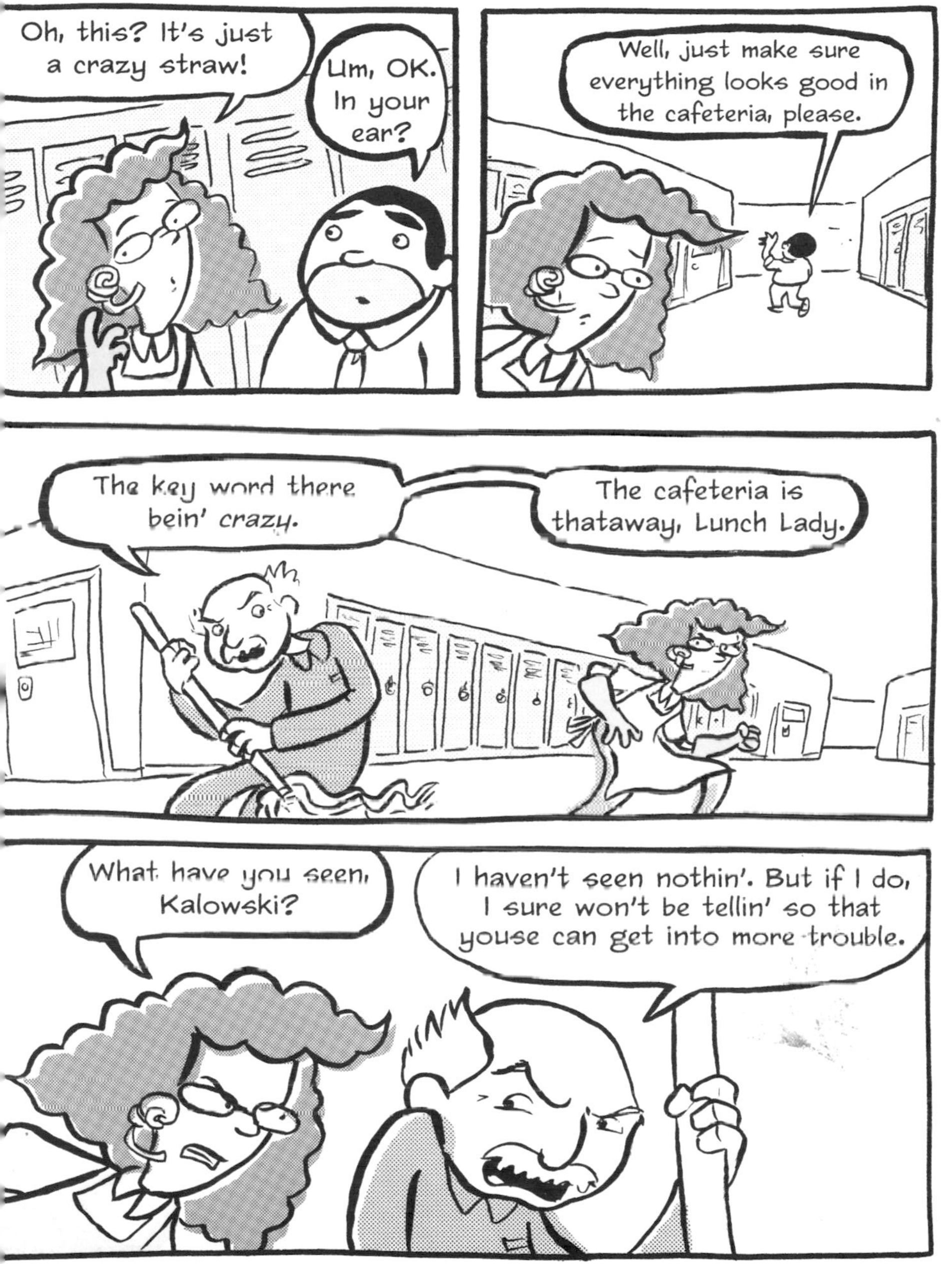
Oh, this? It's just a crazy straw!
Um, OK. In your ear?
Well, just make sure everything looks good in the cafeteria, please.
The key word there bein' crazy.
The cafeteria is thataway, Lunch Lady.
What have you seen, Kalowski?
I haven't seen nothin'. But if I do, I sure won't be tellin' so that youse can get into more trouble.

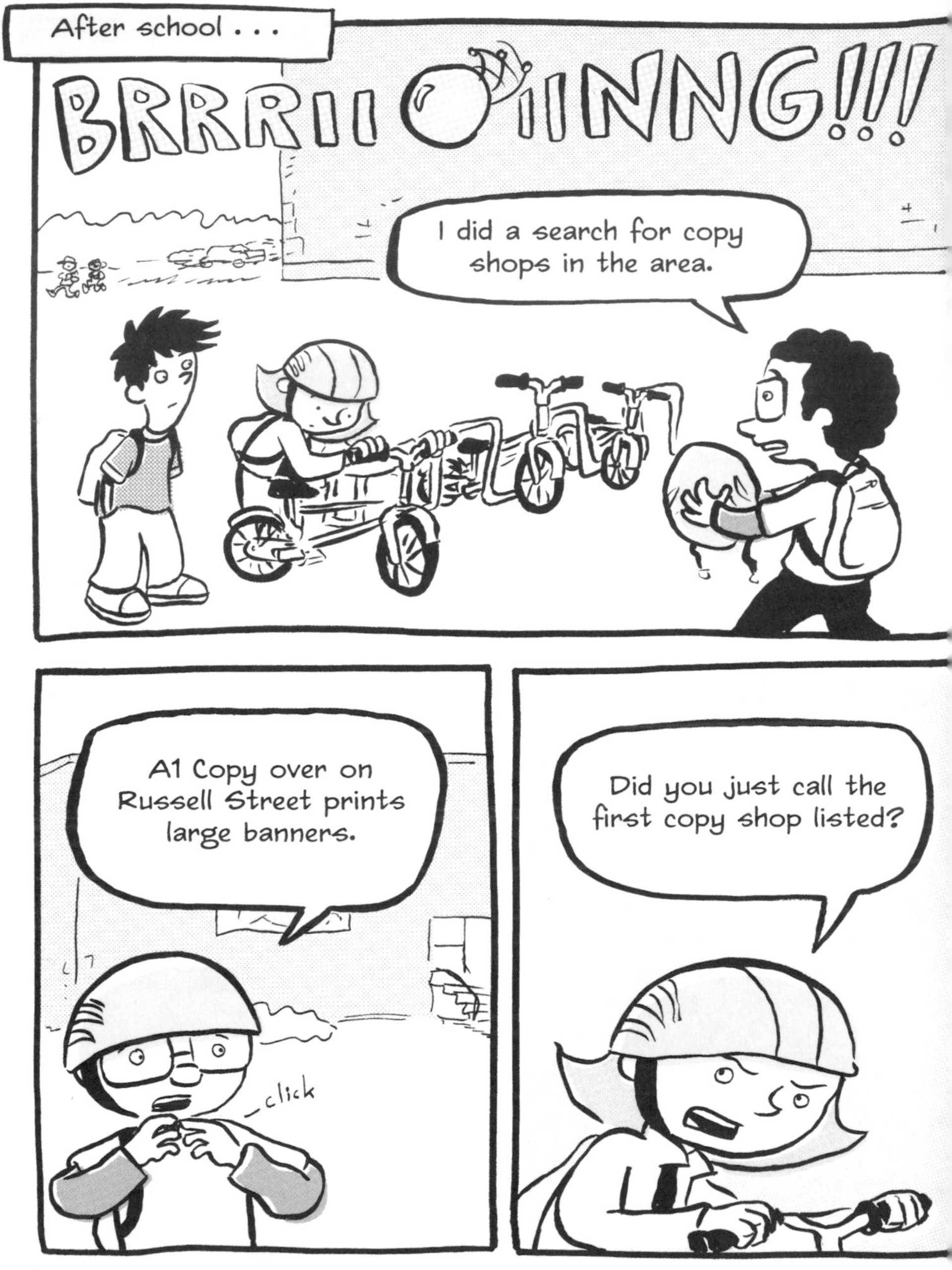
After school . . .
BRRRIIIIINNG!!!
I did a search for copy shops in the area.
A1 Copy over on Russell Street prints large banners.
click
Did you just call the first copy shop listed?

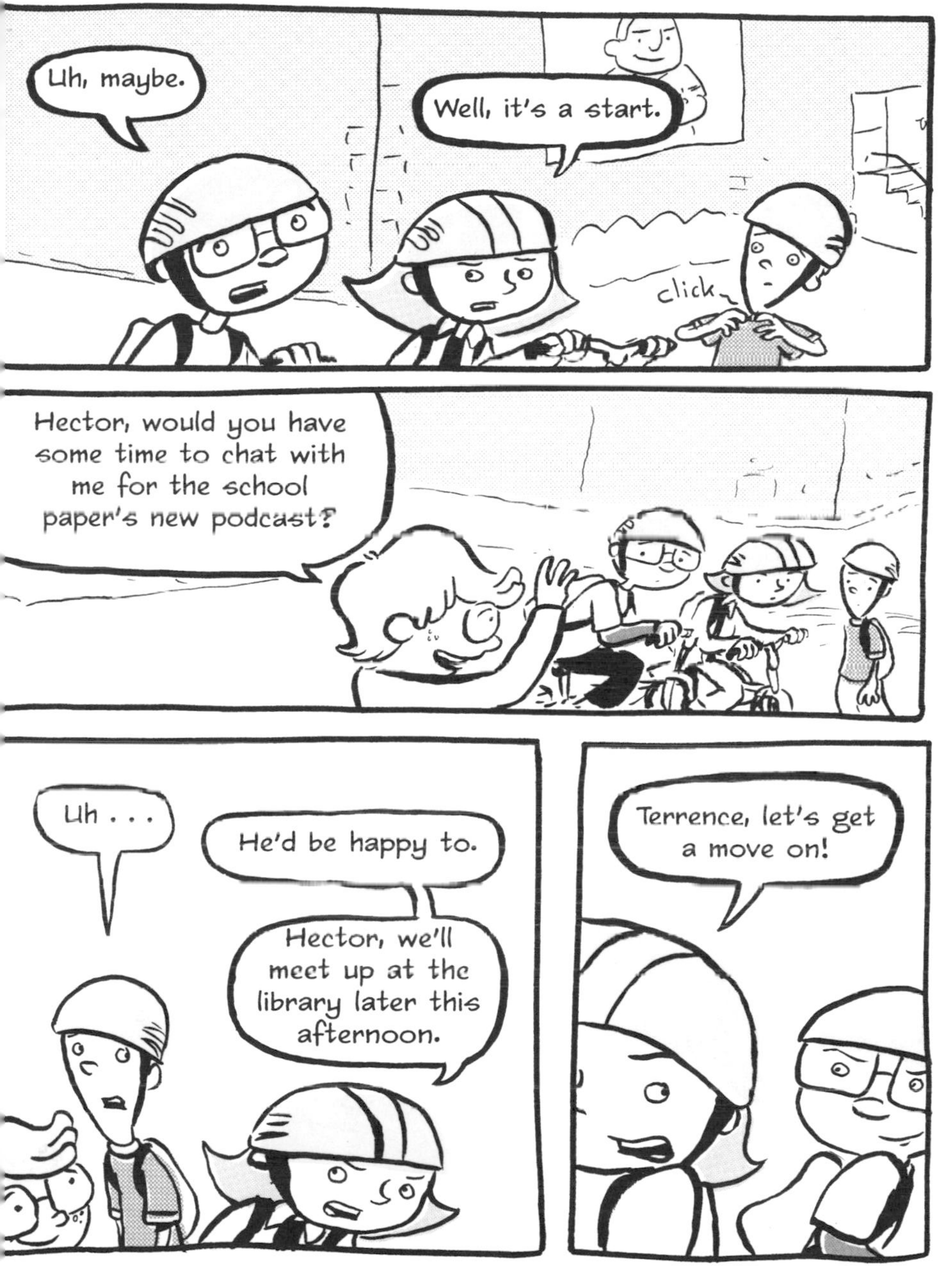
Uh, maybe.
Well, it's a start.
click
Hector, would you have some time to chat with me for the school paper's new podcast?
Uh . . .
He'd be happy to.
Hector, we'll meet up at the library later this afternoon.
Terrence, let's get a move on!

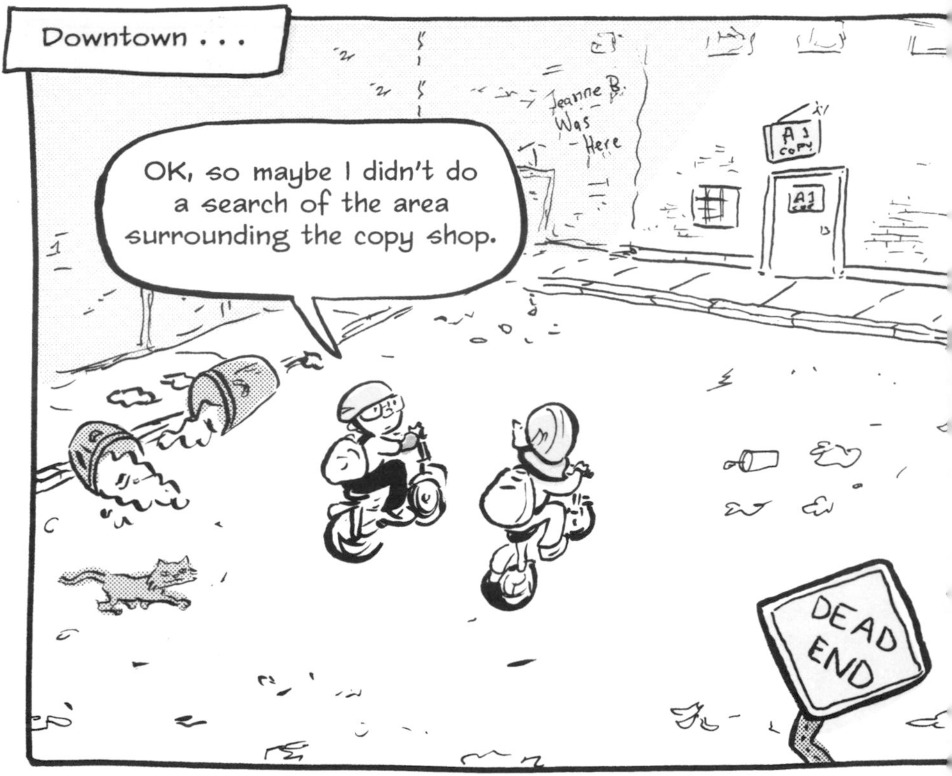
Downtown . . .
Jeanne B. Was Here
A1 COPY
OK, so maybe I didn't do a search of the area surrounding the copy shop.
DEAD END

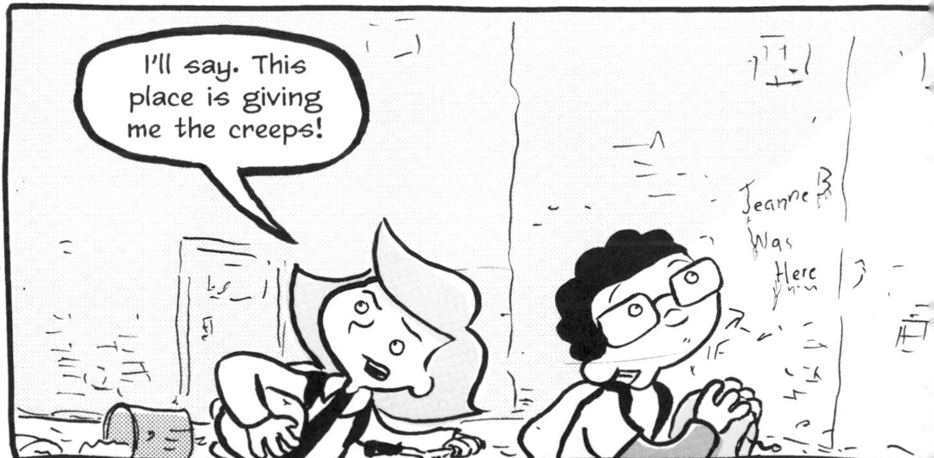
I'll say. This place is giving me the creeps!
Jeanne B. Was Here

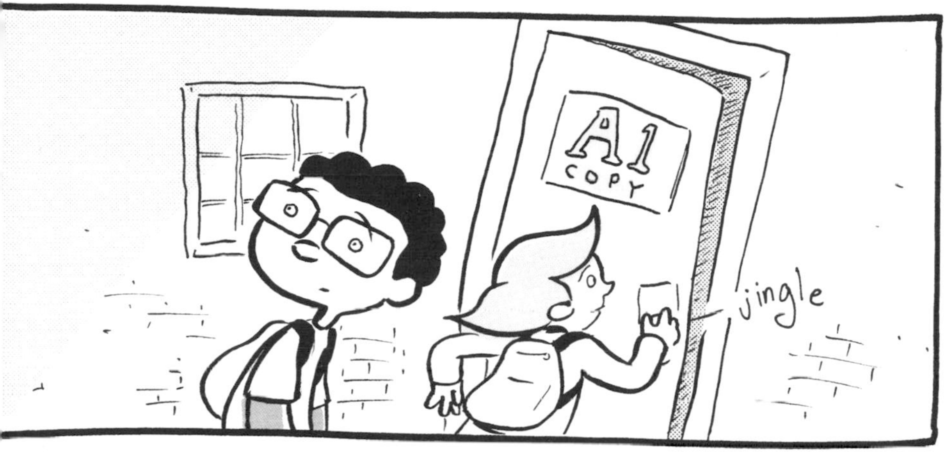
A1
COPY
jingle

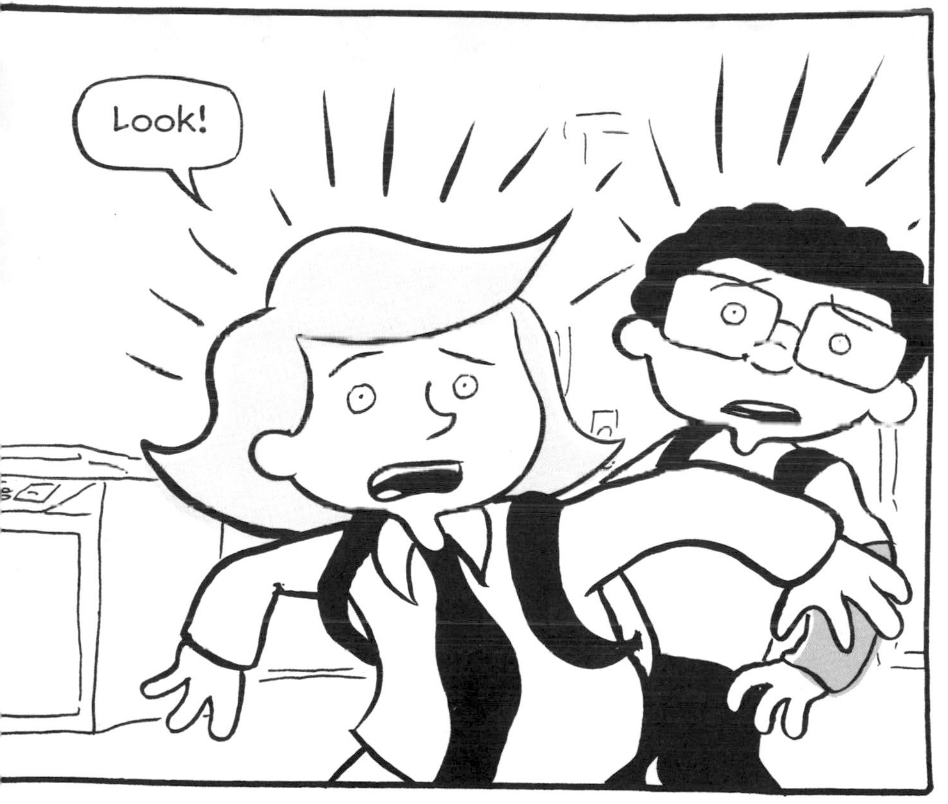
Look!

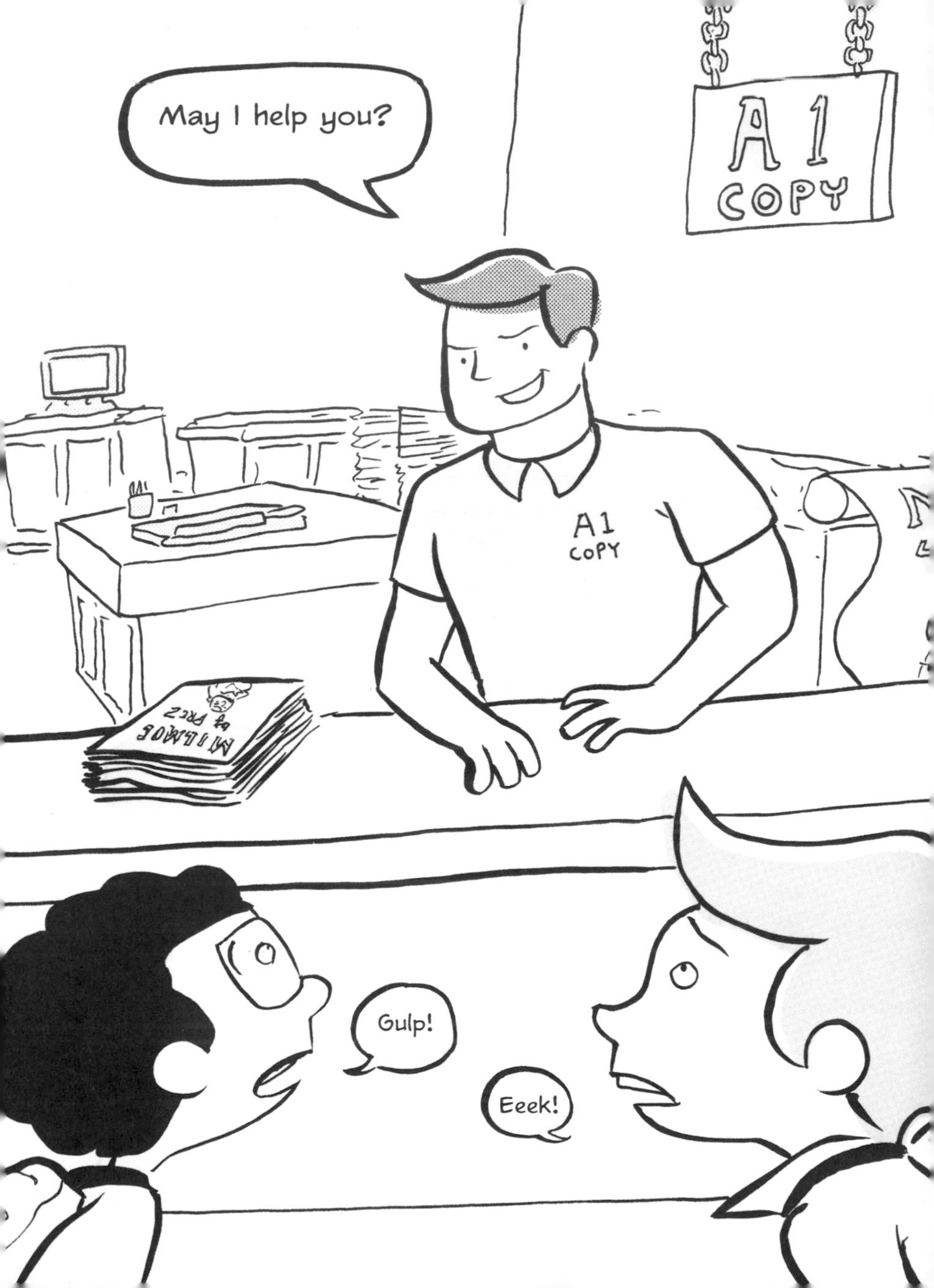
May I help you?
A1 COPY
A1 COPY
Gulp!
Eeek!

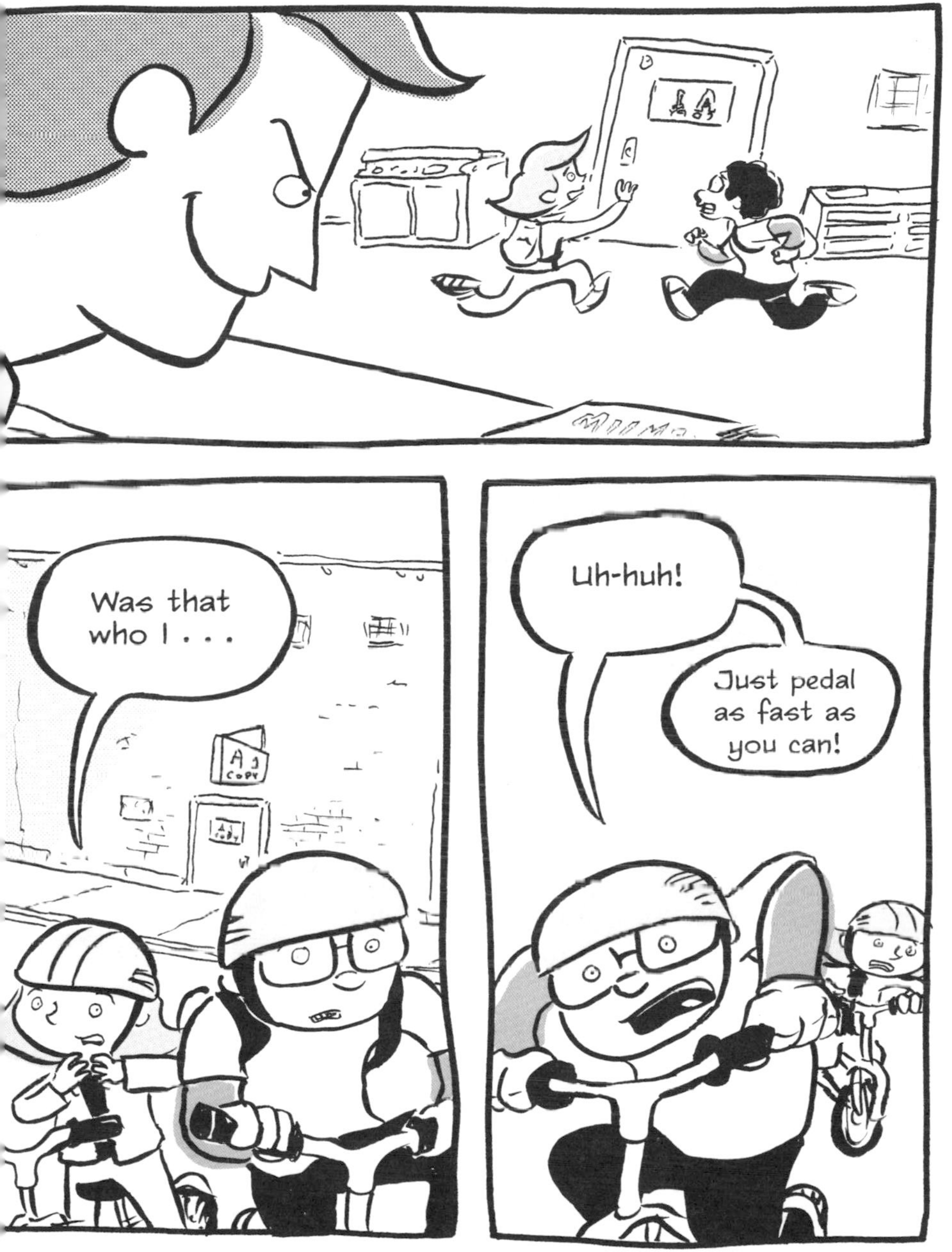
Was that who I . . .
Uh-huh!
Just pedal as fast as you can!

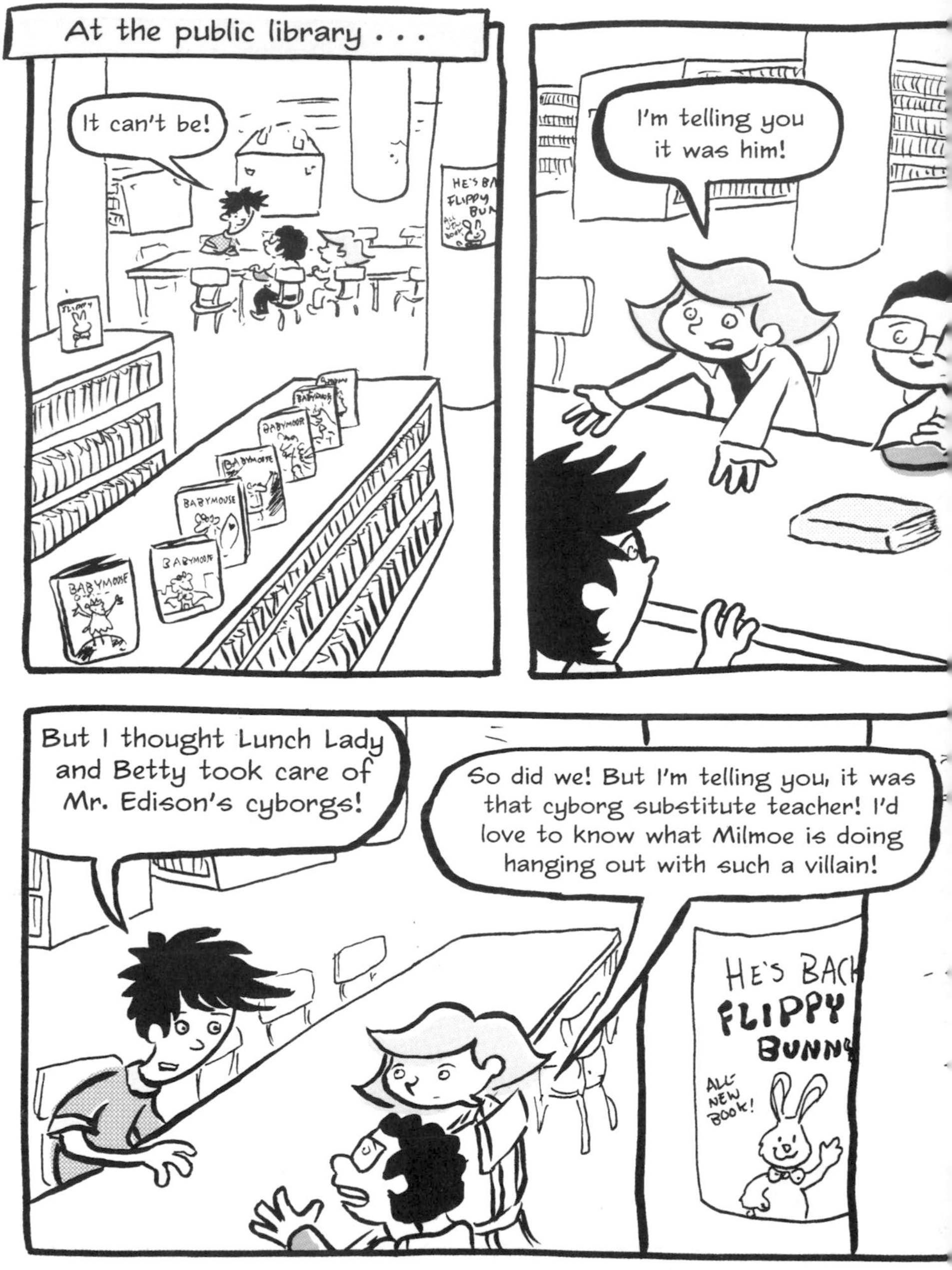
At the public library . . .
It can't be!
BABYMOUSE
I'm telling you it was him!
But I thought Lunch Lady and Betty took care of Mr. Edison's cyborgs!
So did we! But I'm telling you, it was that cyborg substitute teacher! I'd love to know what Milmoe is doing hanging out with such a villain!
HE'S BACK
FLIPPY
BUNN
ALL NEW BOOK!

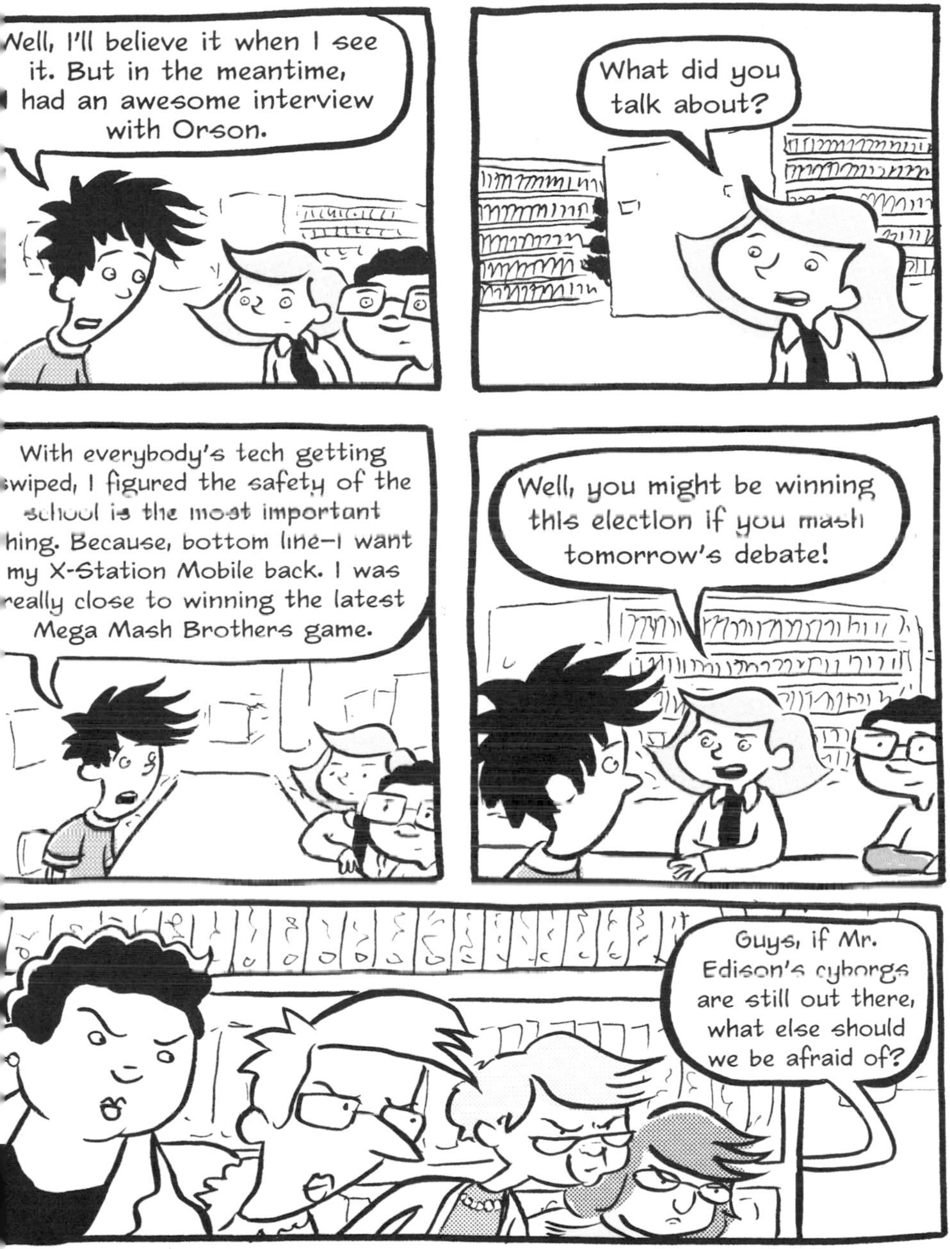
Nell, I'll believe it when I see it. But in the meantime, had an awesome interview with Orson.
What did you talk about?
With everybody's tech getting wiped, I figured the safety of the school is the most important hing. Because, bottom line—I want my X-Station Mobile back. I was eally close to winning the latest Mega Mash Brothers game.
Well, you might be winning this election if you mash tomorrow's debate!
Guys, if Mr. Edison's cyborgs are still out there, what else should we be afraid of?

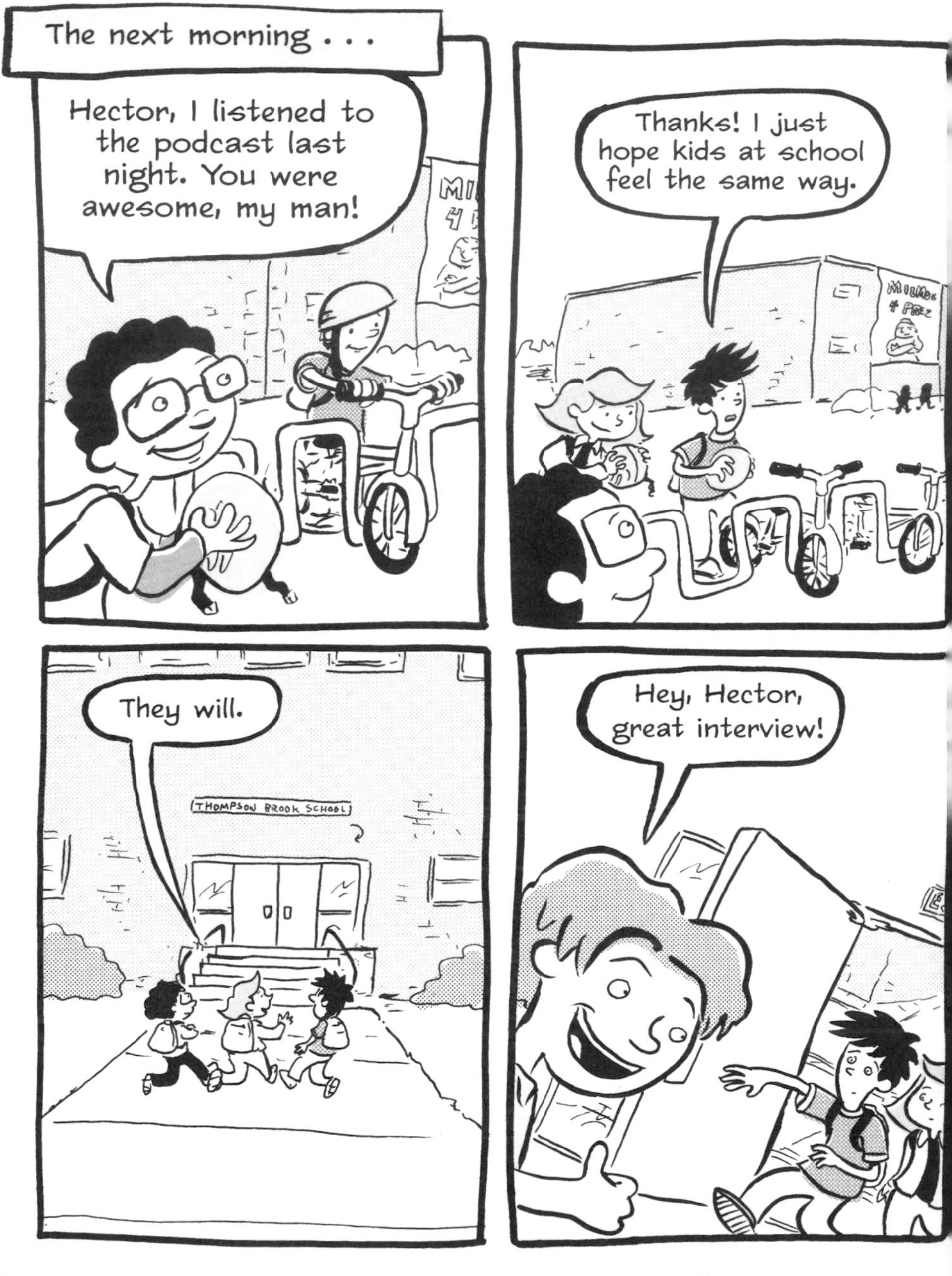

The next morning . . .
Hector, I listened to the podcast last night. You were awesome, my man!
Thanks! I just hope kids at school feel the same way.
They will.
THOMPSON BROOK SCHOOL
Hey, Hector, great interview!

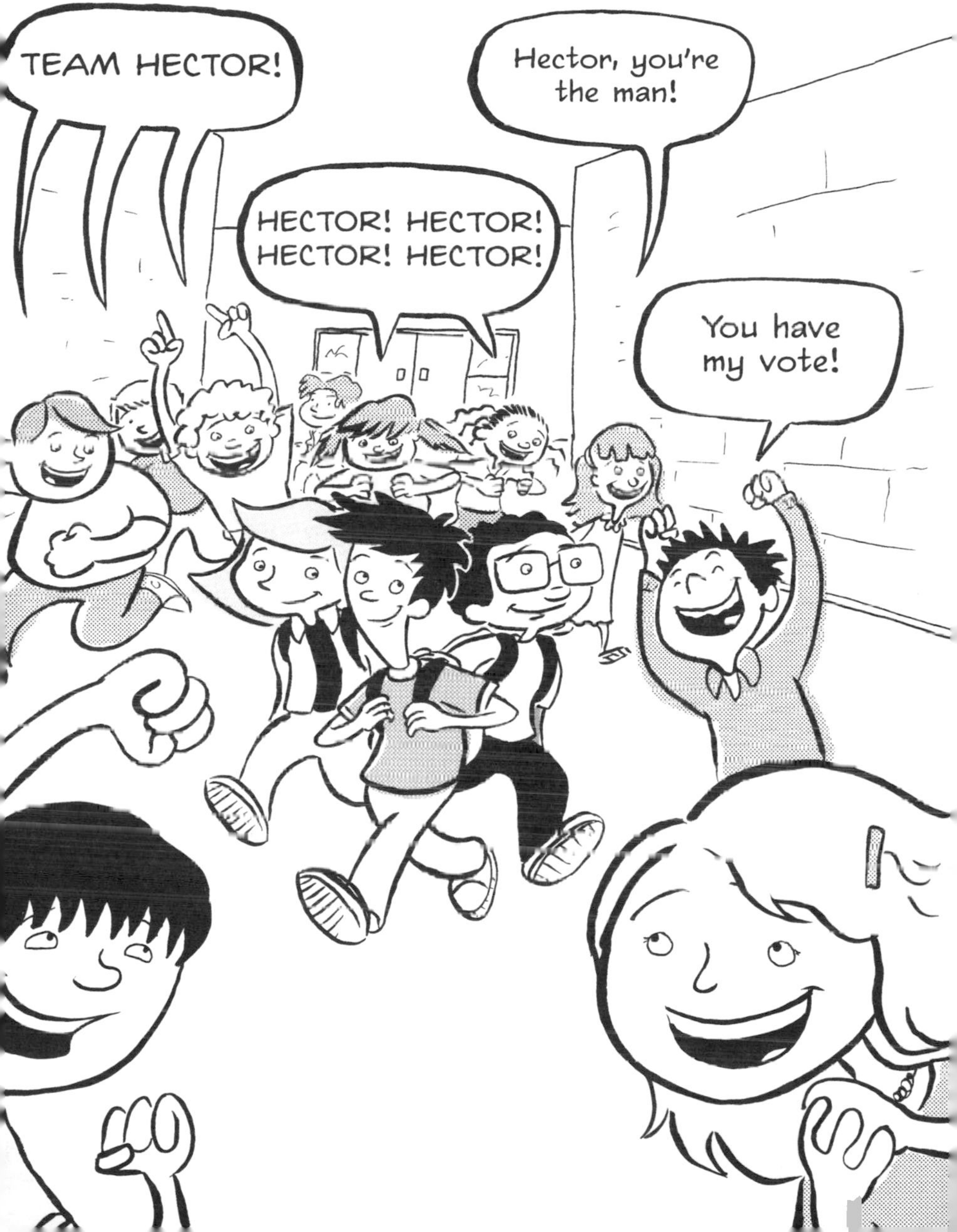
TEAM HECTOR!
HECTOR! HECTOR! HECTOR! HECTOR!
Hector, you're the man!
You have my vote!

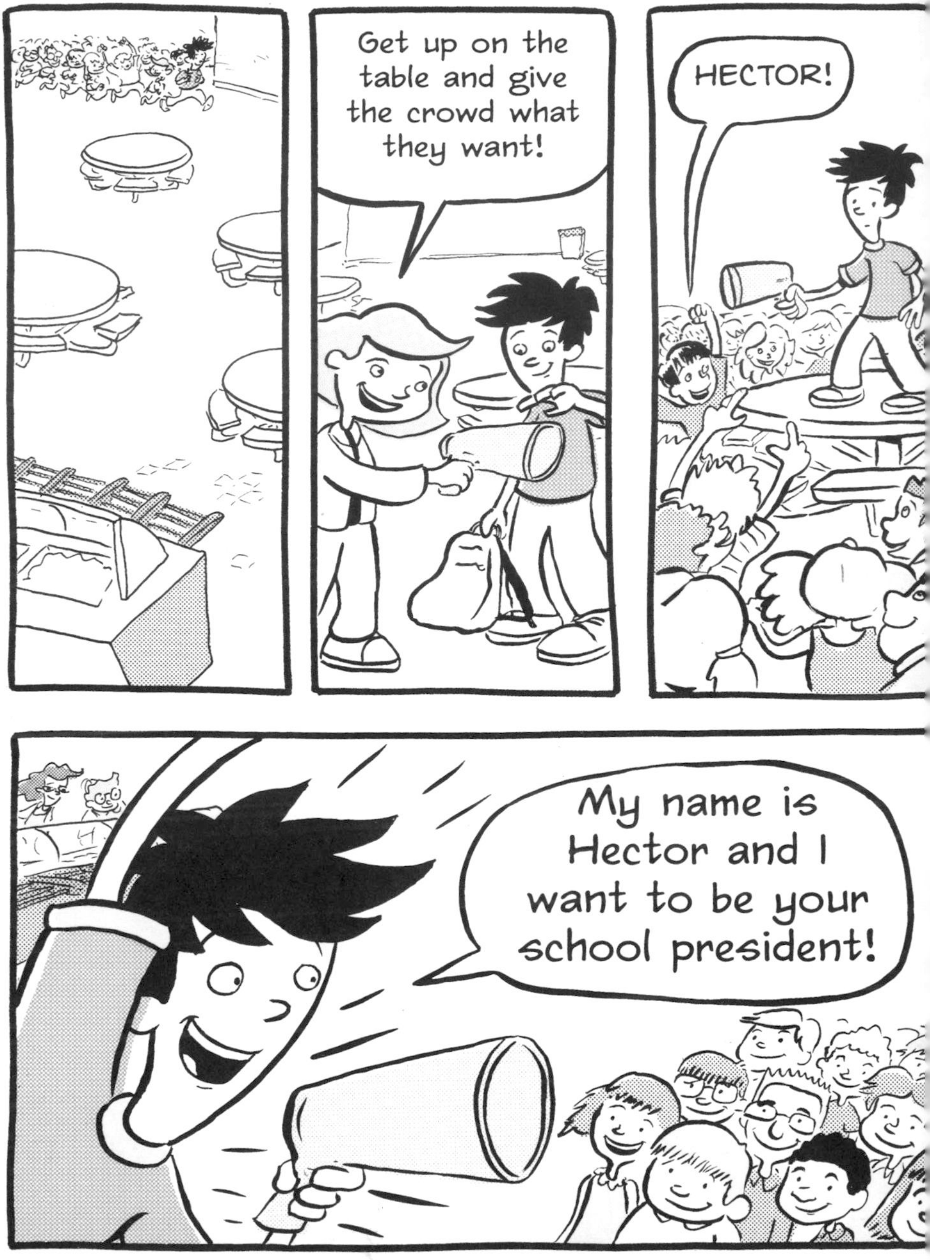
Get up on the table and give the crowd what they want!
HECTOR!
My name is Hector and I want to be your school president!

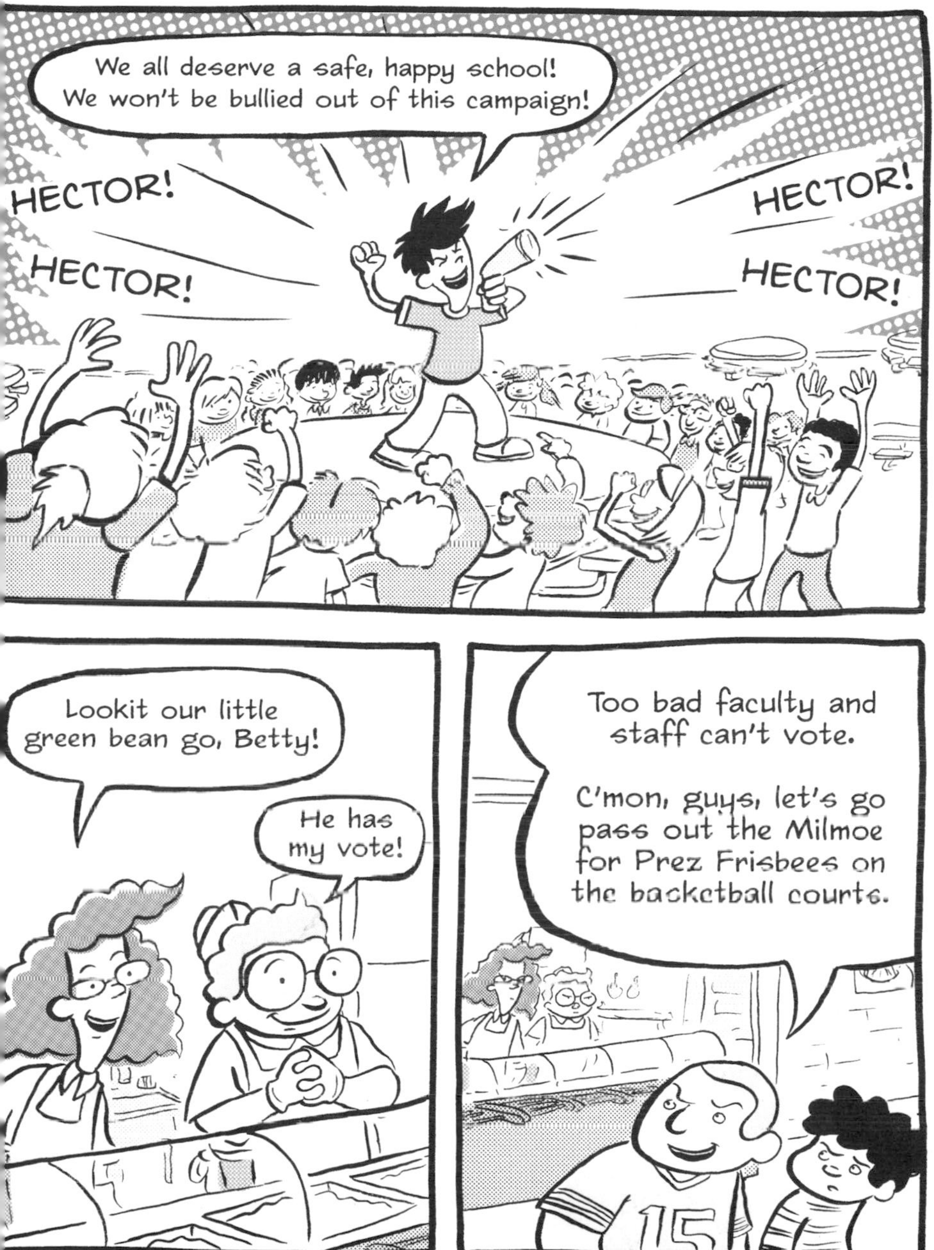
We all deserve a safe, happy school! We won't be bullied out of this campaign!
HECTOR!
HECTOR!
HECTOR!
HECTOR!
Lookit our little green bean go, Betty!
He has my vote!
Too bad faculty and staff can't vote.
C'mon, guys, let's go pass out the Milmoe for Prez Frisbees on the basketball courts.

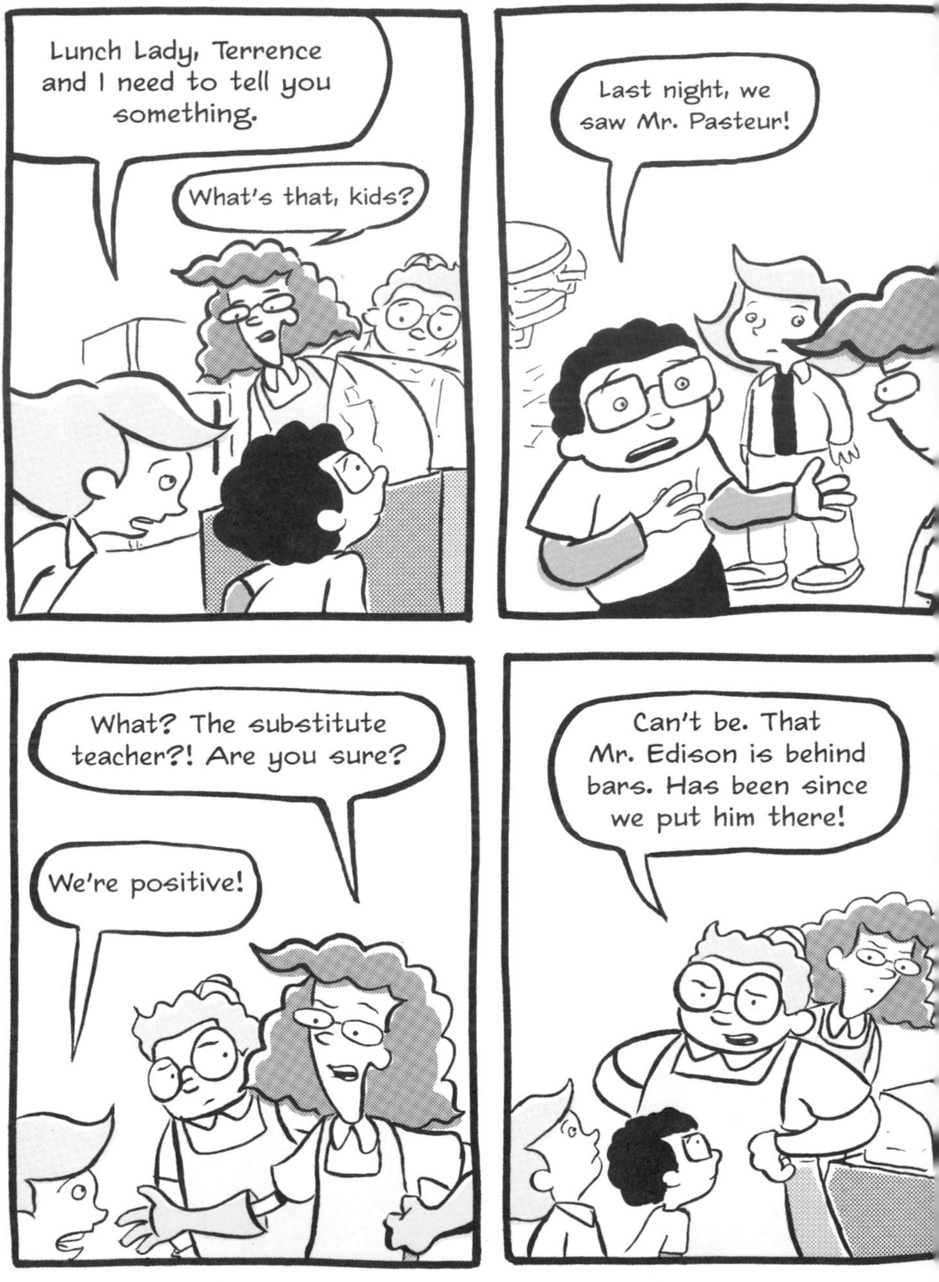
Lunch Lady, Terrence and I need to tell you something.
What's that, kids?
Last night, we saw Mr. Pasteur!
What? The substitute teacher?! Are you sure?
We're positive!
Can't be. That Mr. Edison is behind bars. Has been since we put him there!

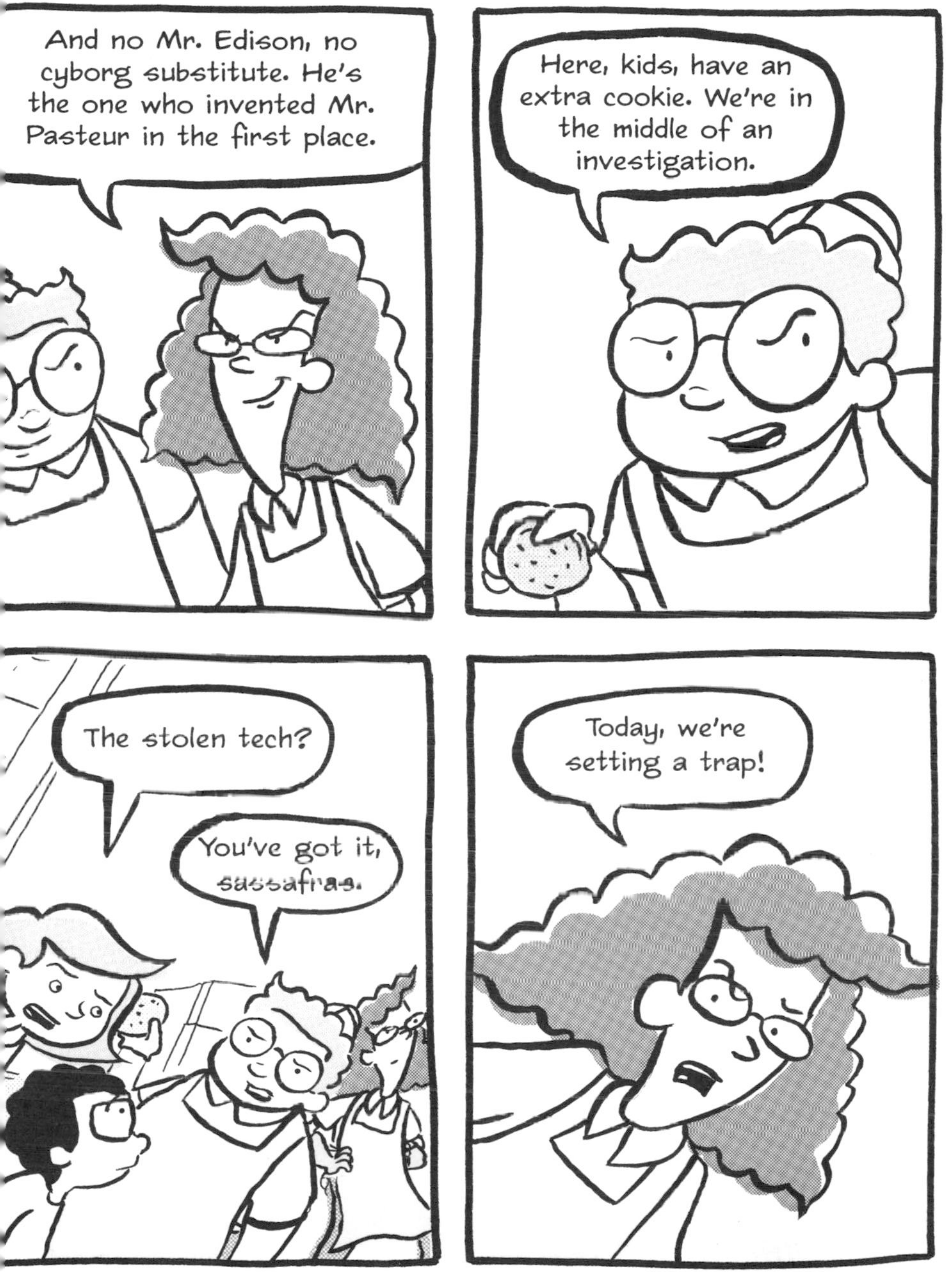
And no Mr. Edison, no cyborg substitute. He's the one who invented Mr. Pasteur in the first place.
Here, kids, have an extra cookie. We're in the middle of an investigation.
The stolen tech?
You've got it, sassafras.
Today, we're setting a trap!

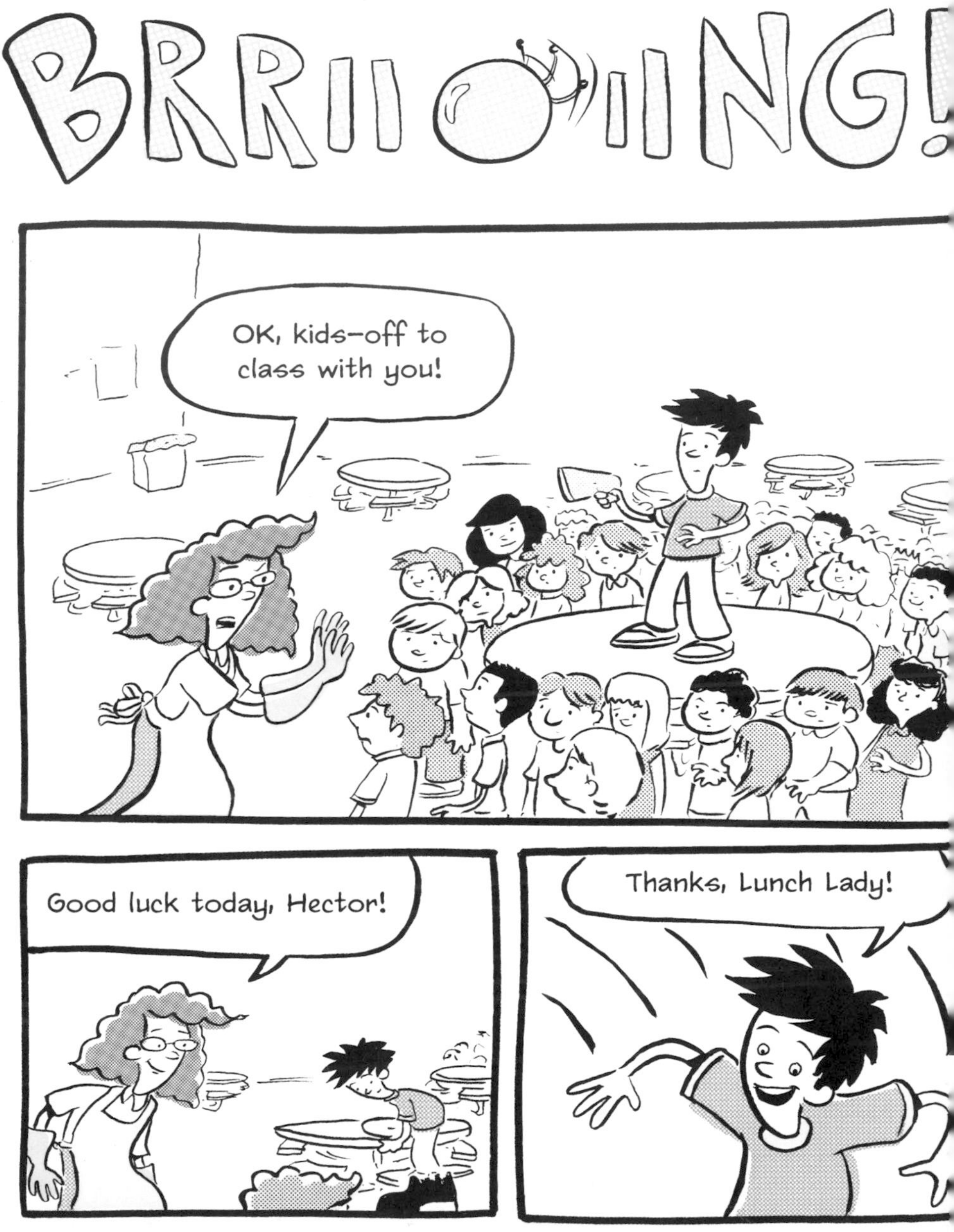
BRRIIIING!
OK, kids–off to class with you!
Good luck today, Hector!
Thanks, Lunch Lady!

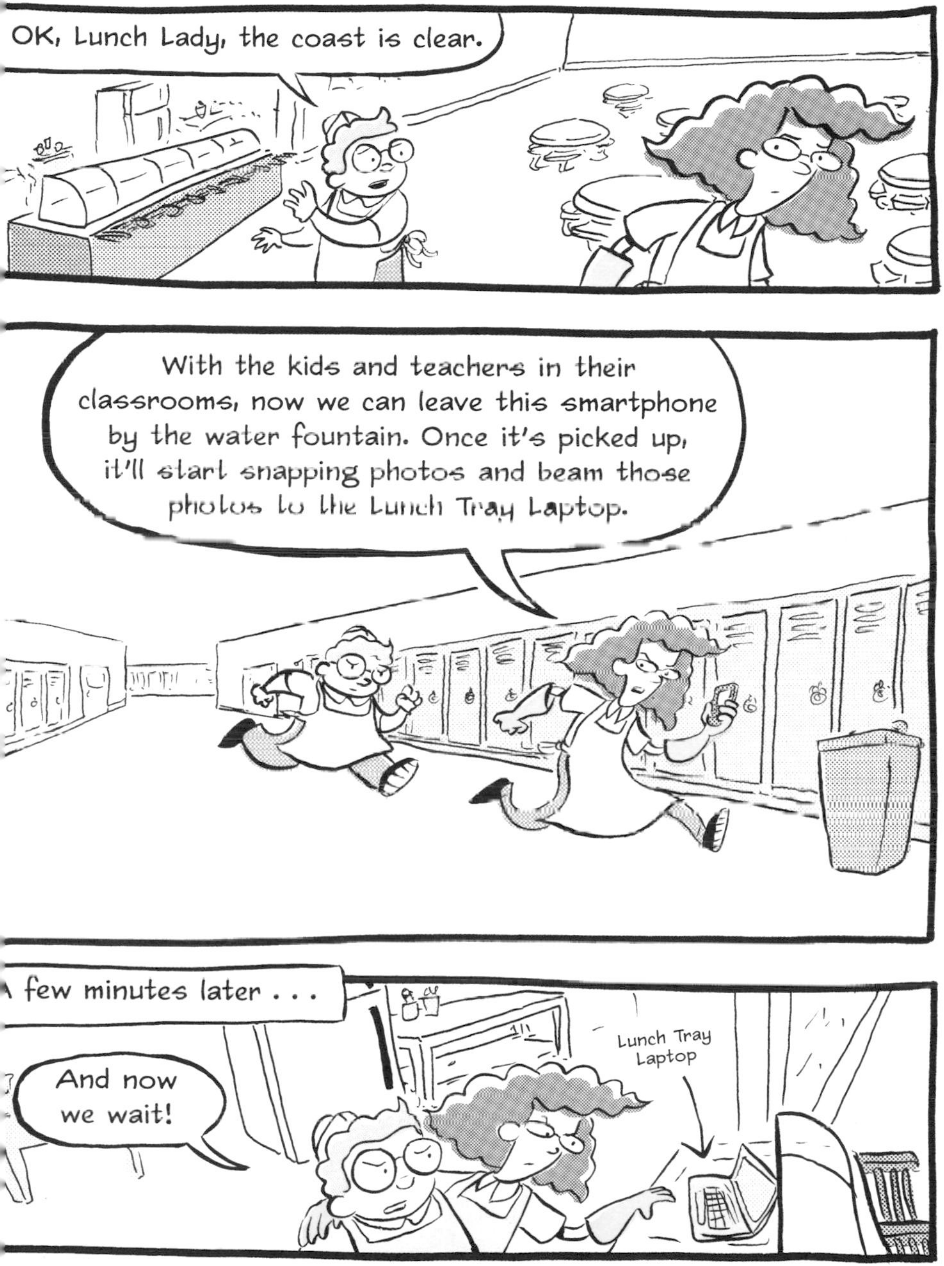
OK, Lunch Lady, the coast is clear.
With the kids and teachers in their classrooms, now we can leave this smartphone by the water fountain. Once it's picked up, it'll start snapping photos and beam those photos to the Lunch Tray Laptop.
A few minutes later . . .
And now we wait!
Lunch Tray Laptop

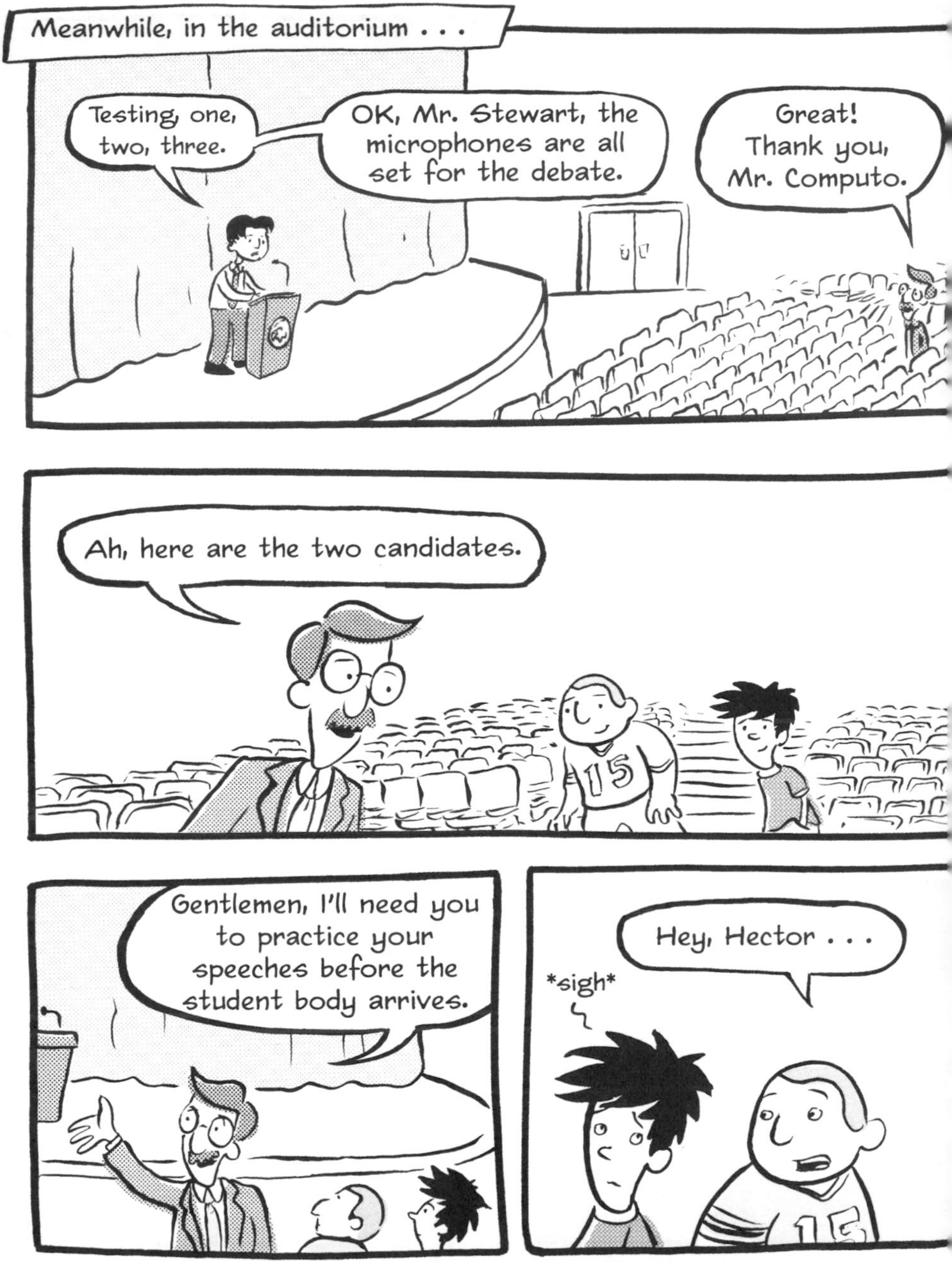
Meanwhile, in the auditorium . . .
Testing, one, two, three.
OK, Mr. Stewart, the microphones are all set for the debate.
Great! Thank you, Mr. Computo.
Ah, here are the two candidates.
Gentlemen, I'll need you to practice your speeches before the student body arrives.
Hey, Hector . . .
sigh

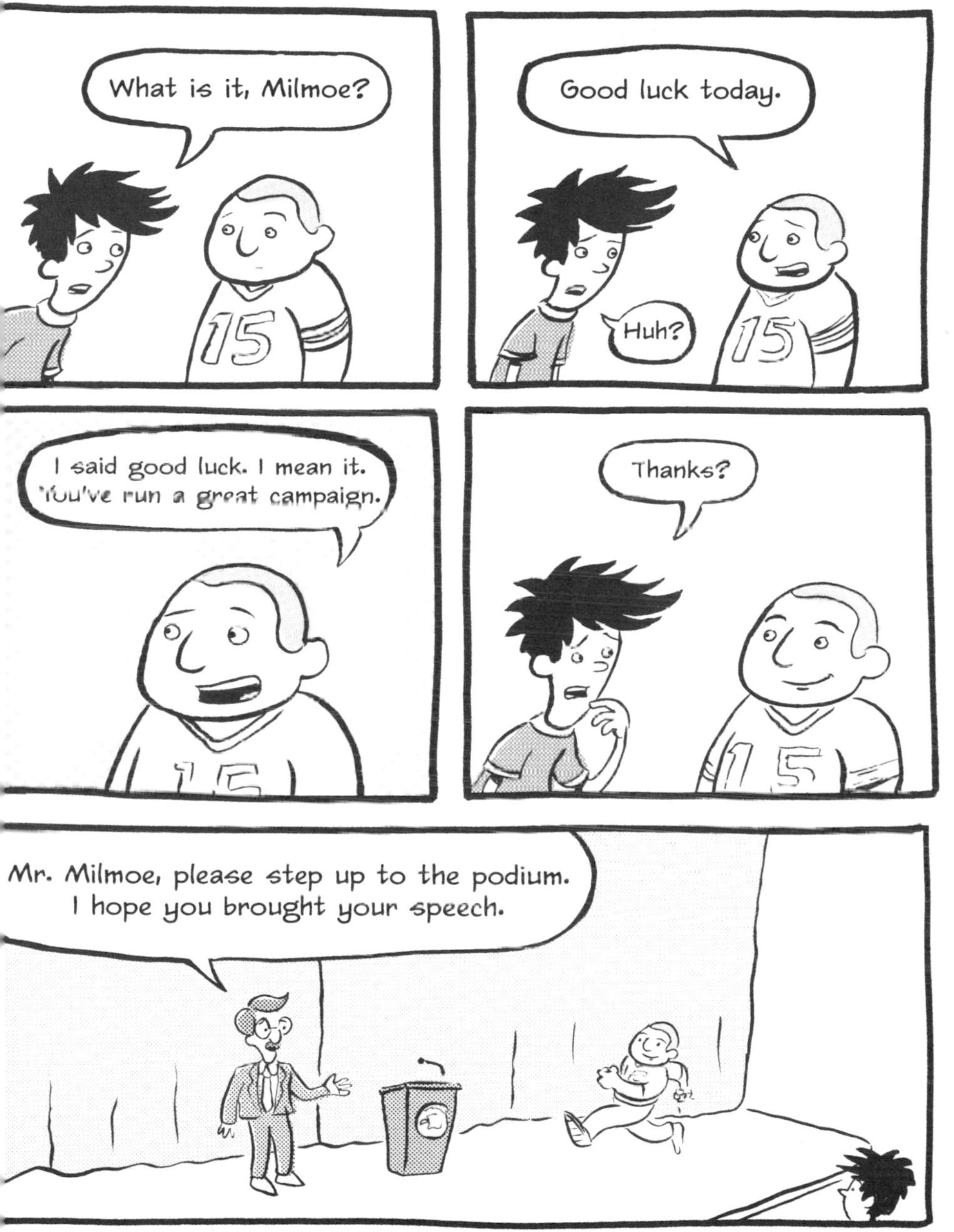
What is it, Milmoe?
Good luck today.
Huh?
I said good luck. I mean it. You've run a great campaign.
Thanks?
Mr. Milmoe, please step up to the podium. I hope you brought your speech.

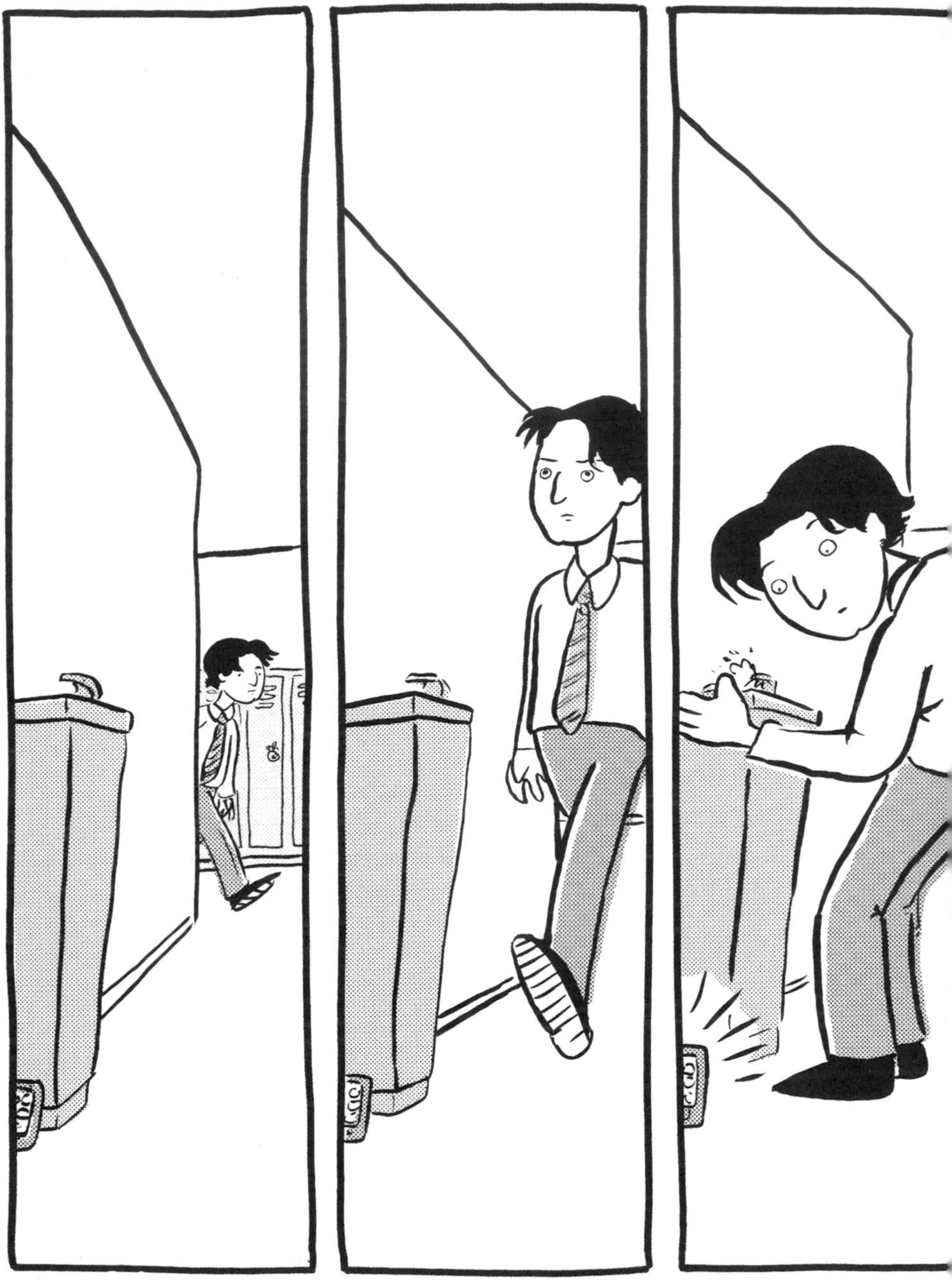

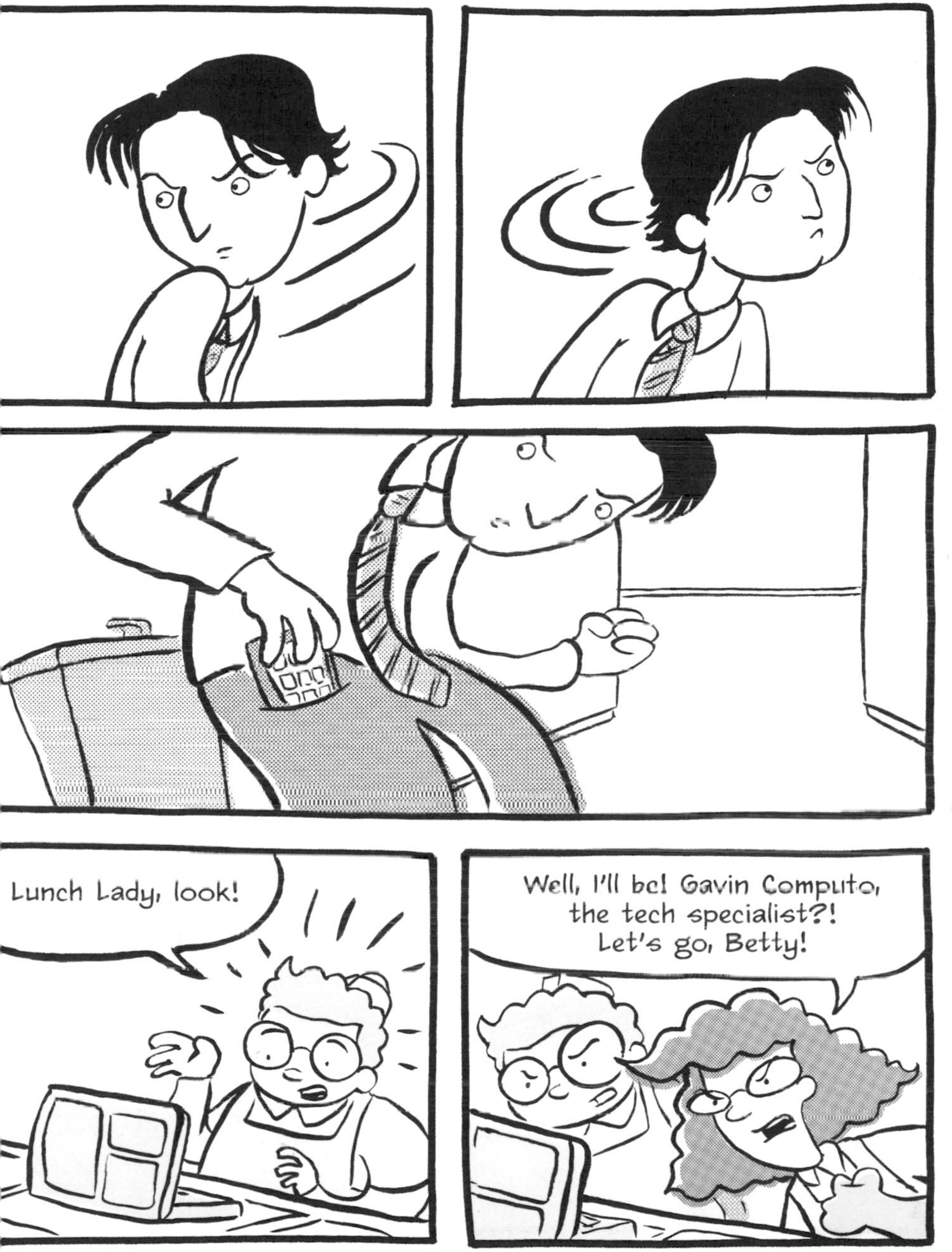
Lunch Lady, look!
Well, I'll be! Gavin Computo, the tech specialist?! Let's go, Betty!

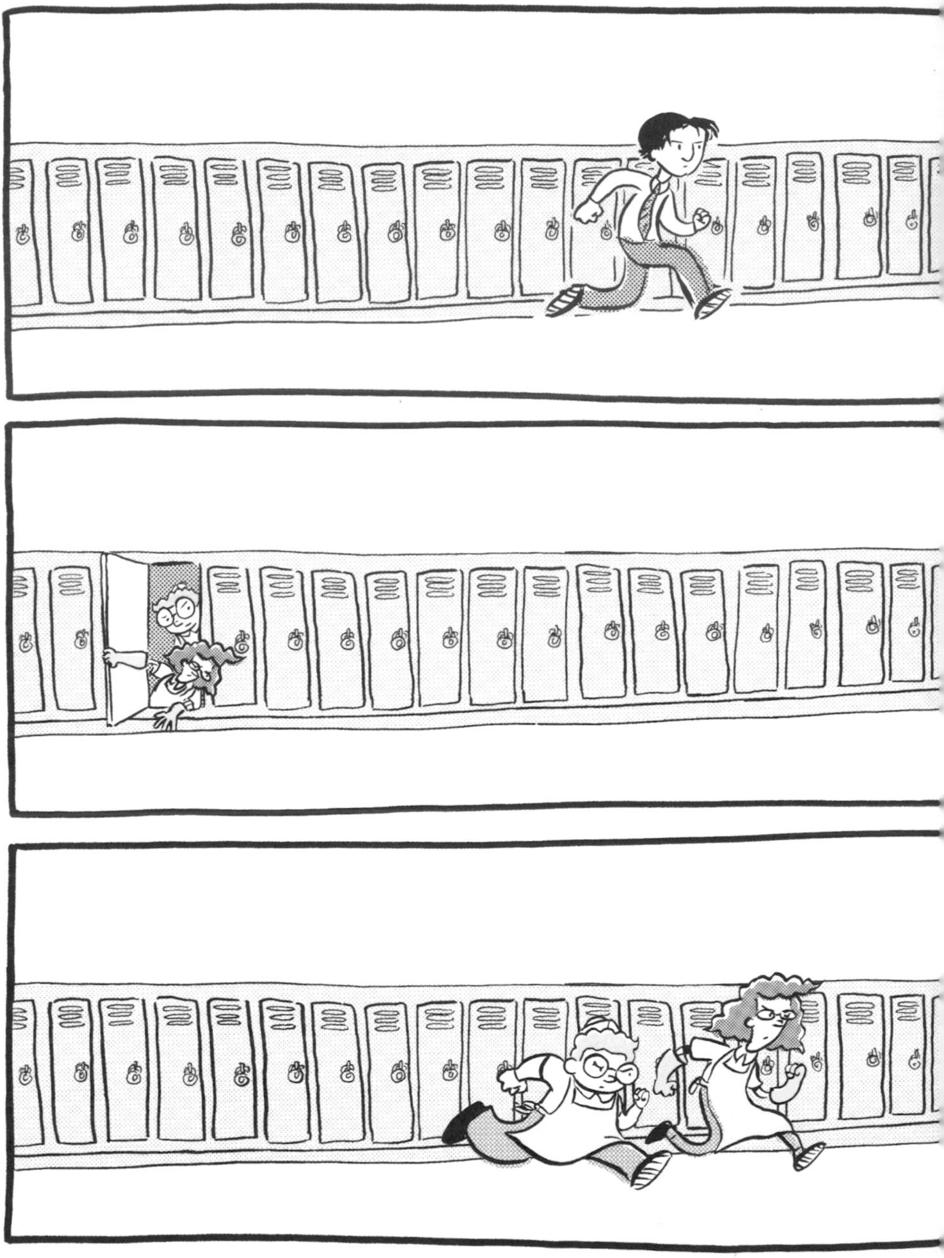

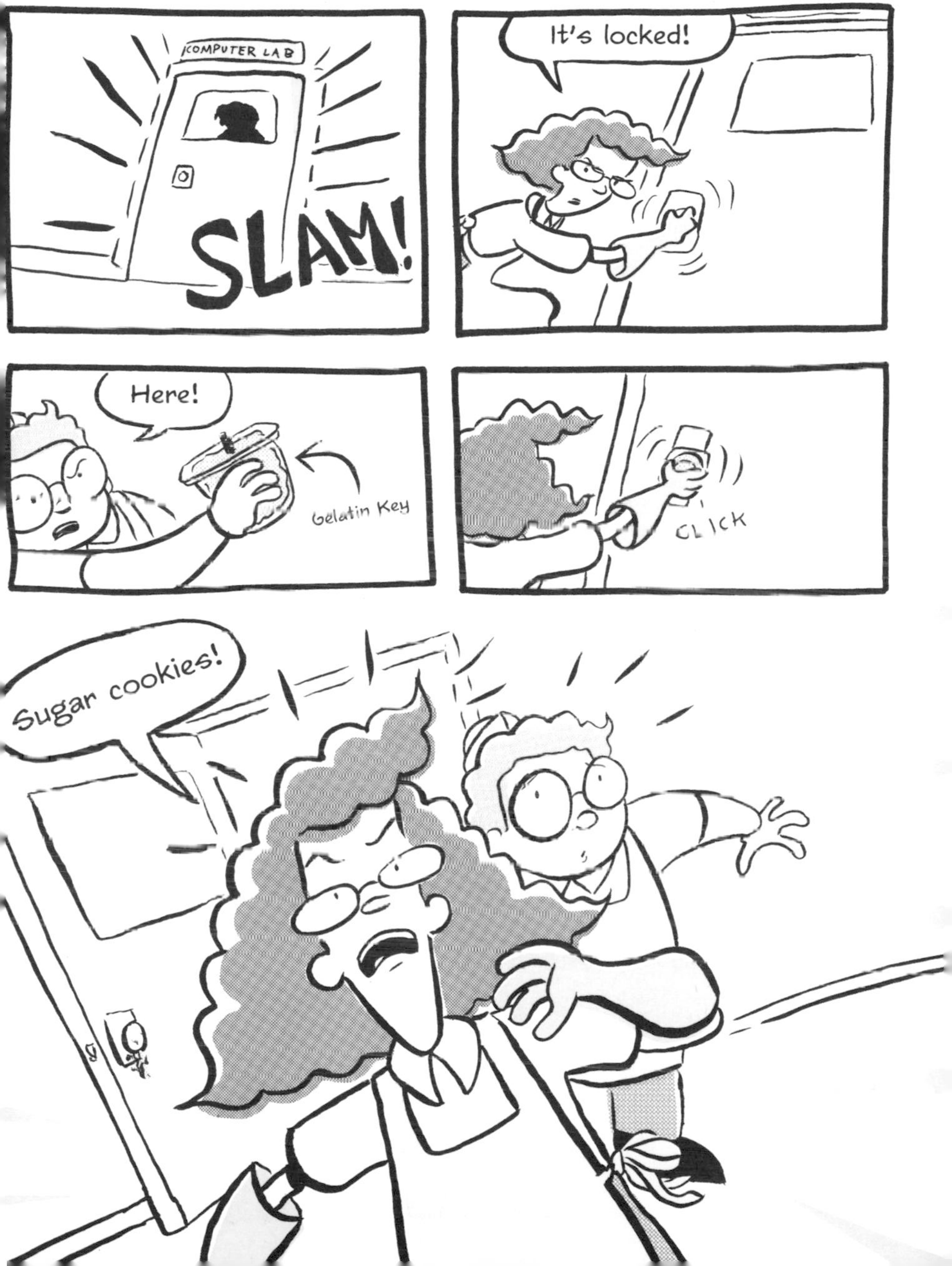
COMPUTER LAB
SLAM!
It's locked!
Here!
Gelatin Key
CLICK
Sugar cookies!

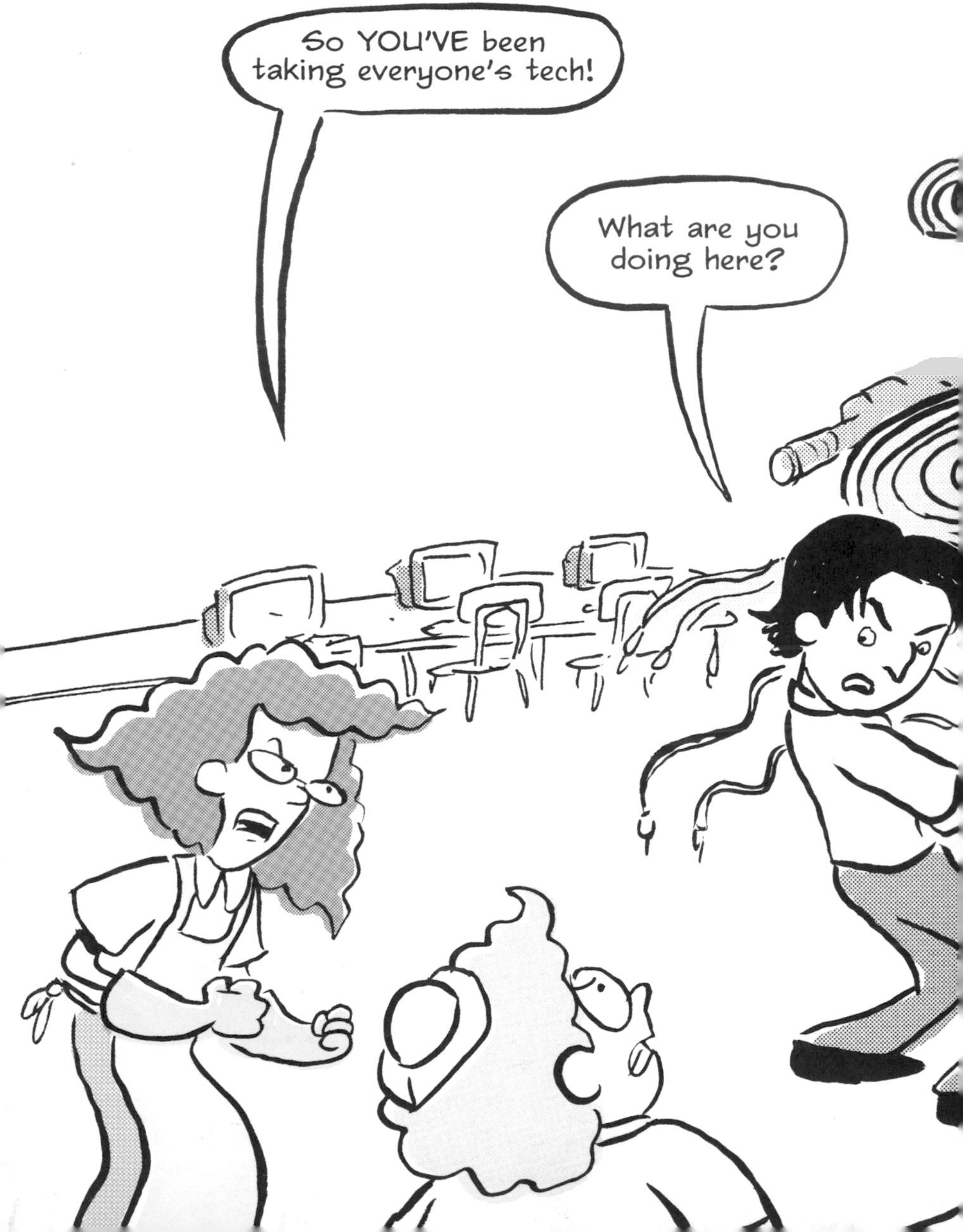
So YOU'VE been taking everyone's tech!
What are you doing here?

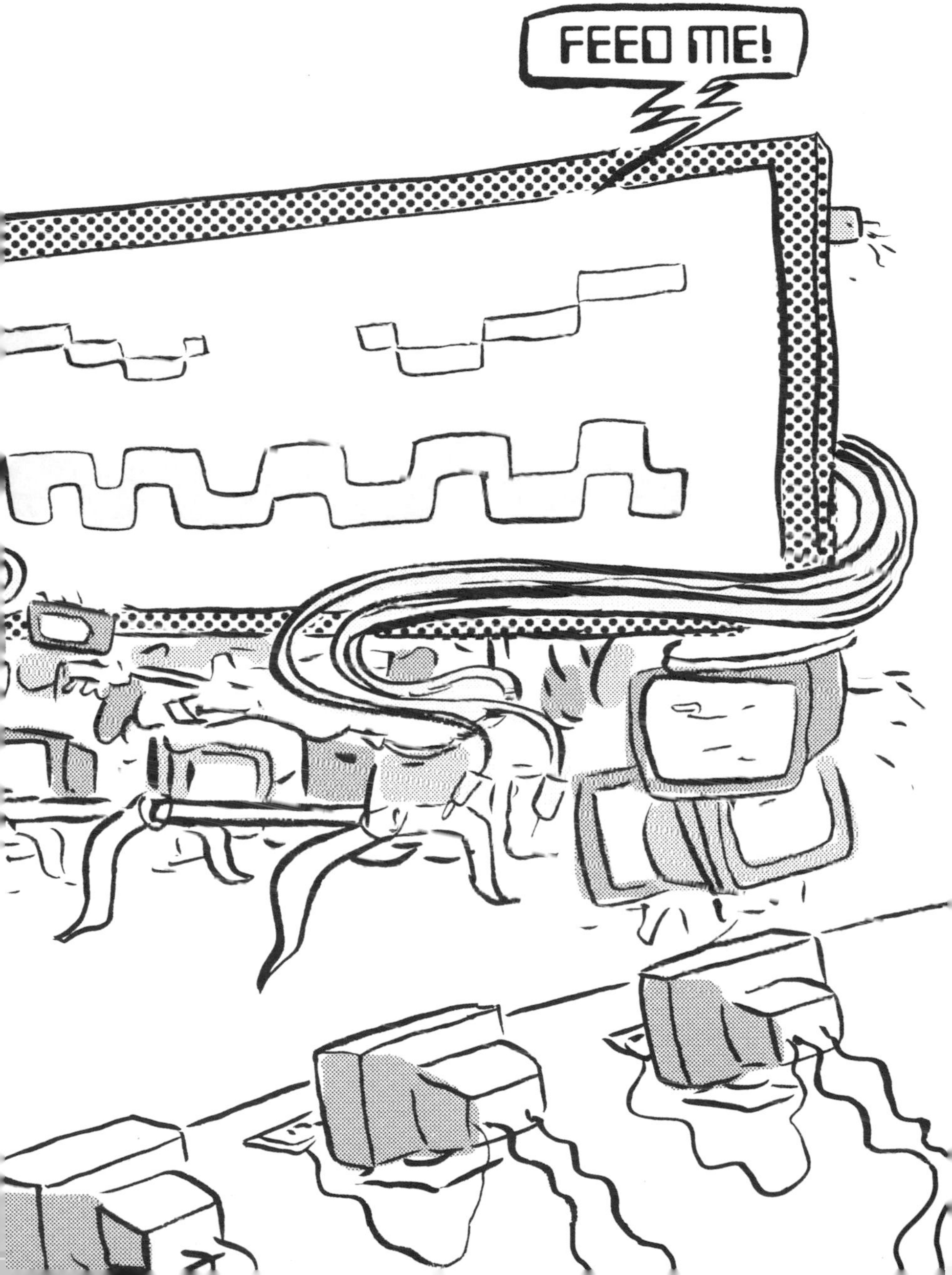
FEED ME!

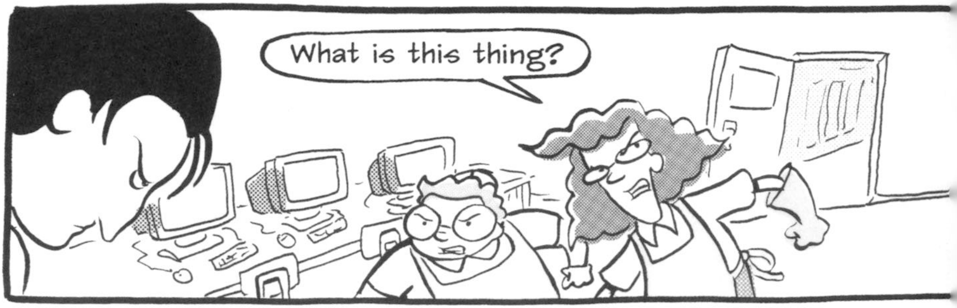
What is this thing?

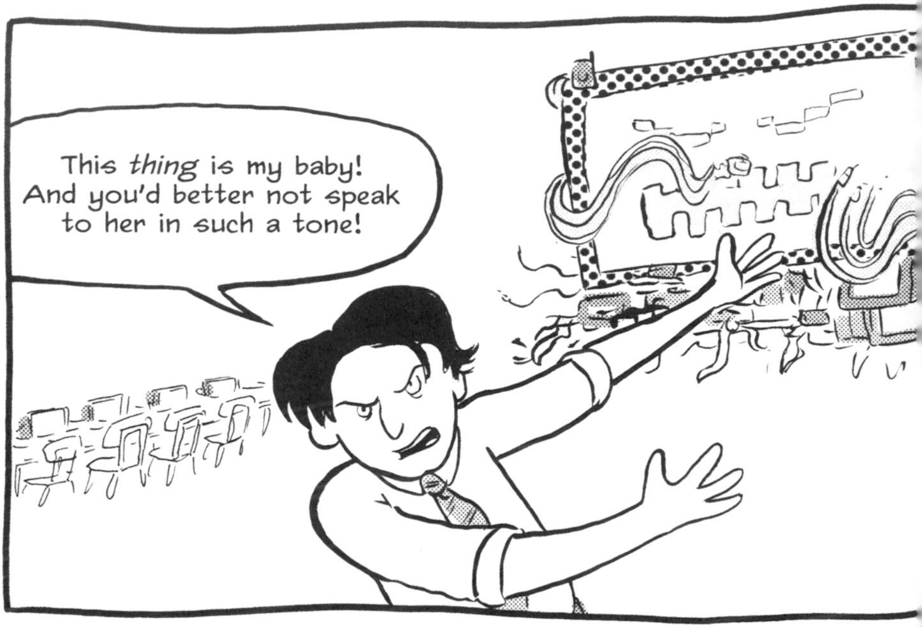
This *thing* is my baby! And you'd better not speak to her in such a tone!

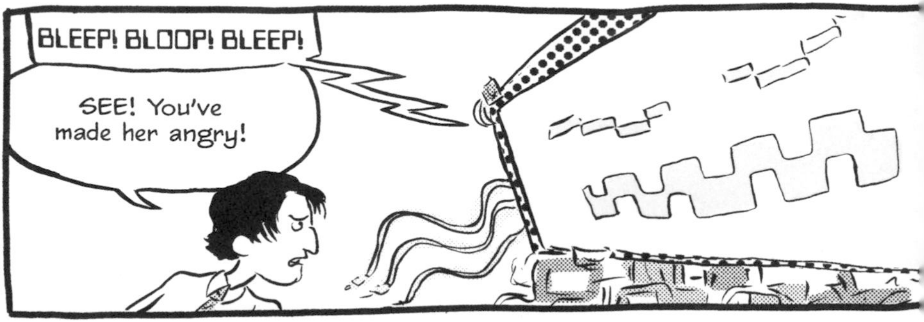
BLEEP! BLOOP! BLEEP!
SEE! You've made her angry!

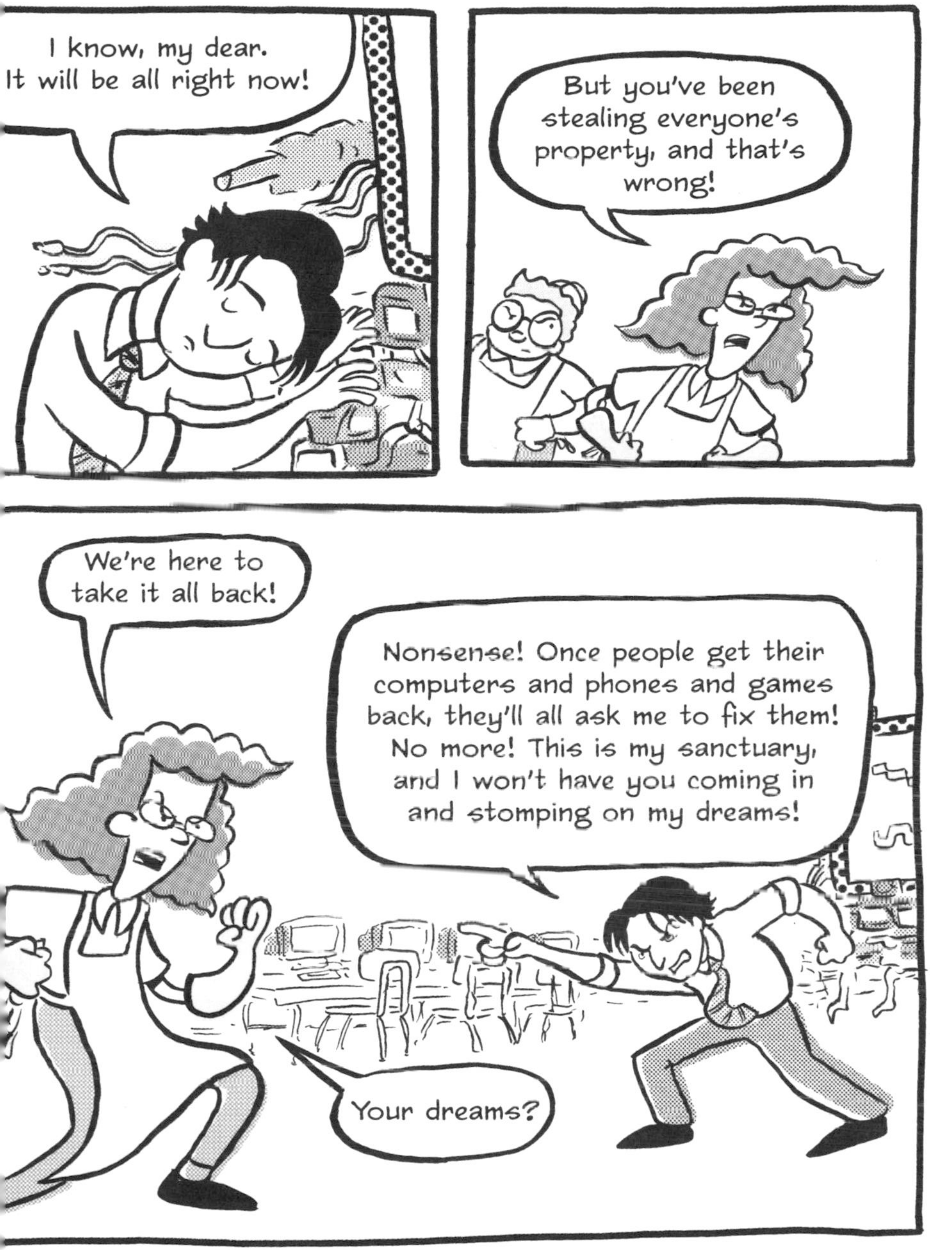
I know, my dear. It will be all right now!
But you've been stealing everyone's property, and that's wrong!
We're here to take it all back!
Nonsense! Once people get their computers and phones and games back, they'll all ask me to fix them! No more! This is my sanctuary, and I won't have you coming in and stomping on my dreams!
Your dreams?

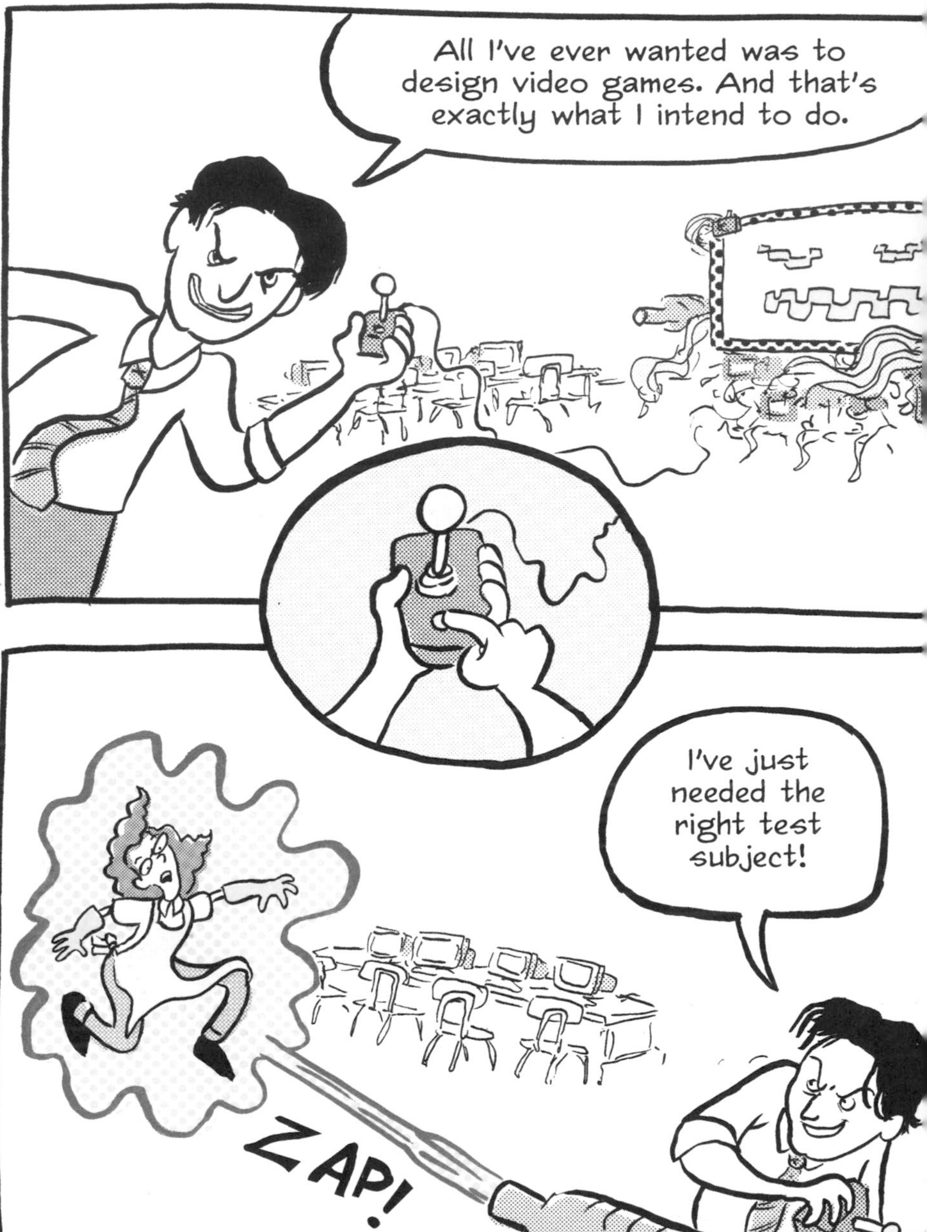
All I've ever wanted was to design video games. And that's exactly what I intend to do.
I've just needed the right test subject!
ZAP!

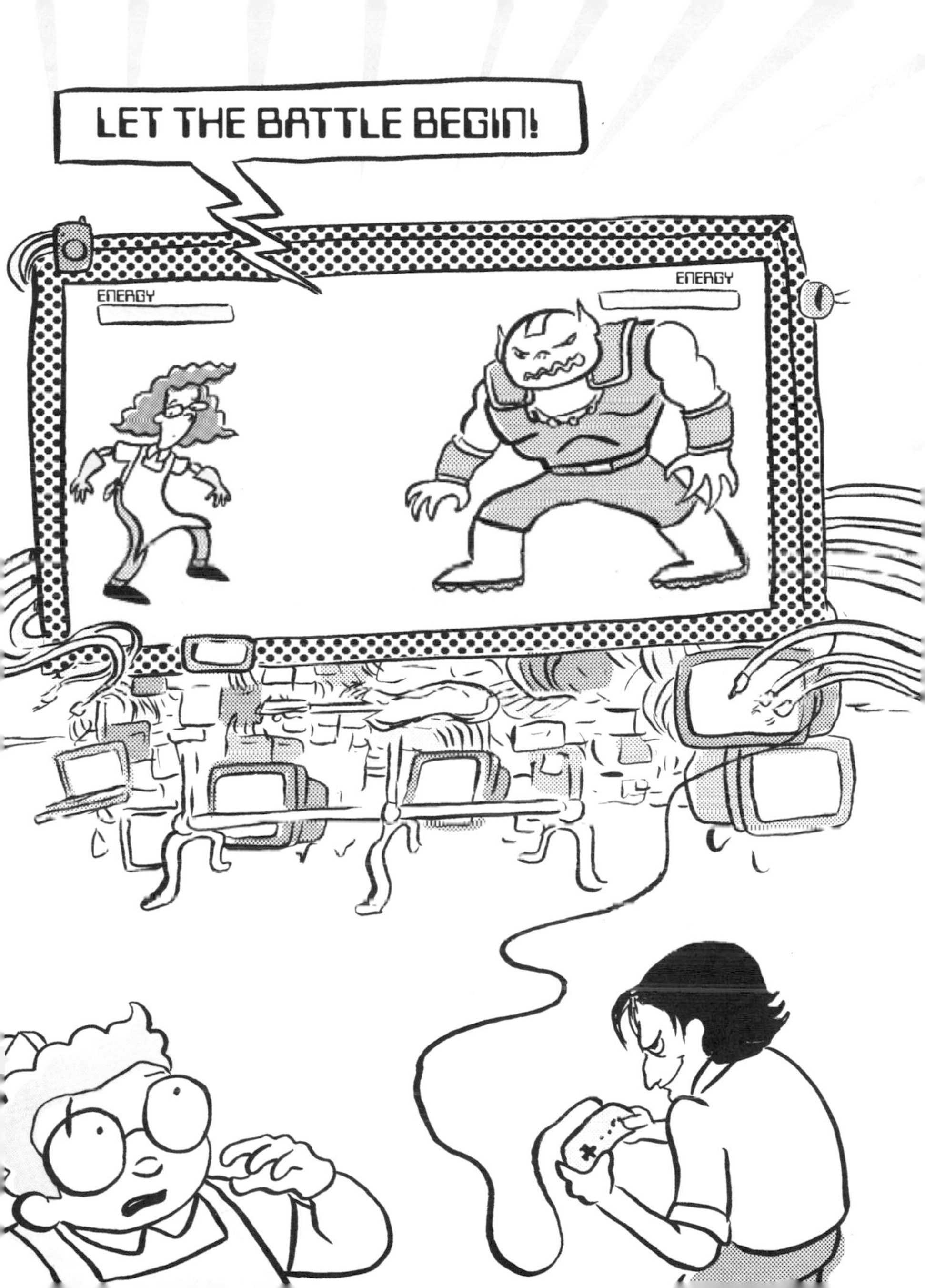
LET THE BATTLE BEGIN!
ENERGY
ENERGY

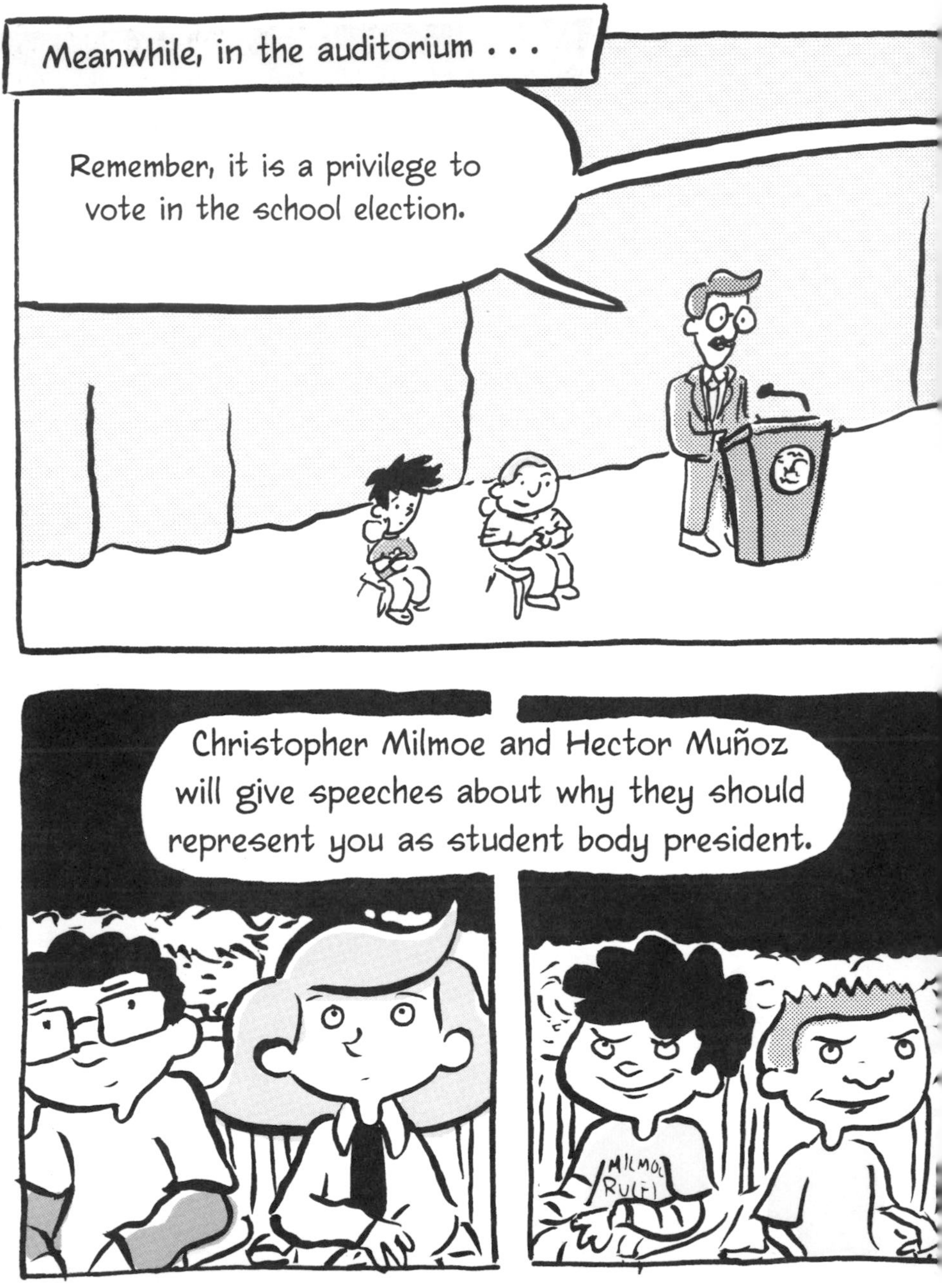
Meanwhile, in the auditorium . . .
Remember, it is a privilege to vote in the school election.
Christopher Milmoe and Hector Muñoz will give speeches about why they should represent you as student body president.

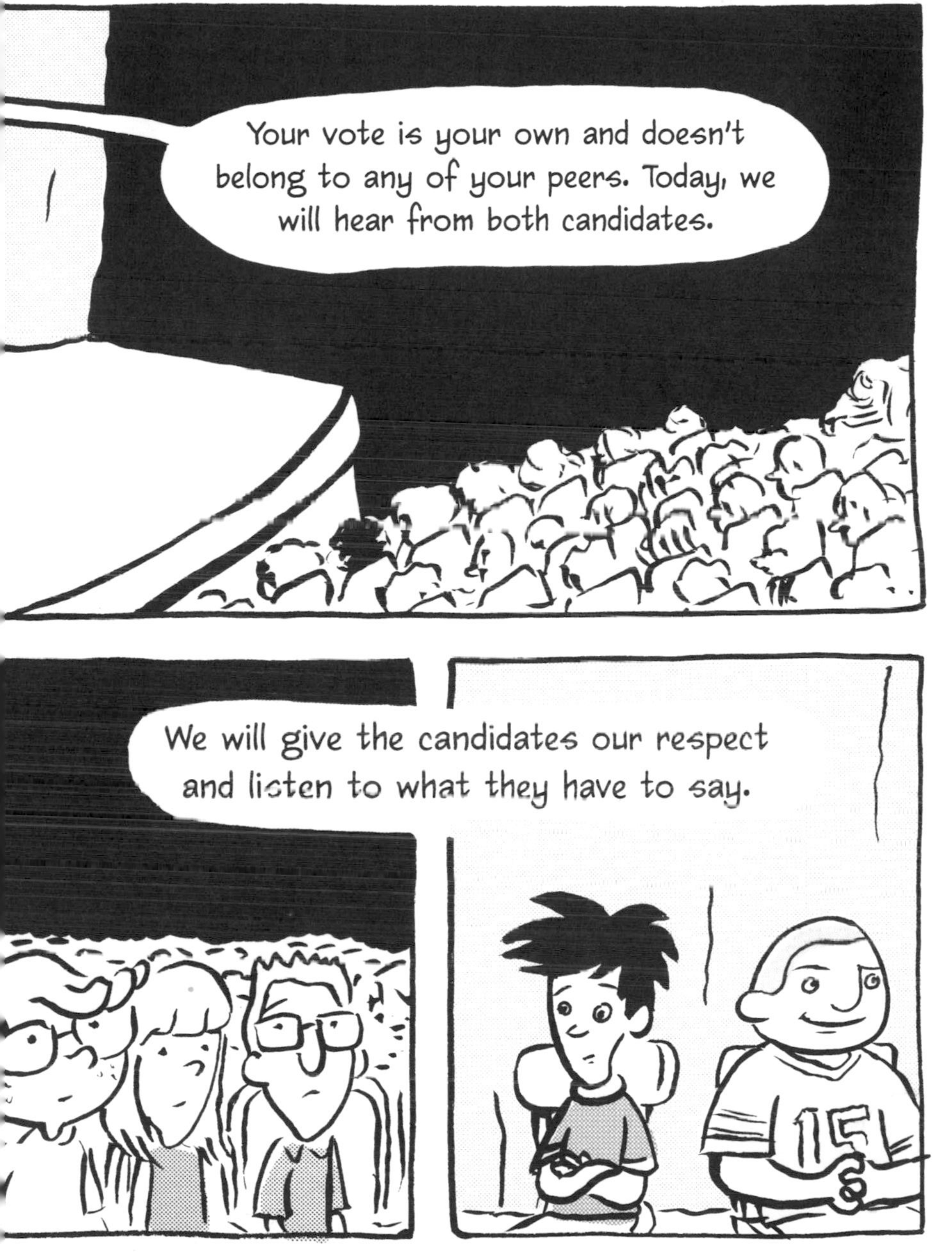
Your vote is your own and doesn't belong to any of your peers. Today, we will hear from both candidates.
We will give the candidates our respect and listen to what they have to say.
15

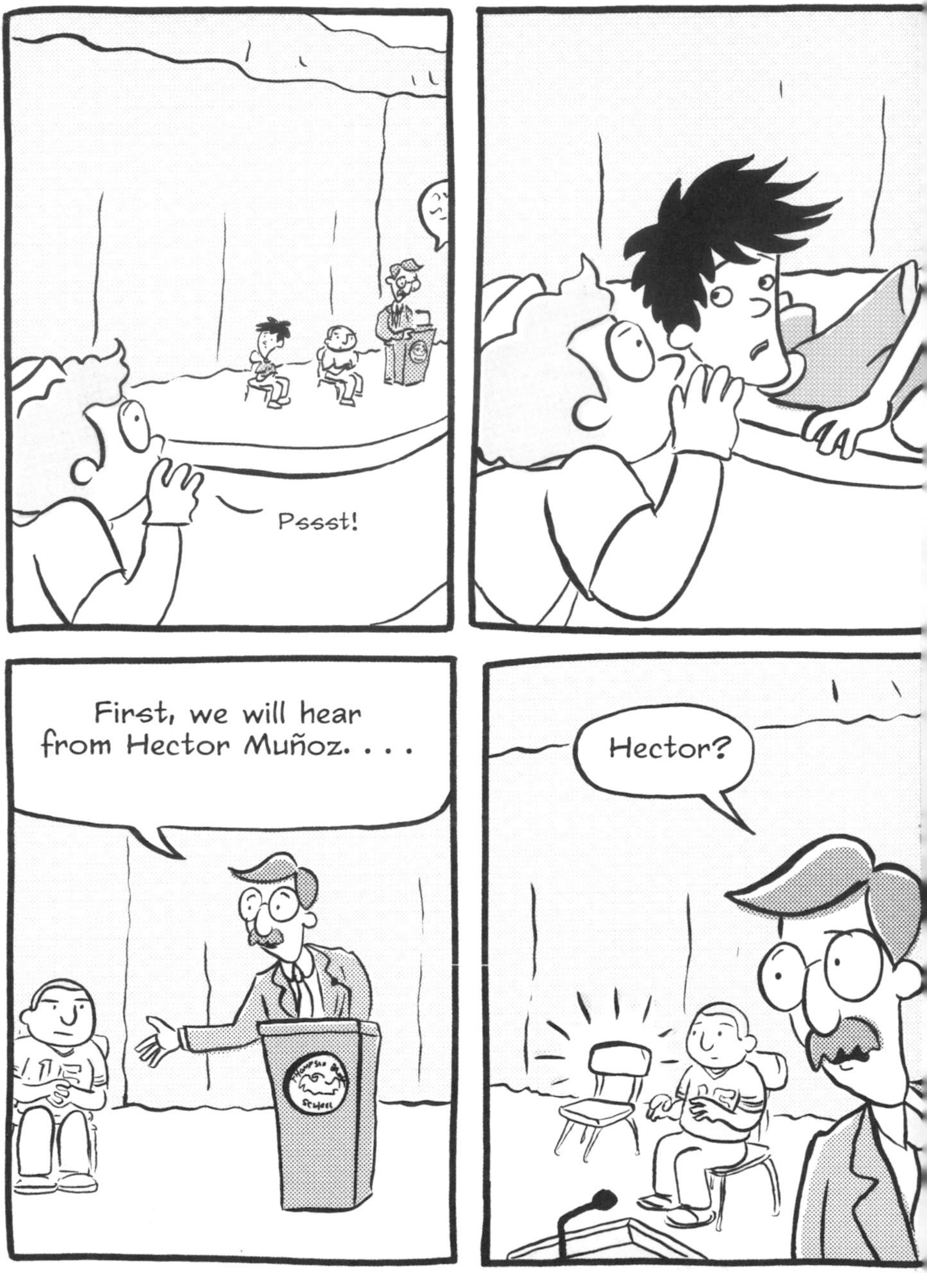
Pssst!
First, we will hear from Hector Muñoz. . . .
Hector?

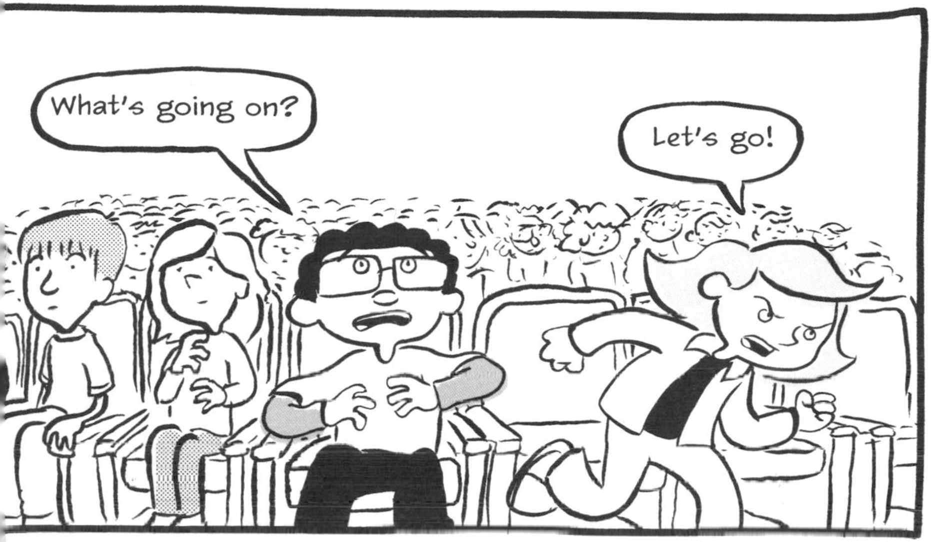
What's going on?
Let's go!

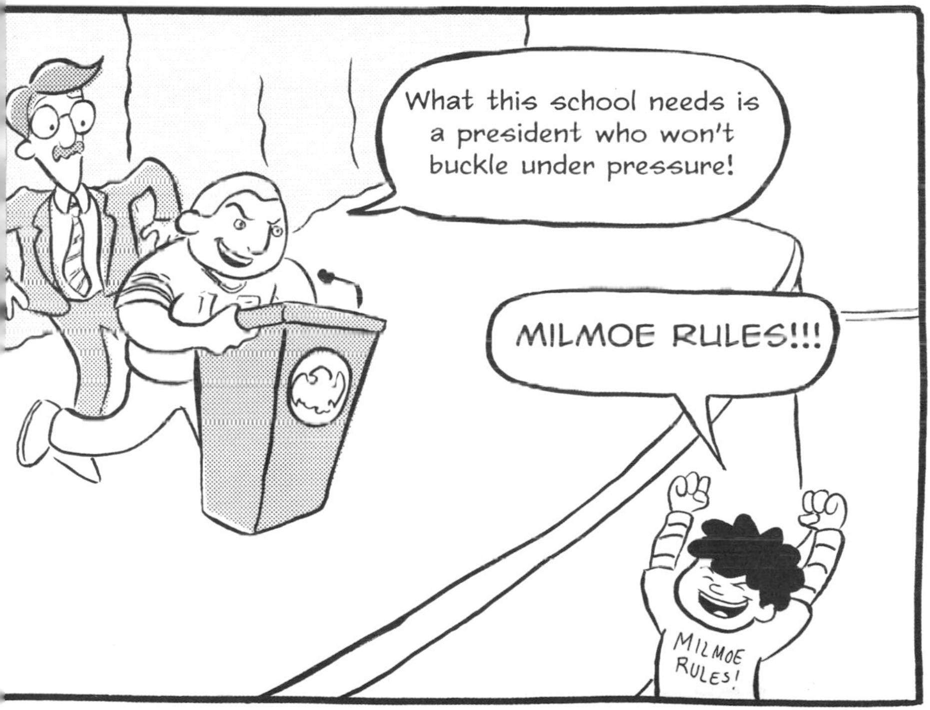
What this school needs is a president who won't buckle under pressure!
MILMOE RULES!!!
MILMOE RULES!

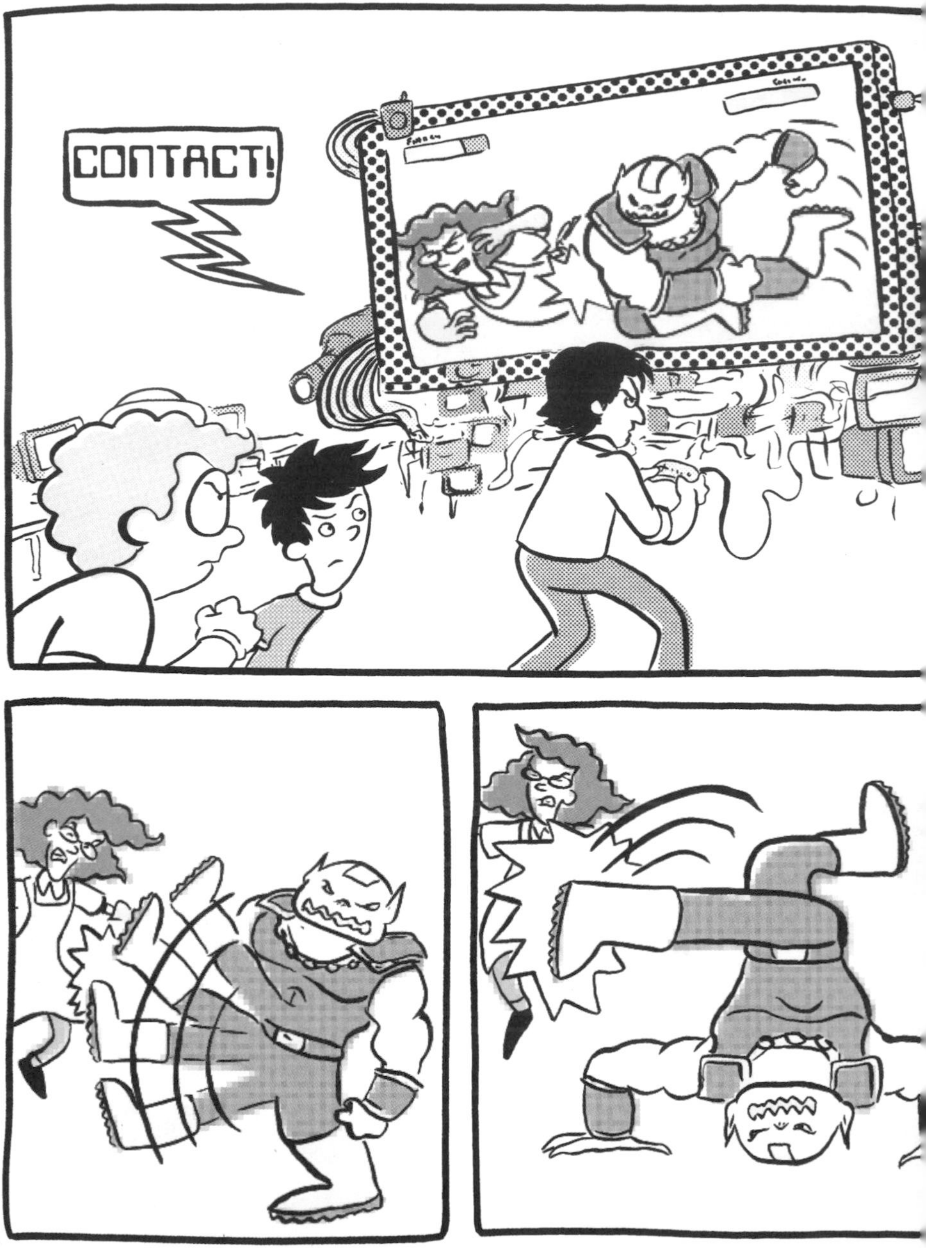
CONTACT!

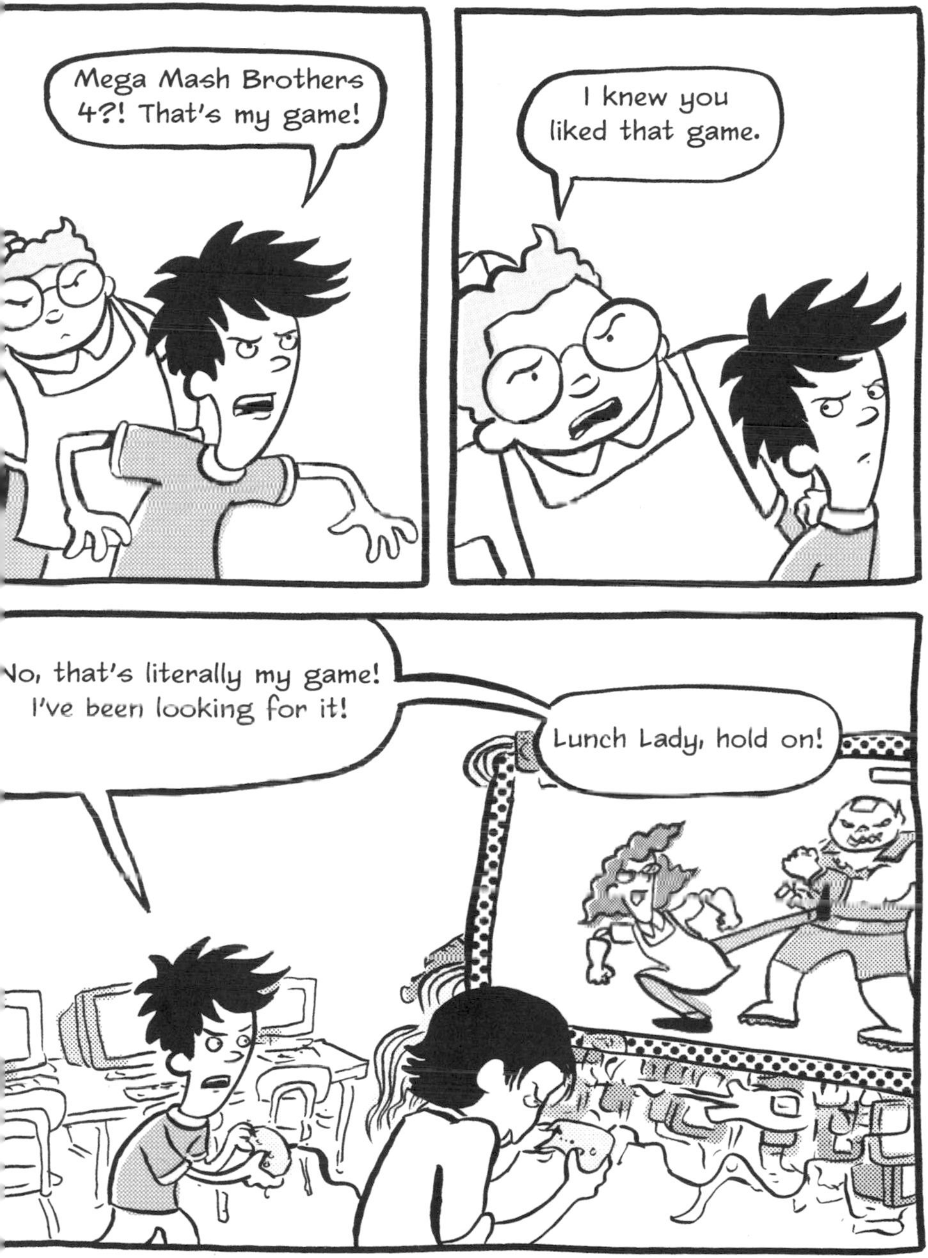
Mega Mash Brothers 4?! That's my game!
I knew you liked that game.
No, that's literally my game! I've been looking for it!
Lunch Lady, hold on!

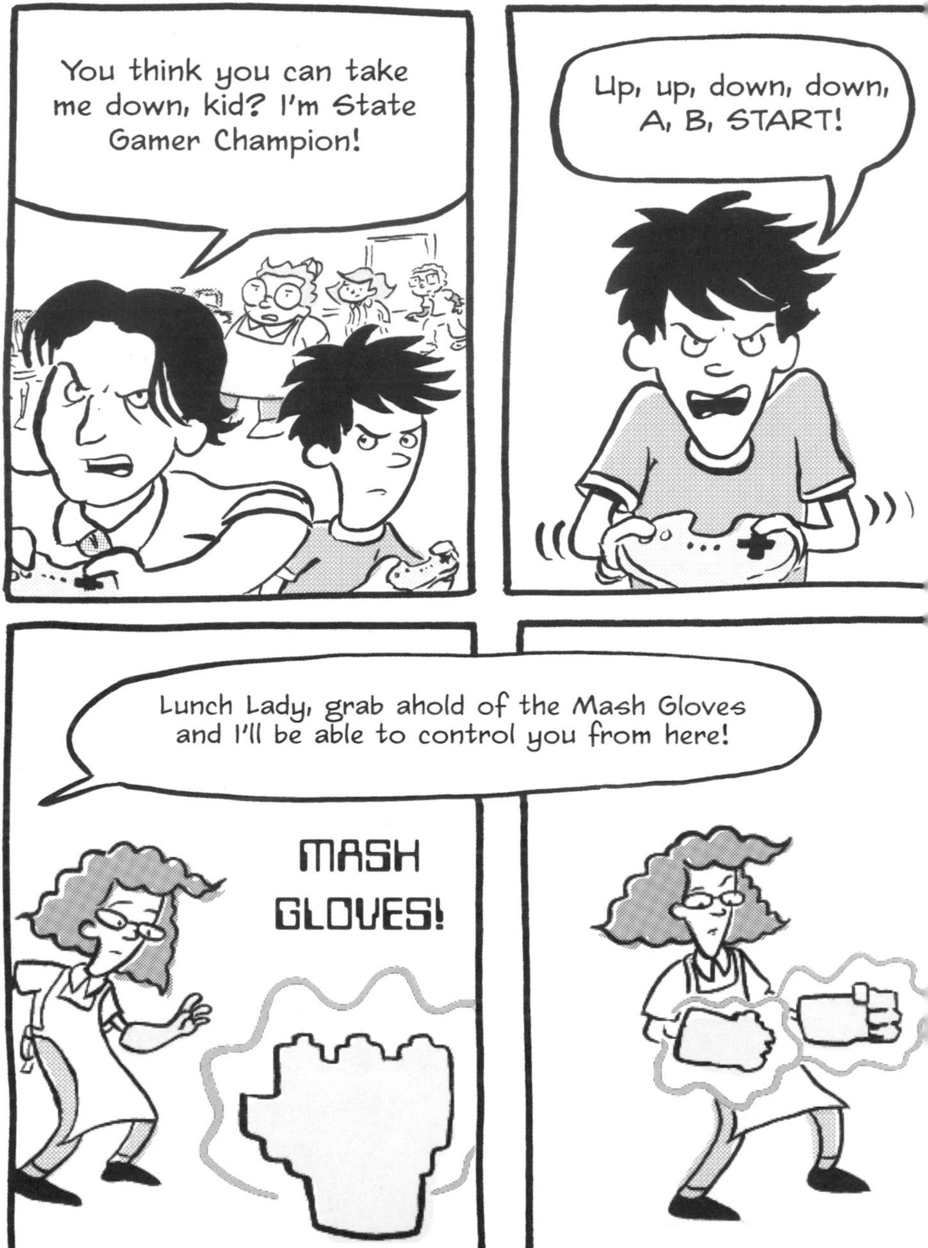
You think you can take me down, kid? I'm State Gamer Champion!
Up, up, down, down, A, B, START!
Lunch Lady, grab ahold of the Mash Gloves and I'll be able to control you from here!
MASH GLOVES!

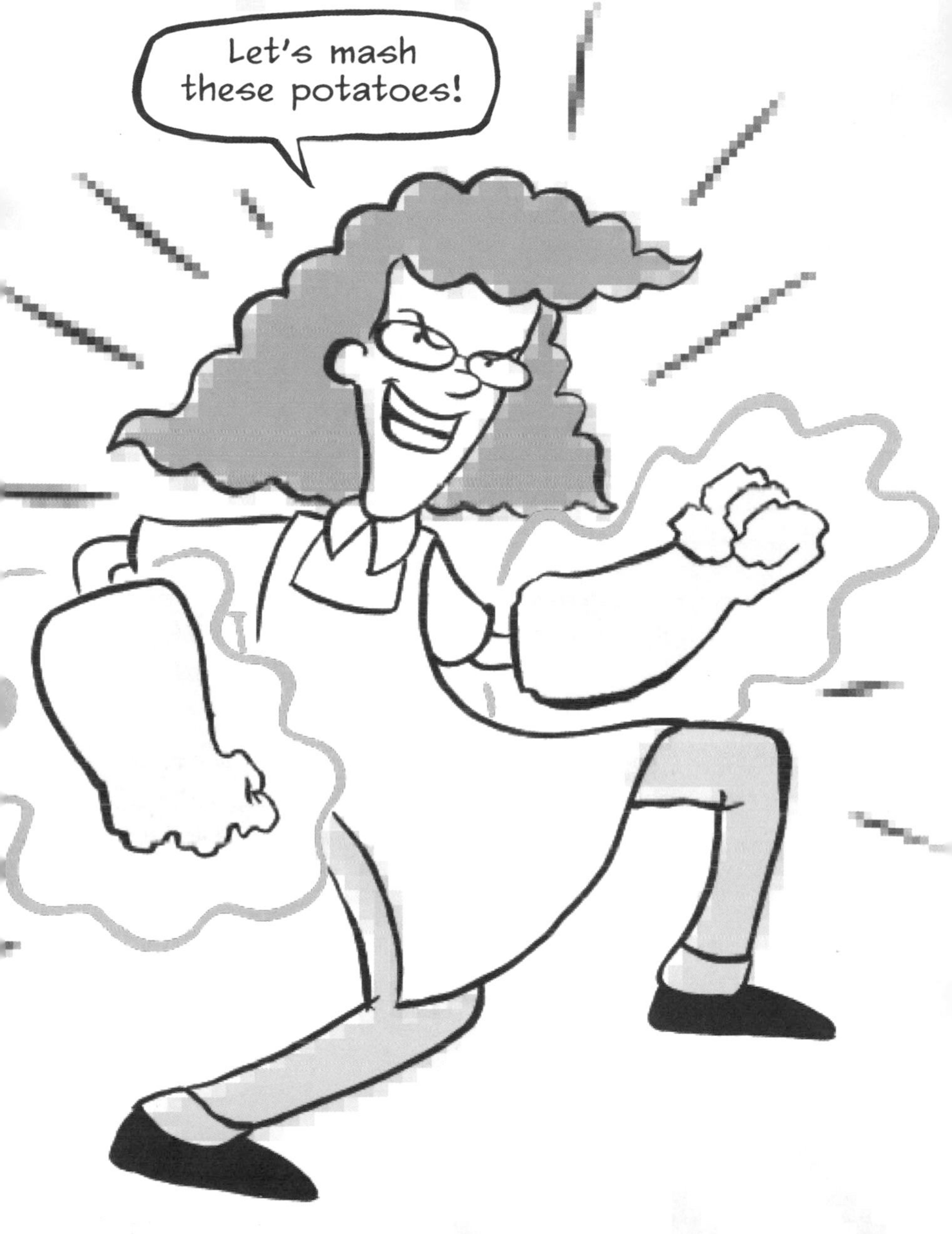
Let's mash these potatoes!

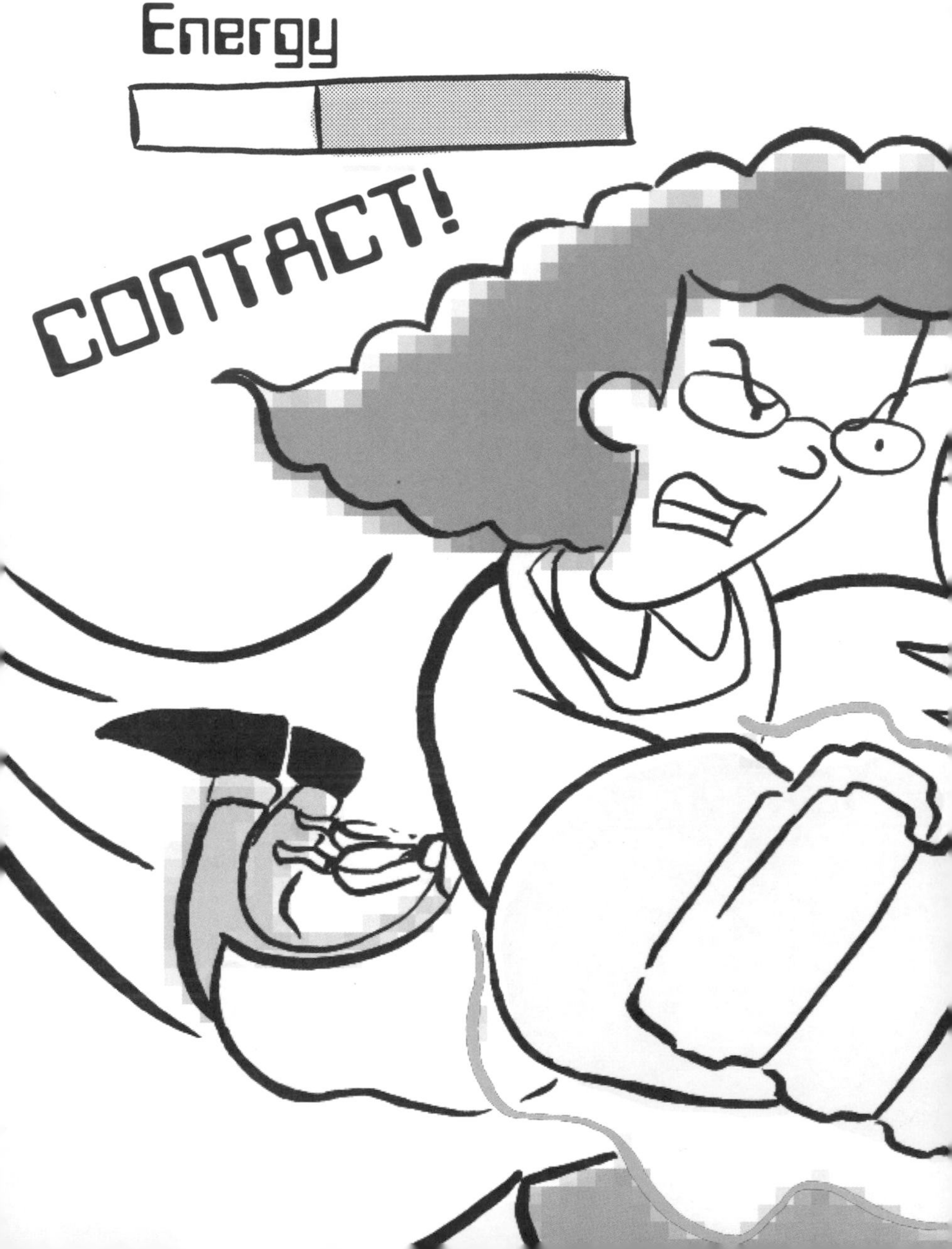
Energy
CONTACT!

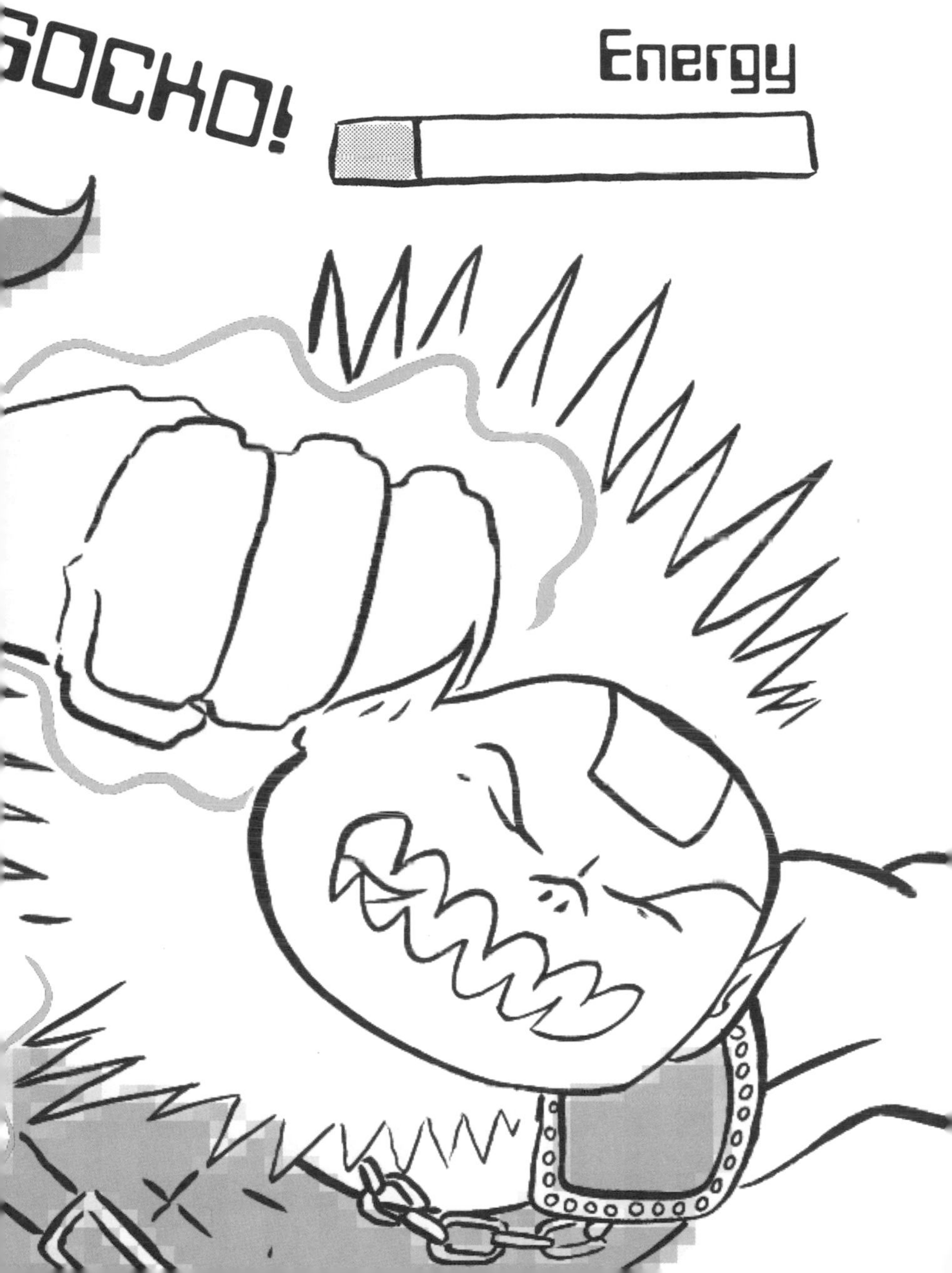

SOCKO!
Energy

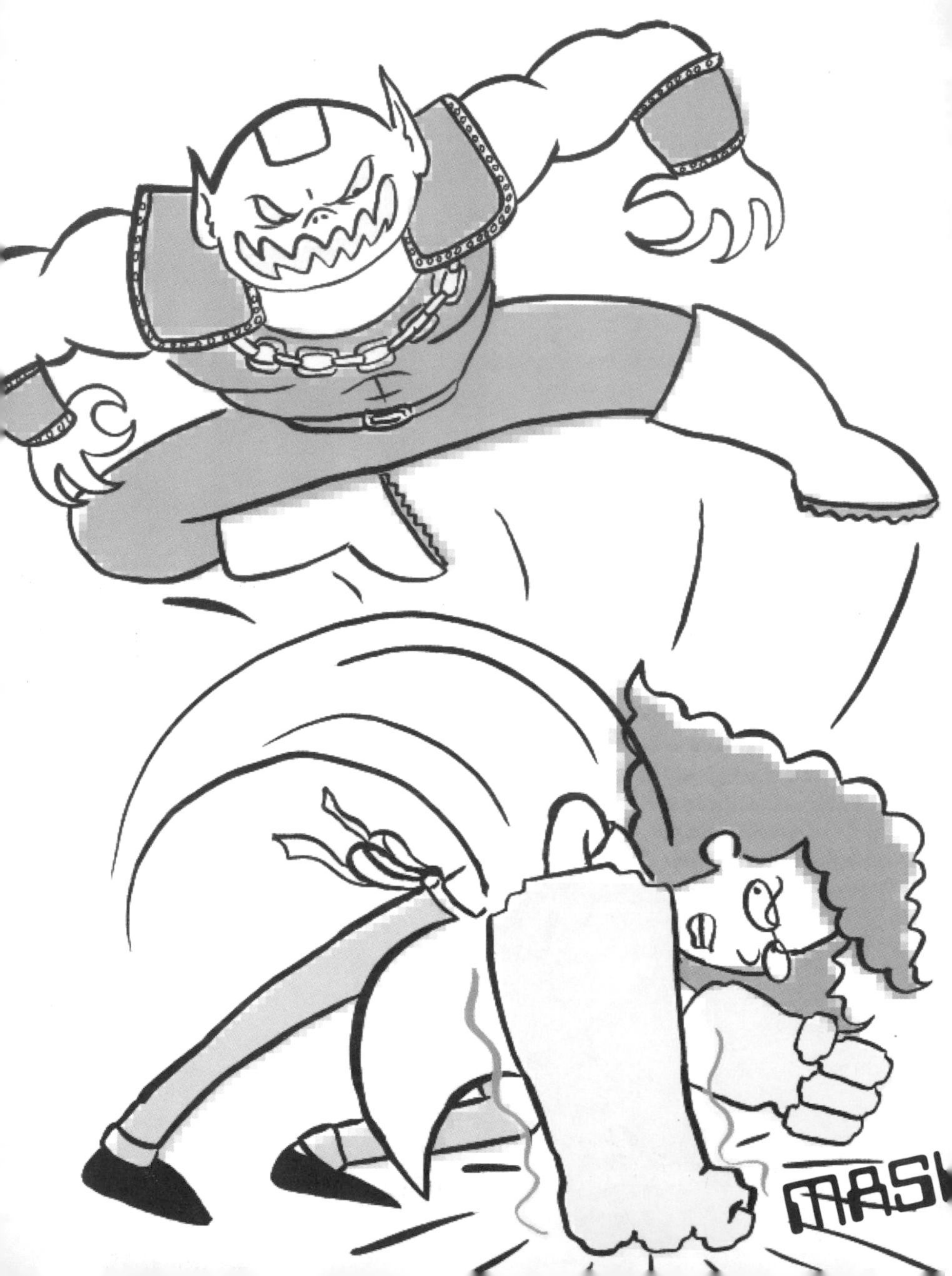

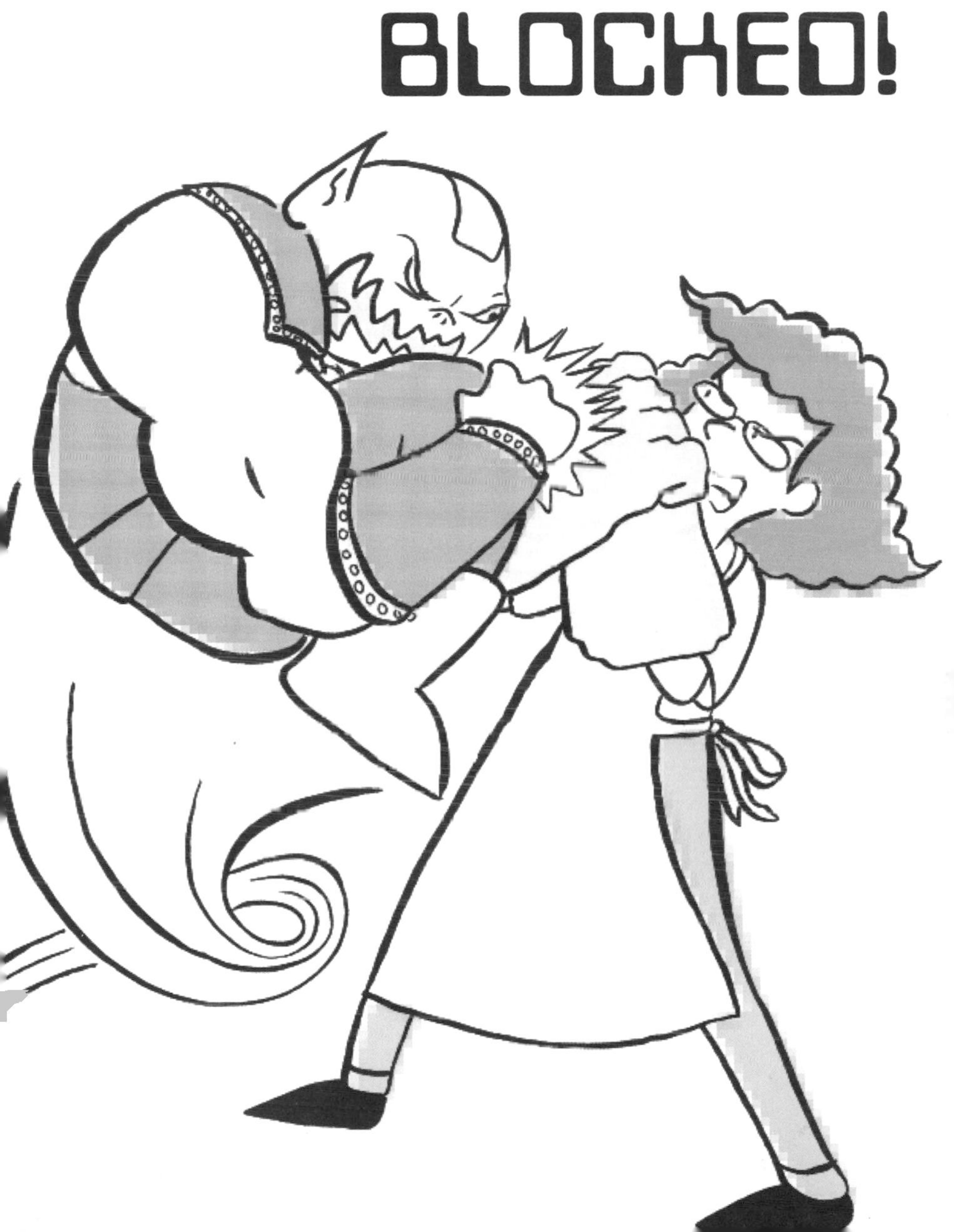
BLOCKED!

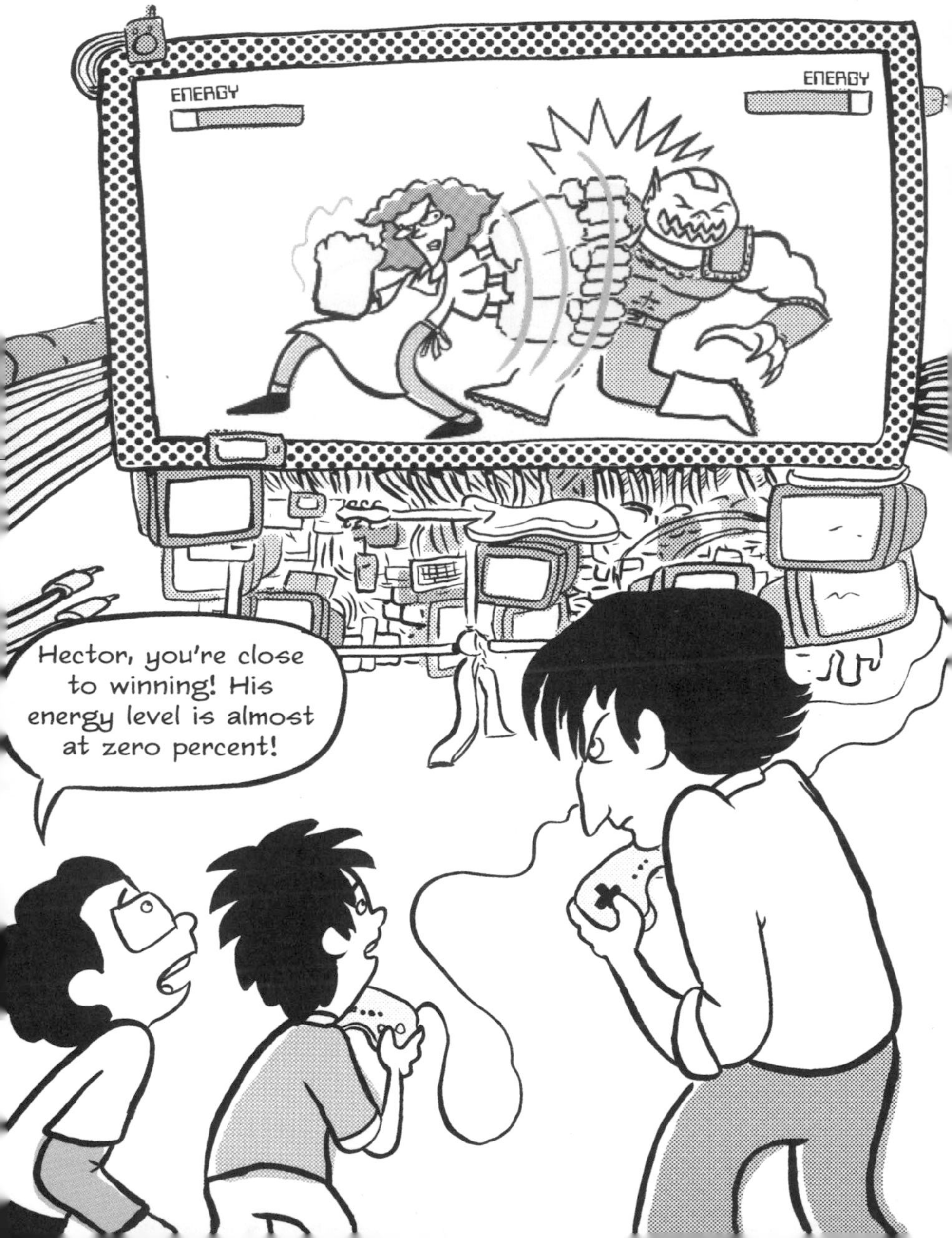
ENERGY
ENERGY
Hector, you're close to winning! His energy level is almost at zero percent!

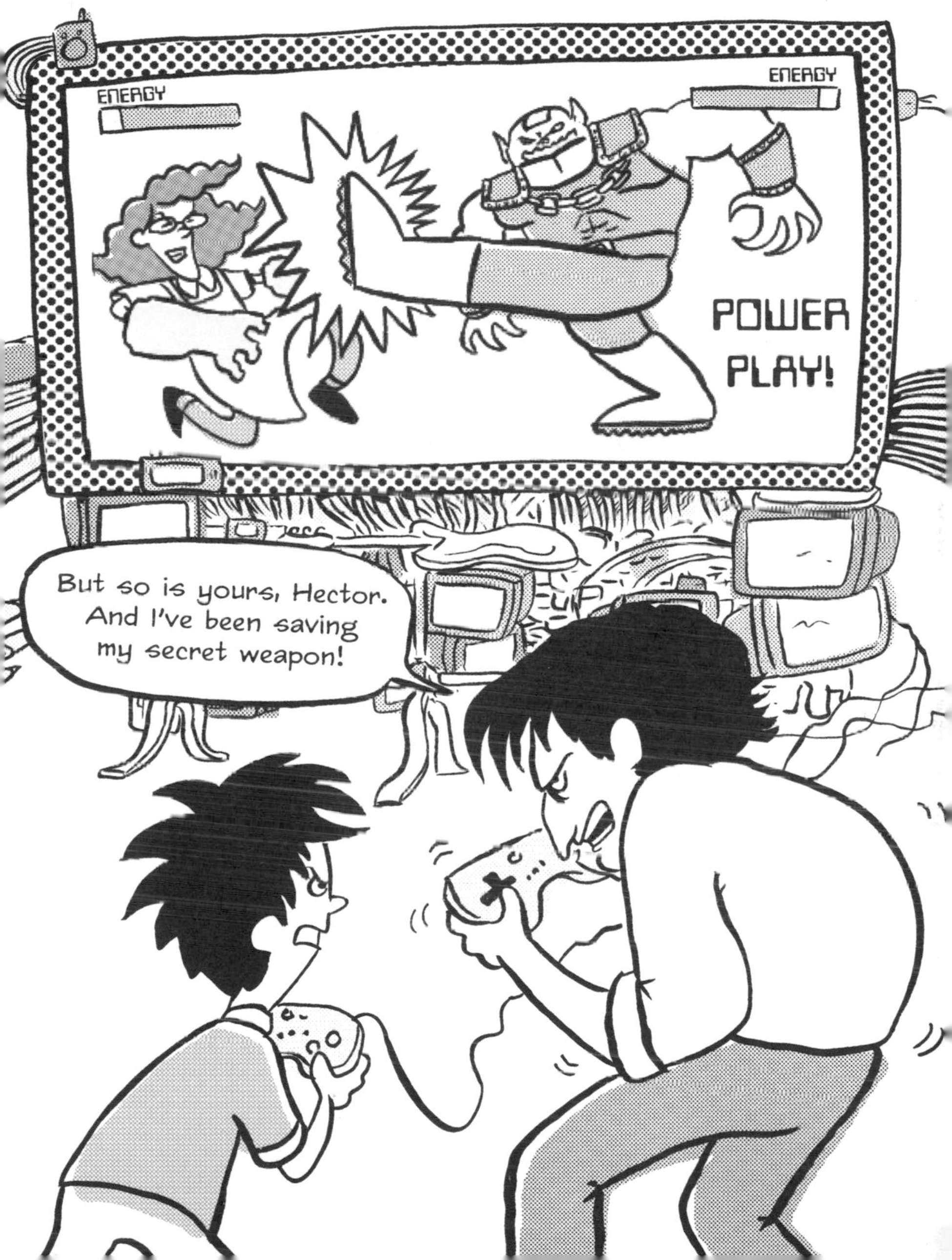

ENERGY
ENERGY
POWER PLAY!
But so is yours, Hector. And I've been saving my secret weapon!

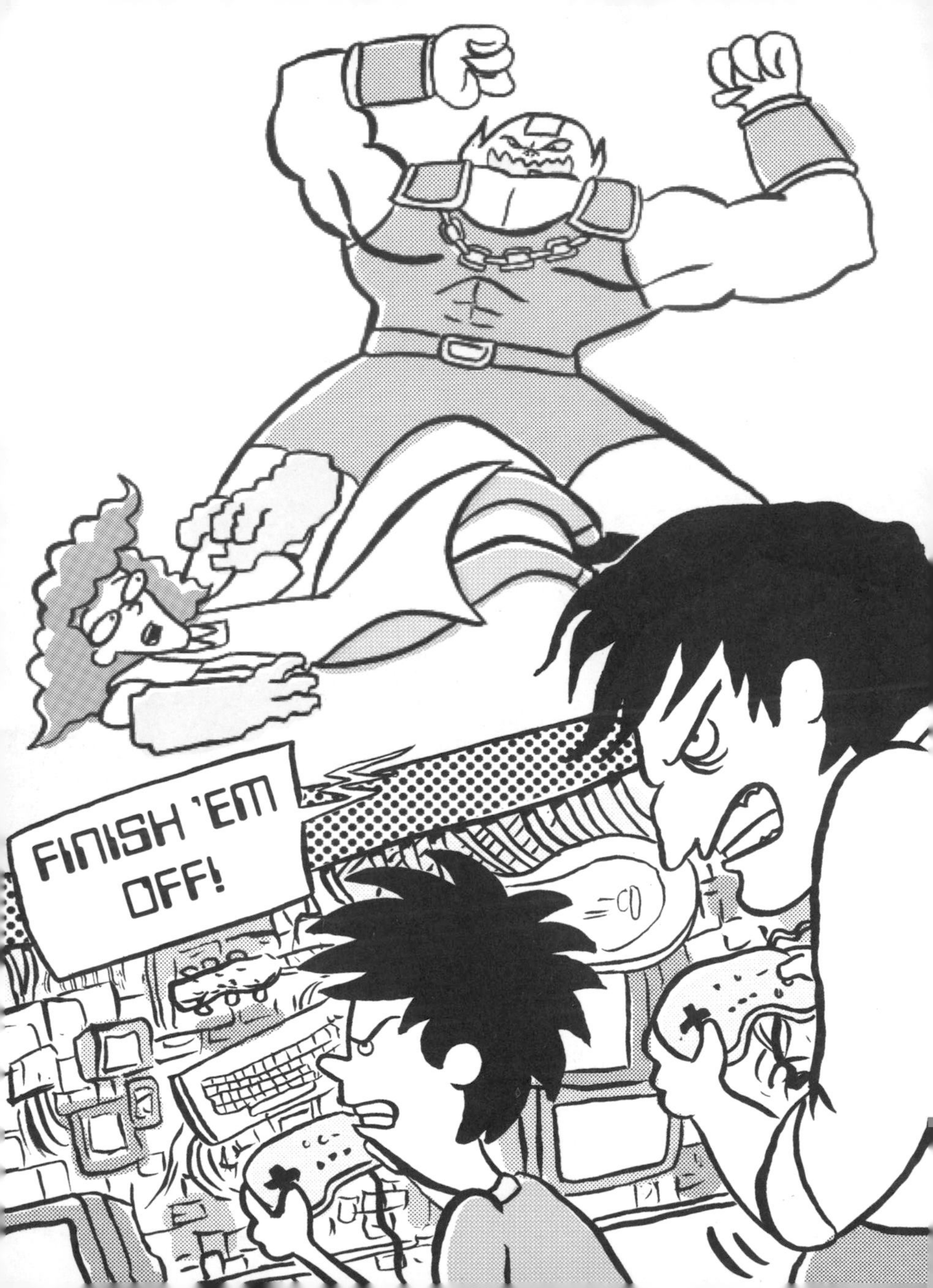
FINISH 'EM OFF!

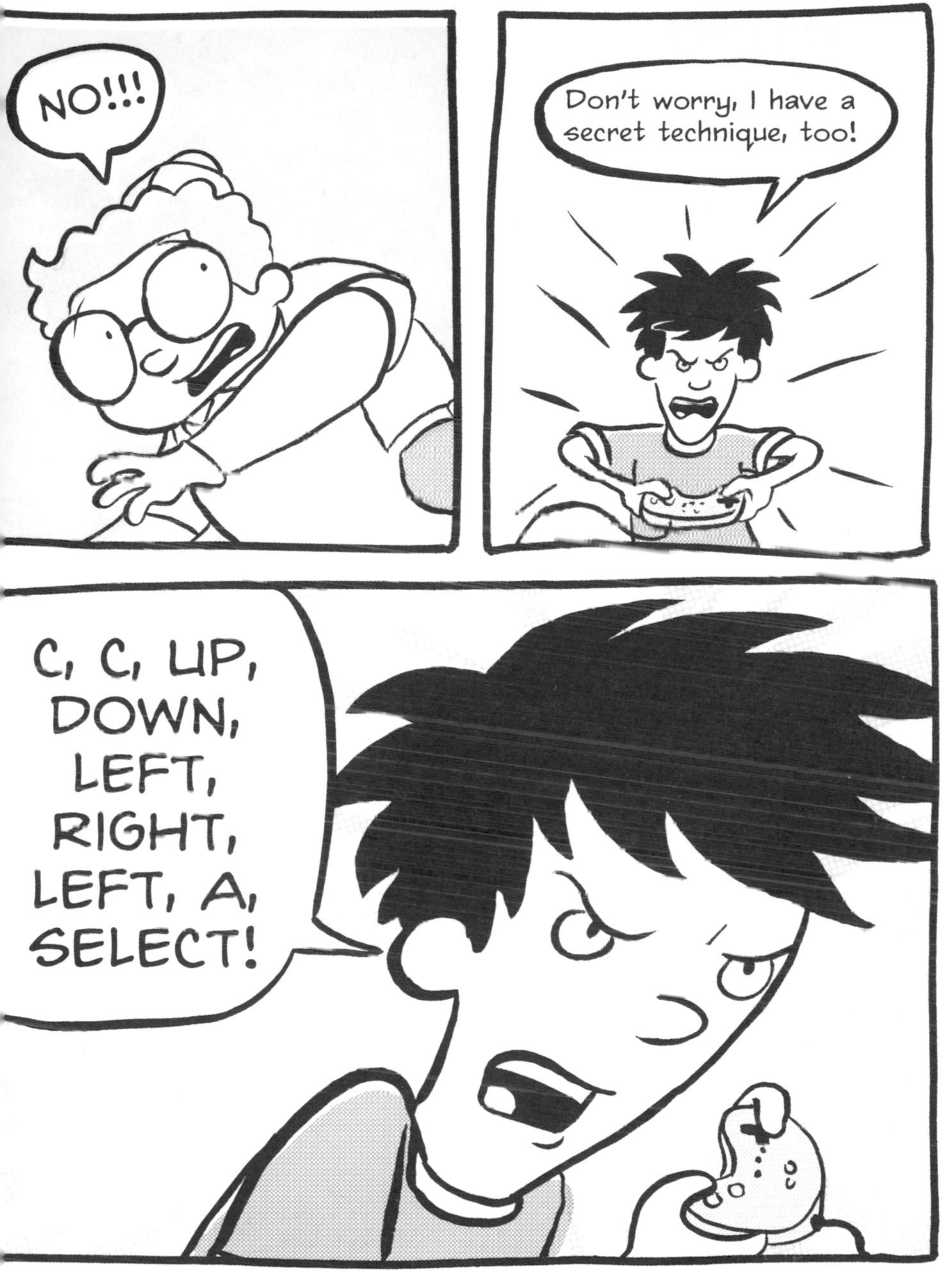
NO!!!
Don't worry, I have a secret technique, too!
C, C, UP, DOWN, LEFT, RIGHT, LEFT, A, SELECT!

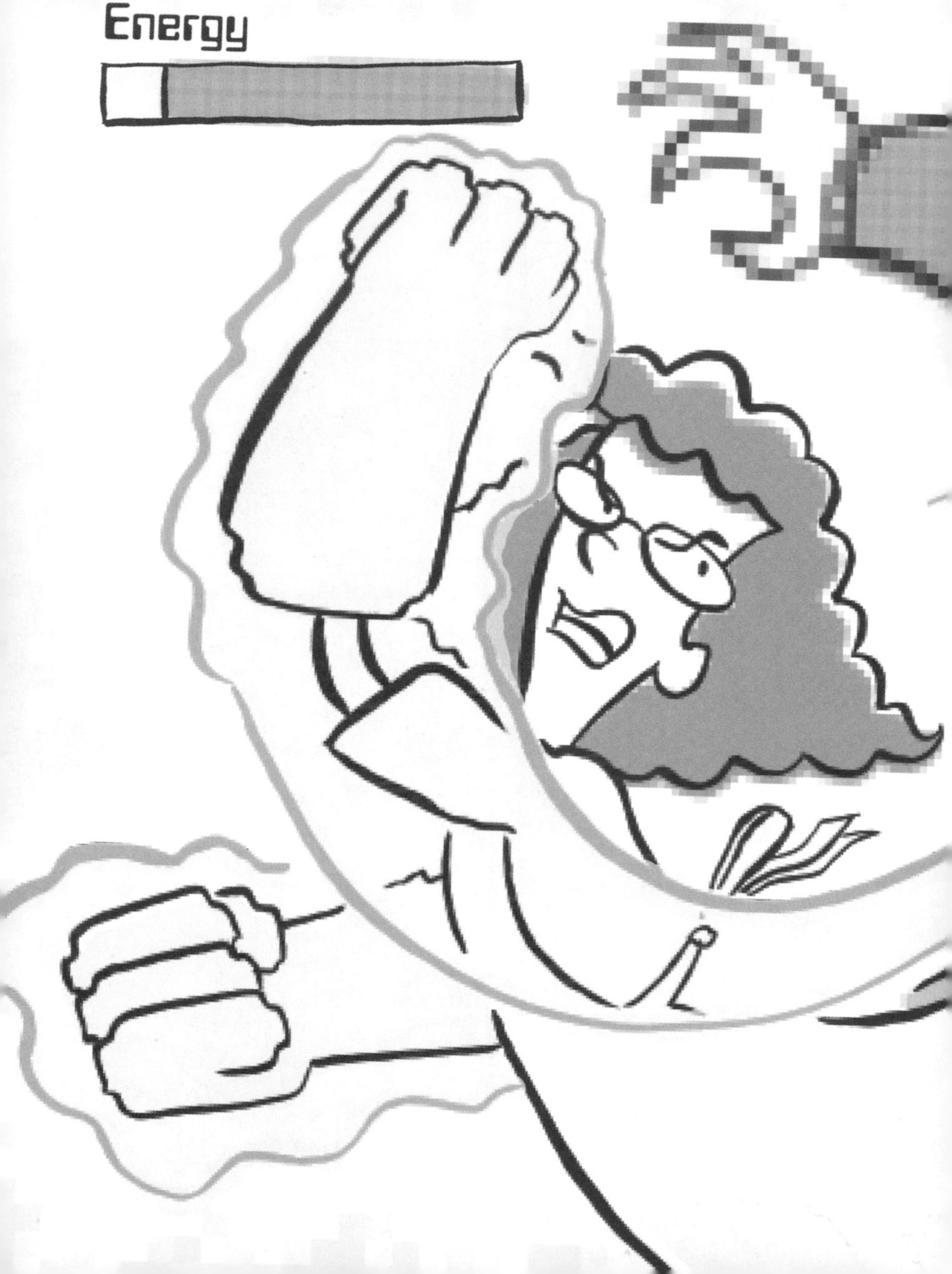
Energy

Energy
ANNIHILATION!

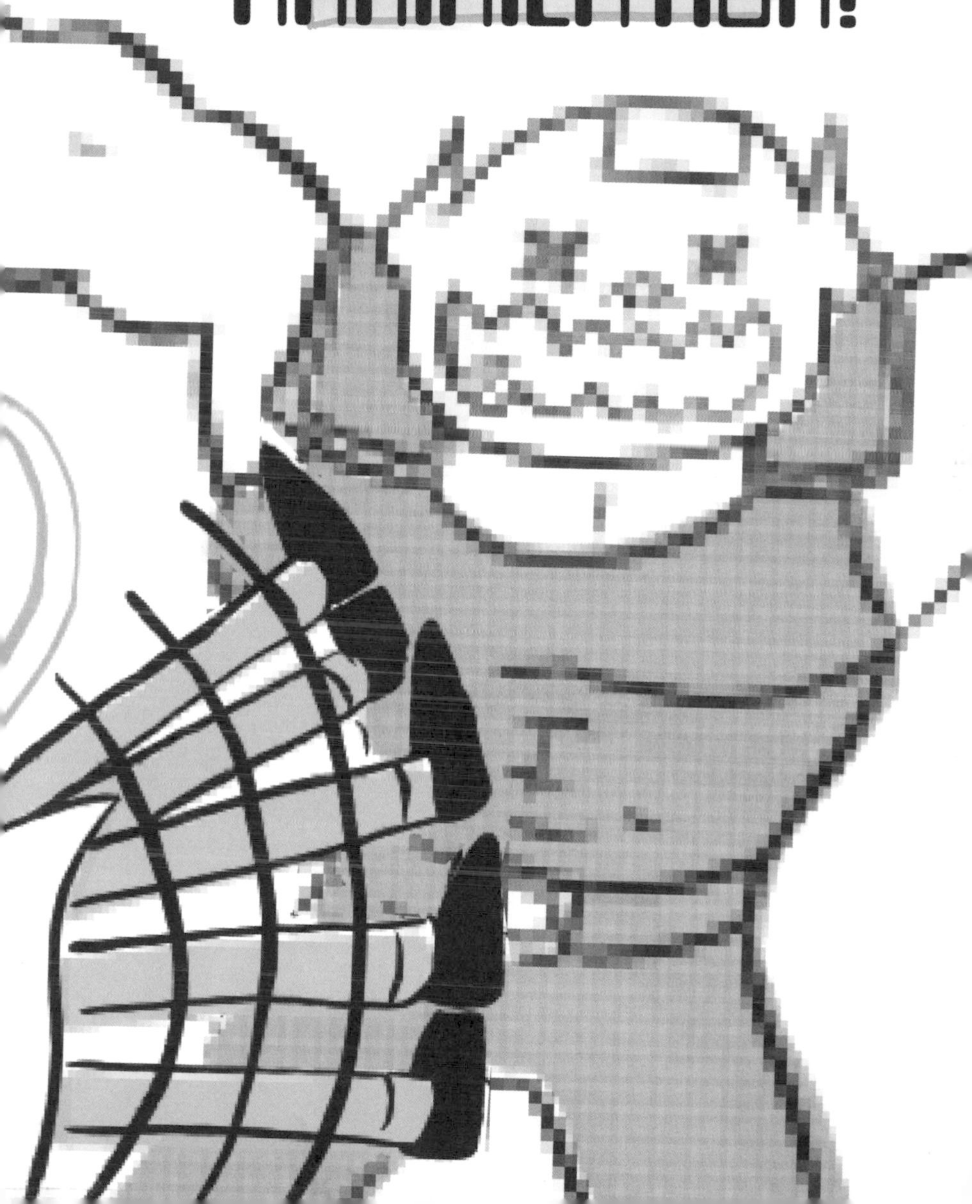

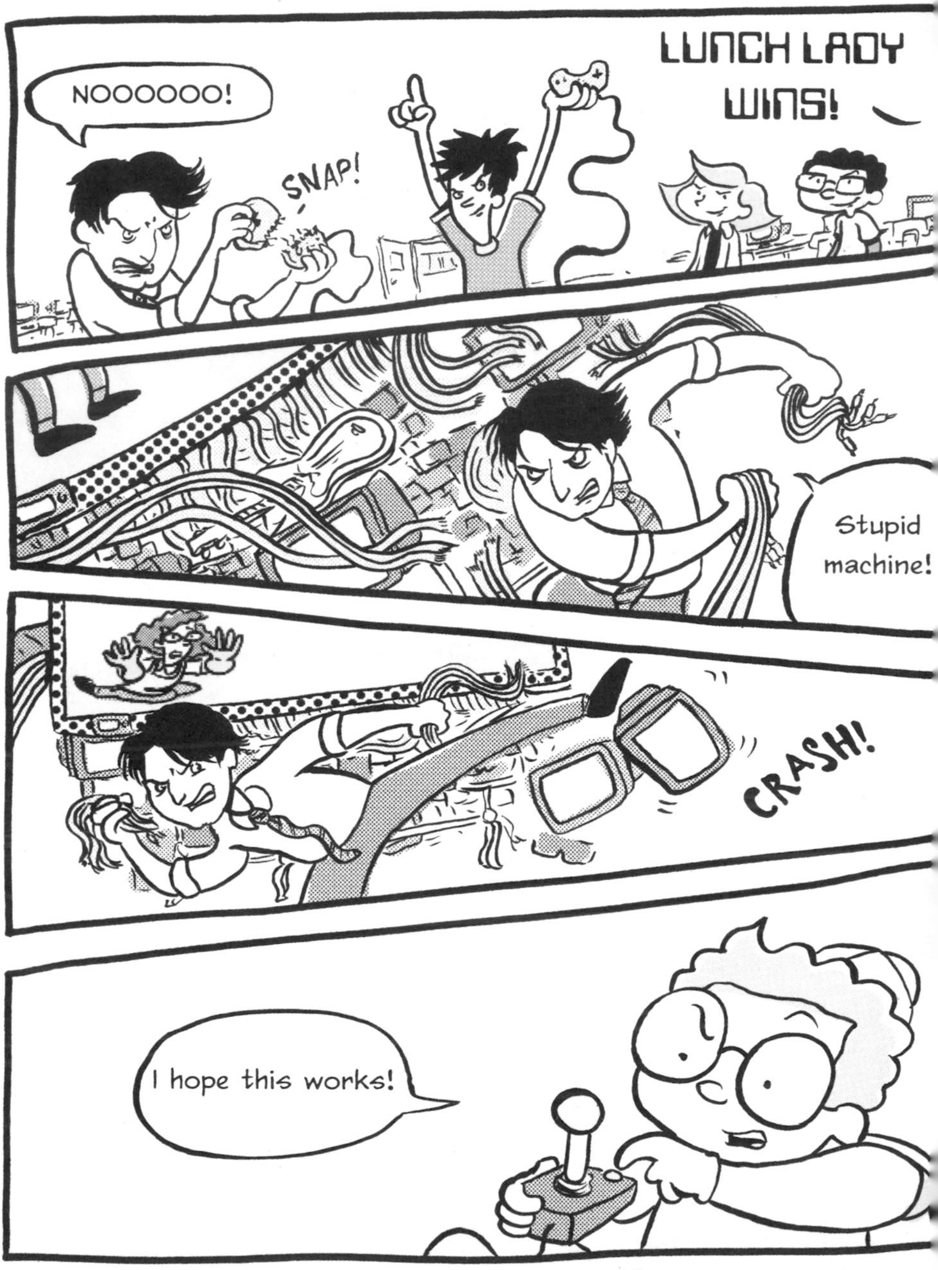
NOOOOOO!
SNAP!
LUNCH LADY WINS!
Stupid machine!
CRASH!
I hope this works!

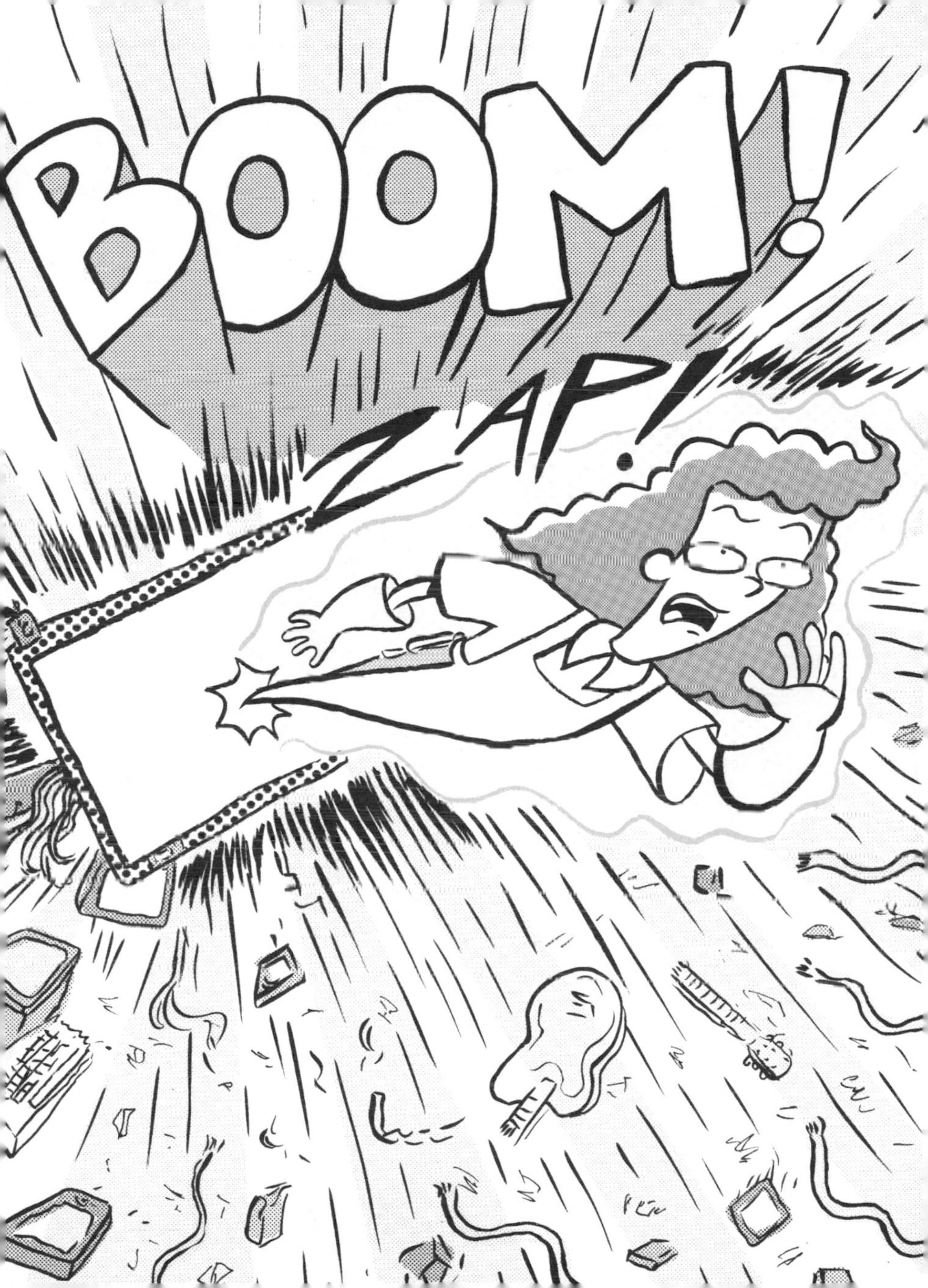
BOOM!
ZAP!

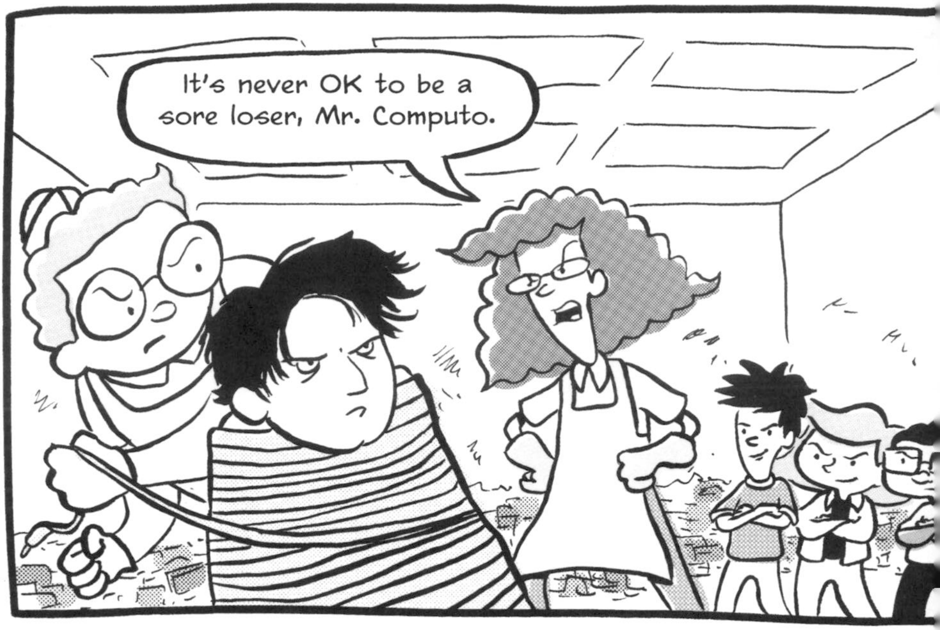
It's never OK to be a sore loser, Mr. Computo.

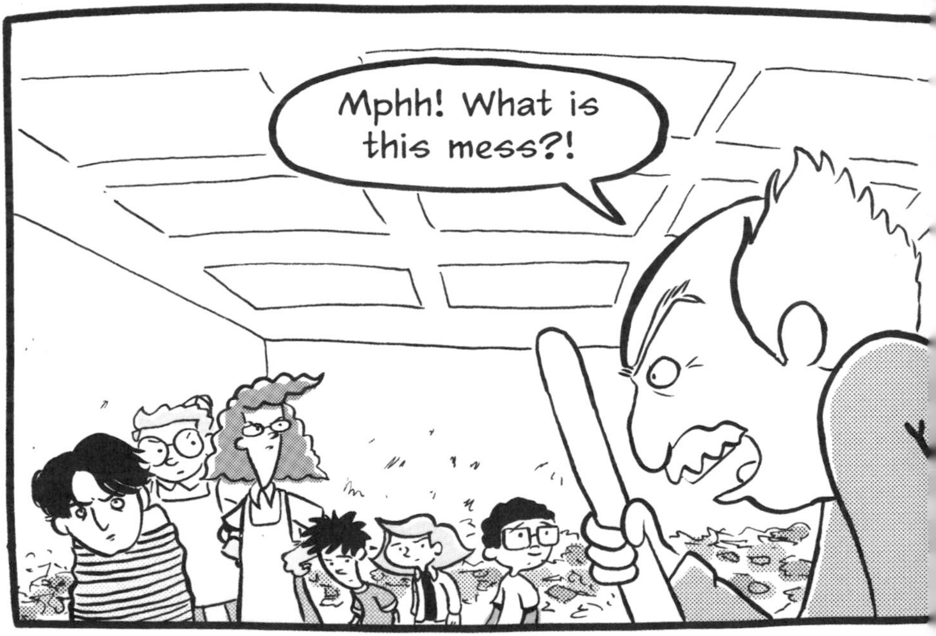
Mphh! What is this mess?!

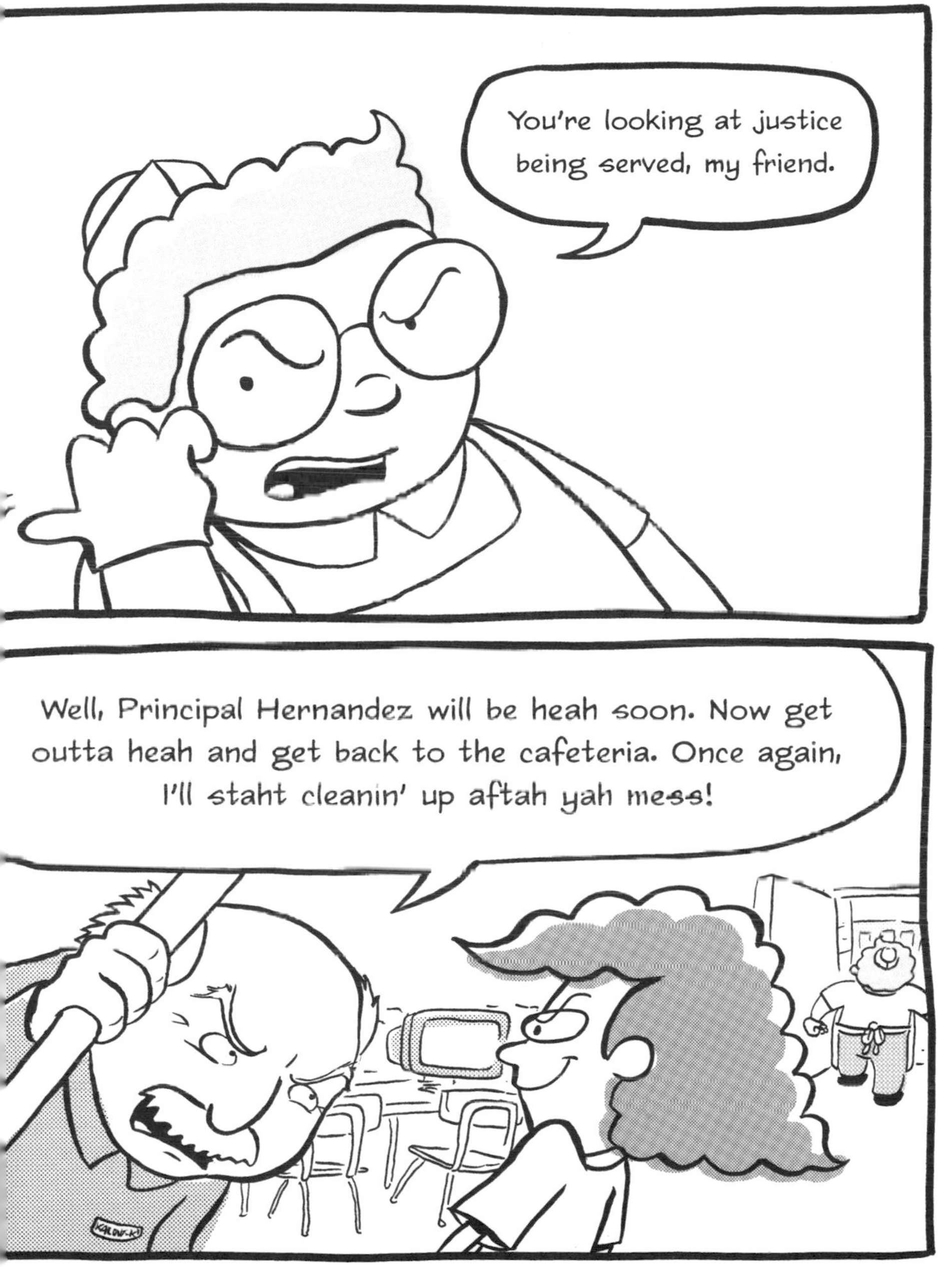
You're looking at justice being served, my friend.
Well, Principal Hernandez will be heah soon. Now get outta heah and get back to the cafeteria. Once again, I'll staht cleanin' up aftah yah mess!

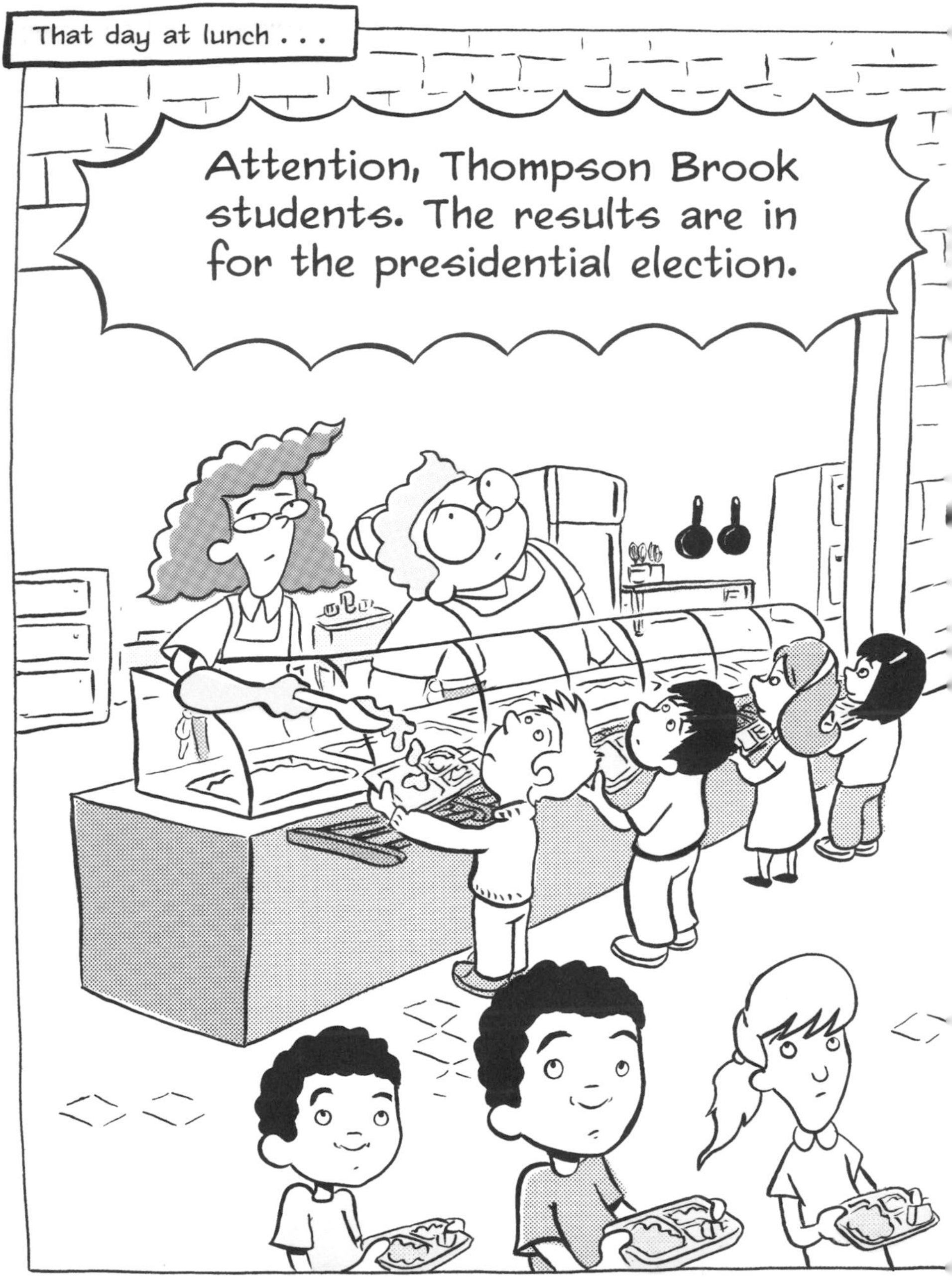
That day at lunch . . .
Attention, Thompson Brook students. The results are in for the presidential election.

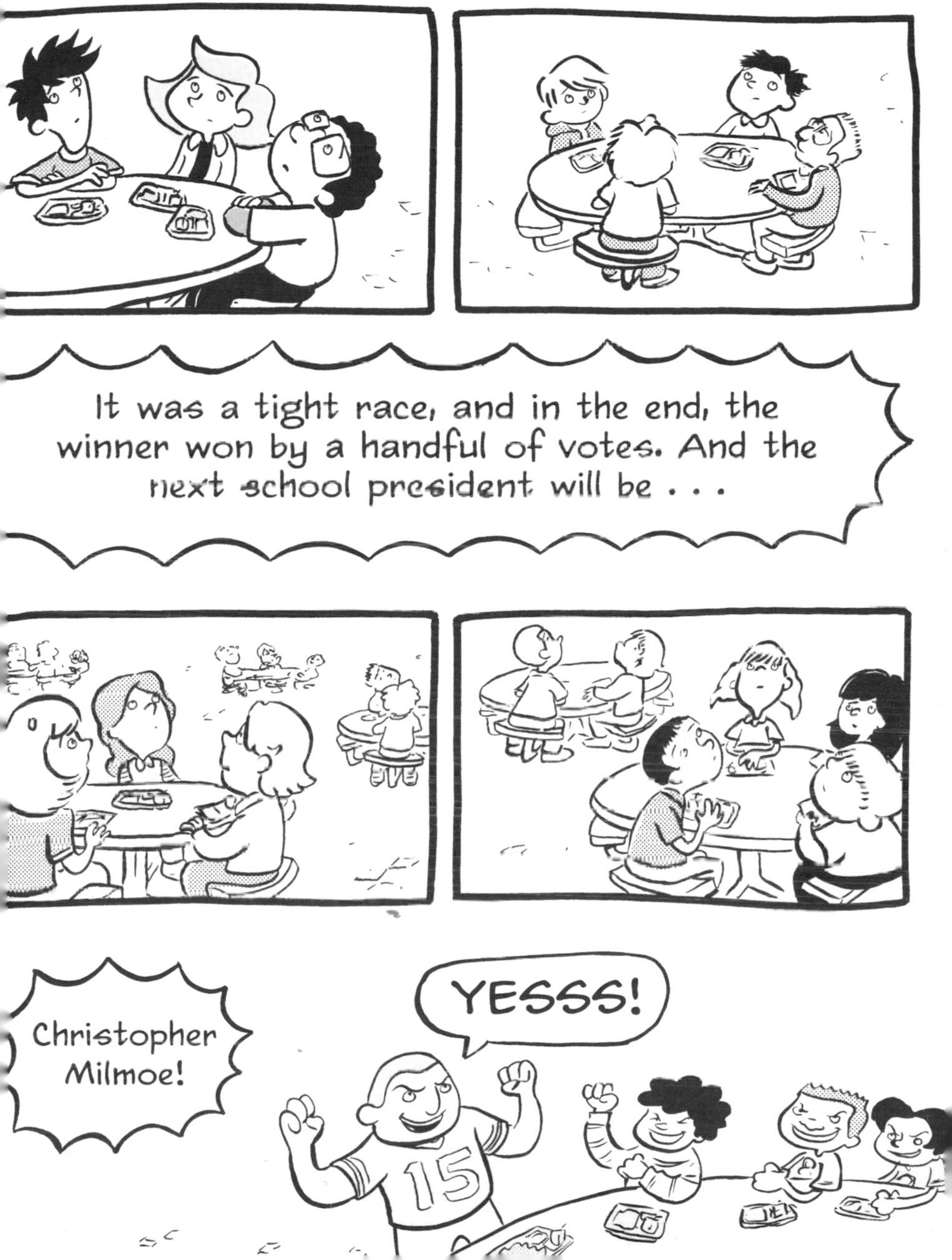
It was a tight race, and in the end, the winner won by a handful of votes. And the next school president will be . . .
Christopher Milmoe!
YESSS!
15

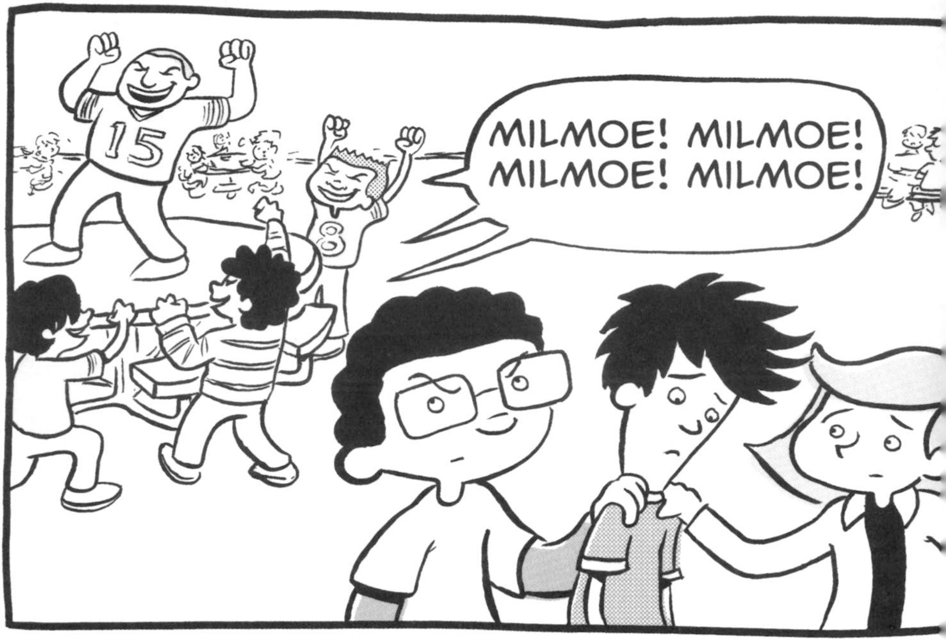
MILMOE! MILMOE! MILMOE! MILMOE!

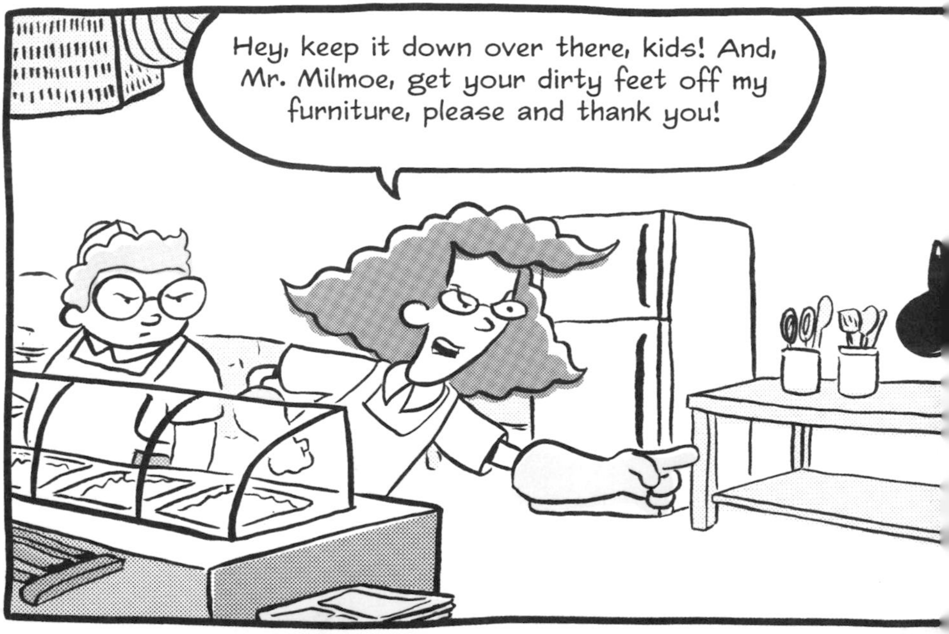
Hey, keep it down over there, kids! And, Mr. Milmoe, get your dirty feet off my furniture, please and thank you!

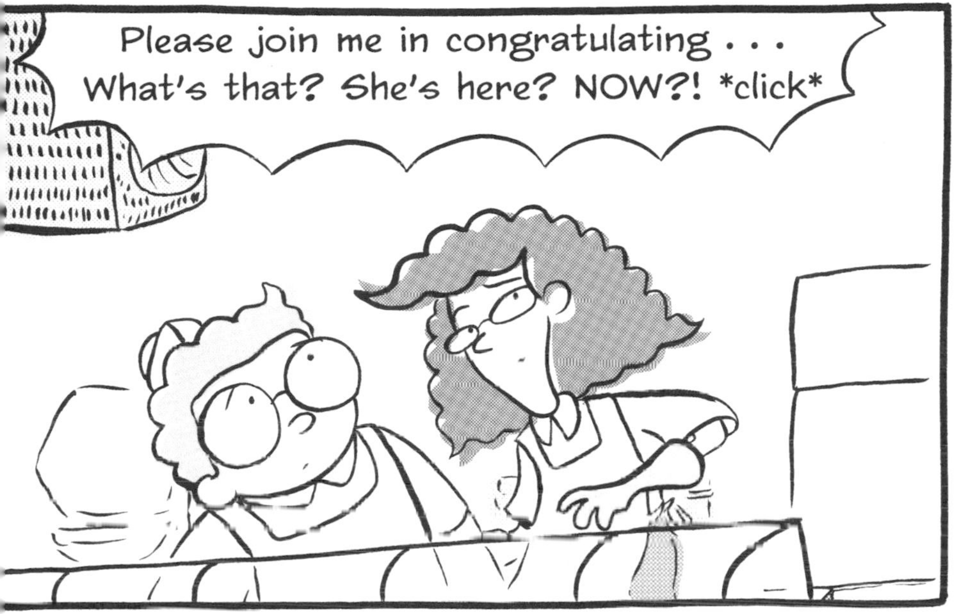
Please join me in congratulating . . . What's that? She's here? NOW?! *click*

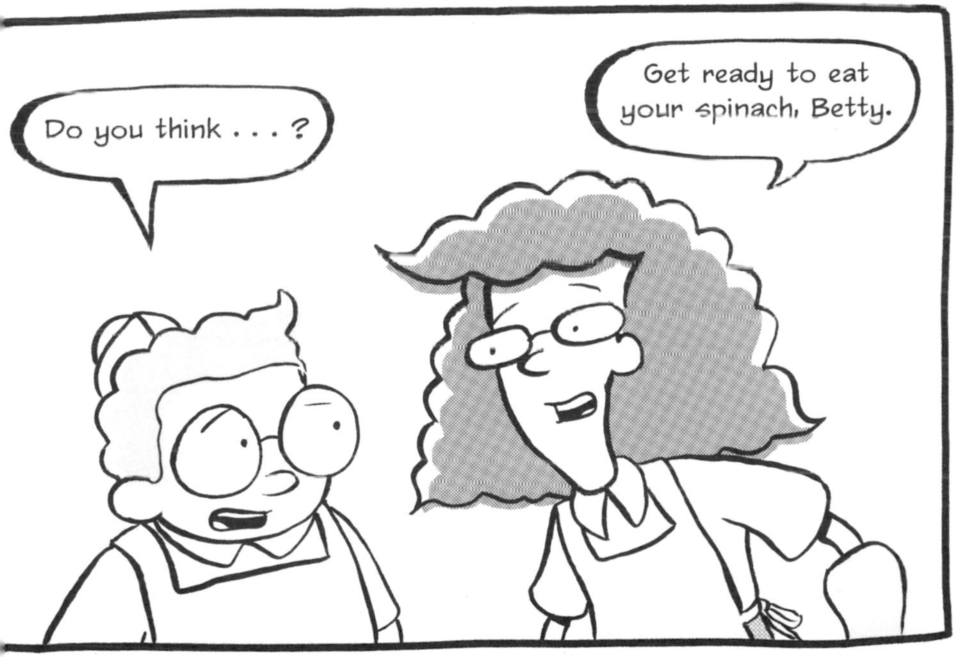
Do you think . . . ?
Get ready to eat your spinach, Betty.

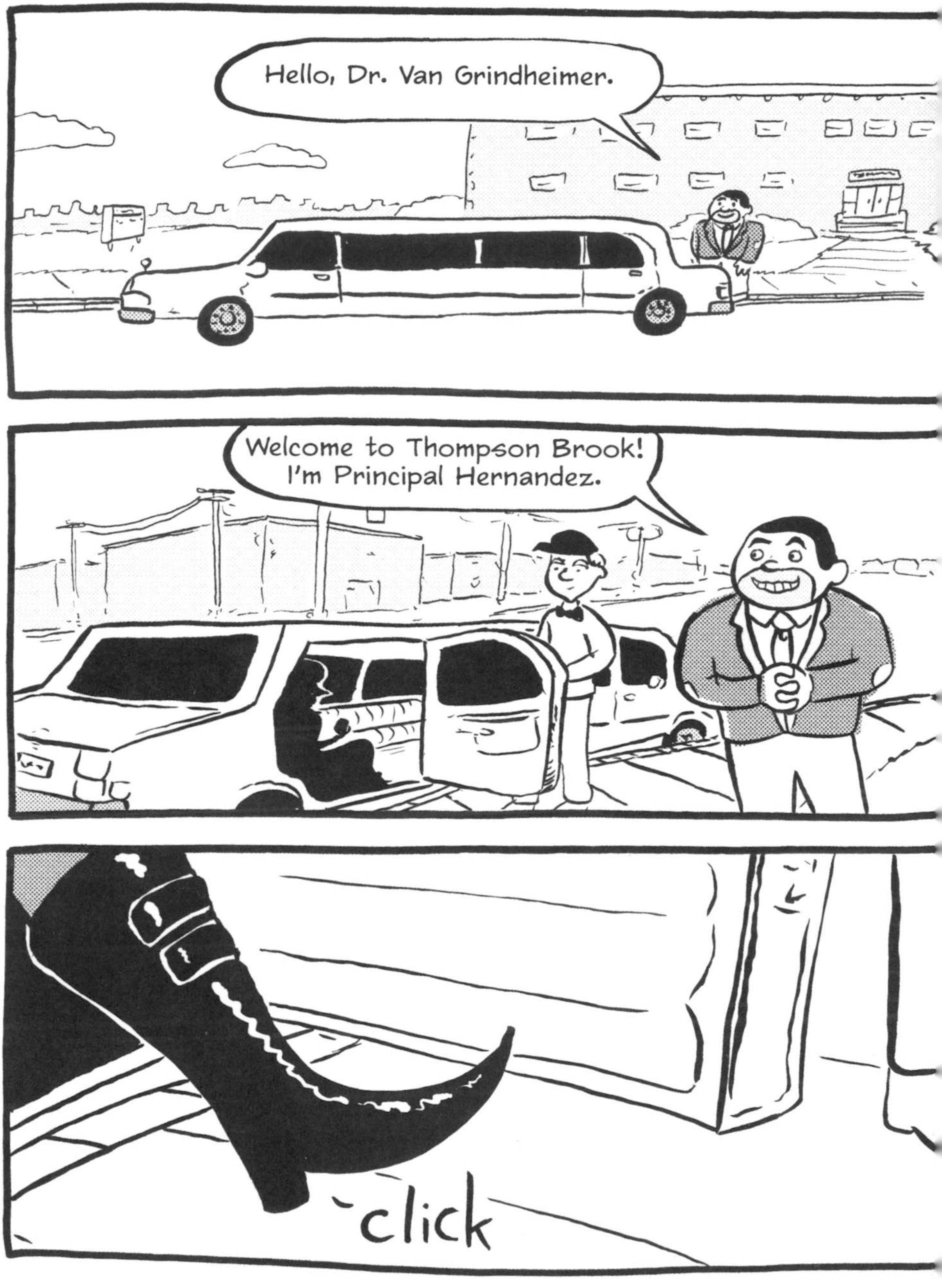
Hello, Dr. Van Grindheimer.
Welcome to Thompson Brook! I'm Principal Hernandez.
click

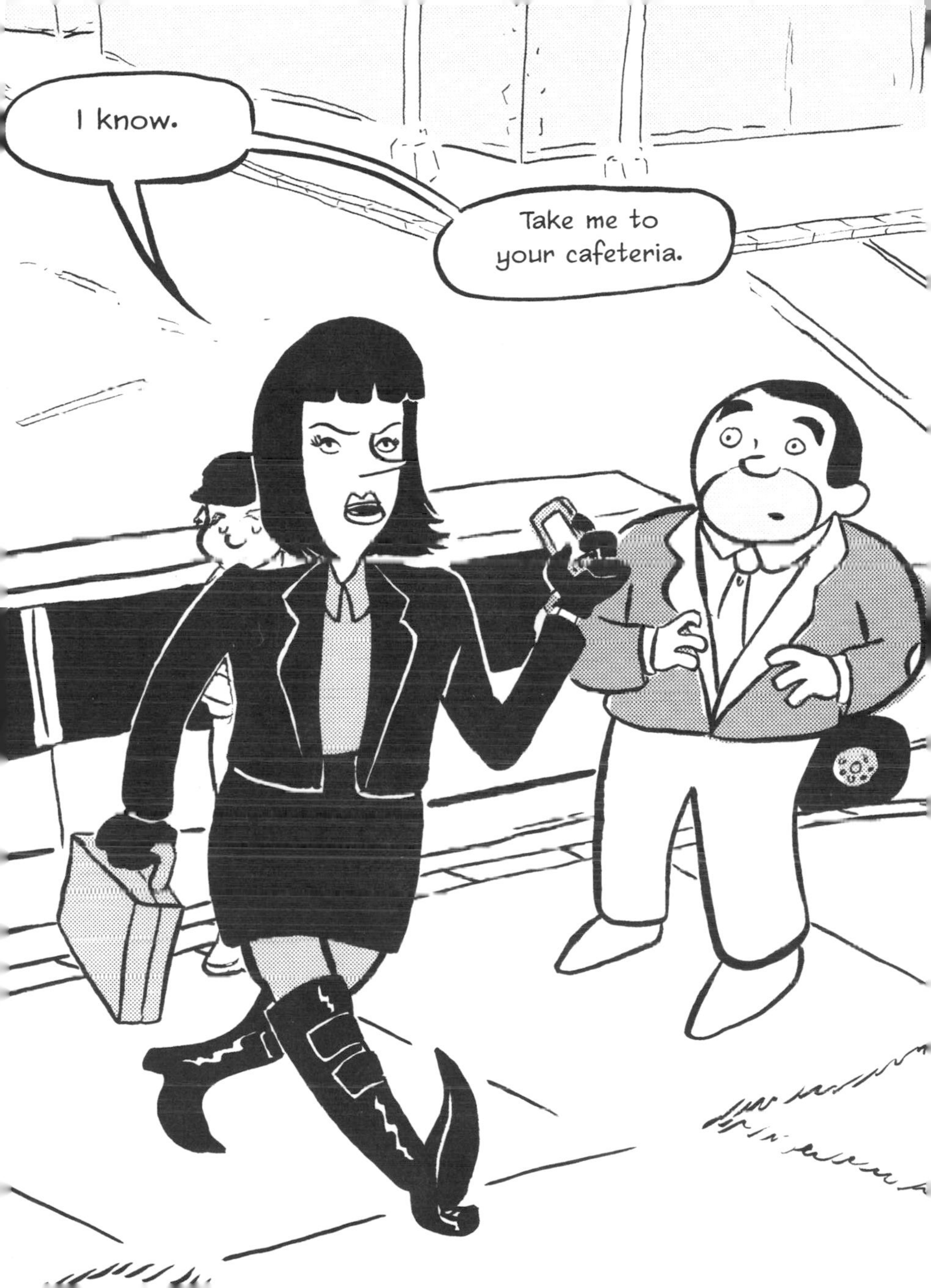
I know.
Take me to your cafeteria.

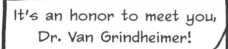
It's an honor to meet you, Dr. Van Grindheimer!

Hmph.

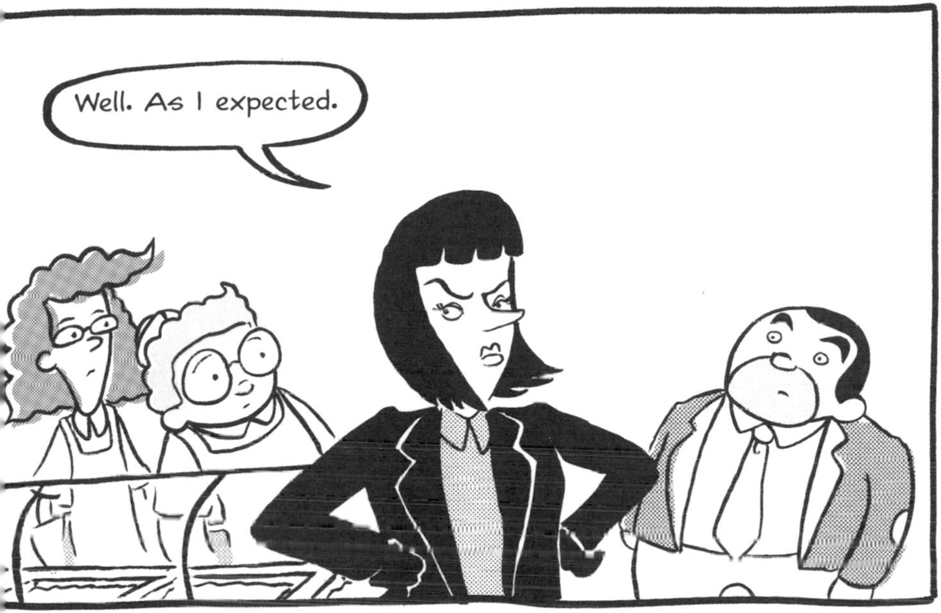
Well. As I expected.

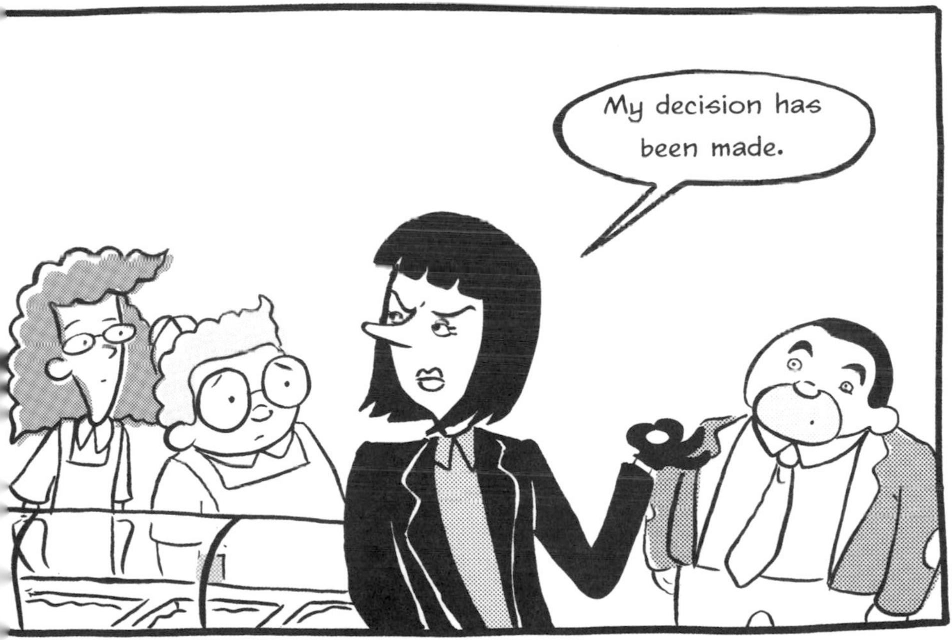
My decision has been made.

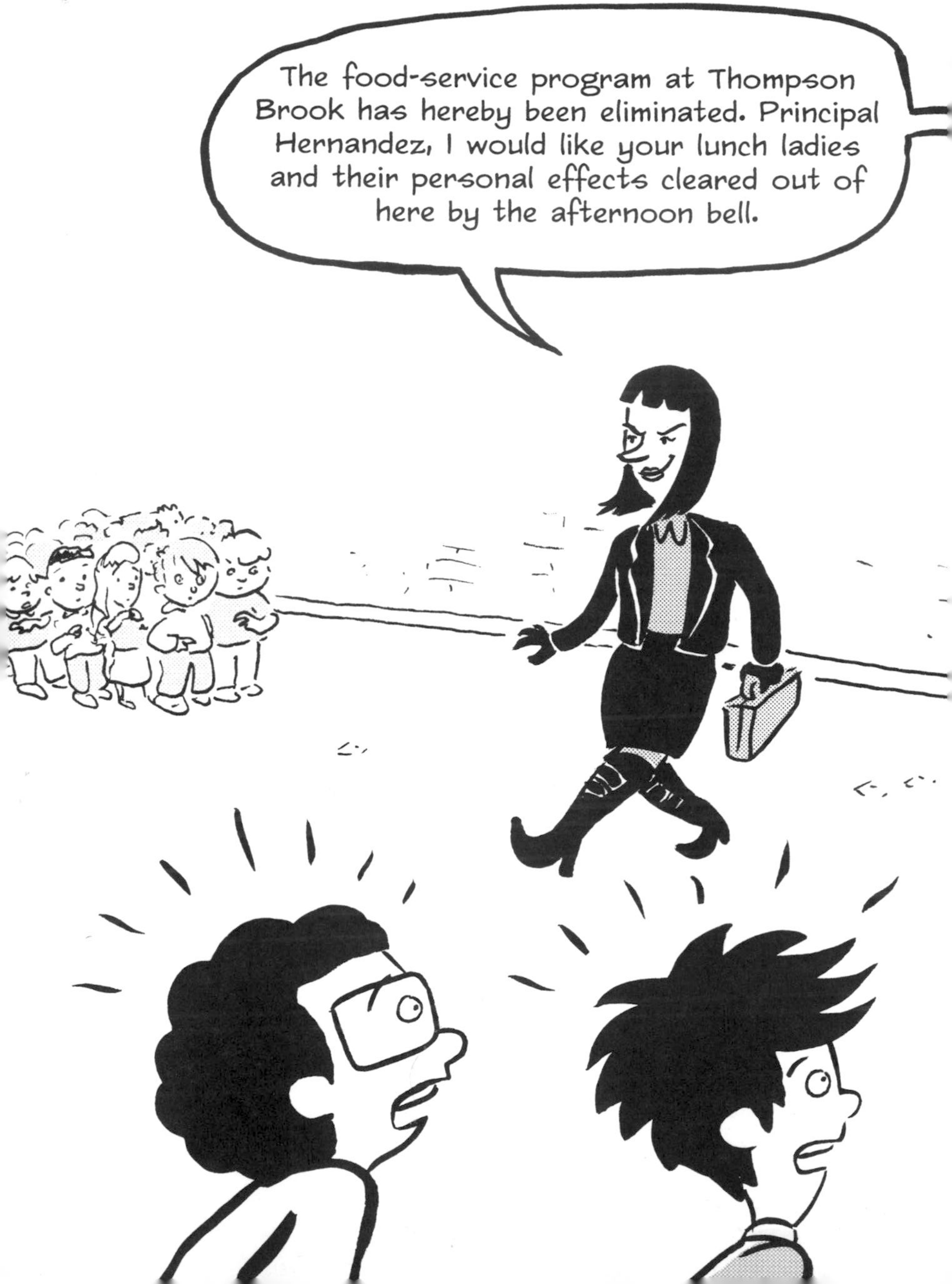
The food-service program at Thompson Brook has hereby been eliminated. Principal Hernandez, I would like your lunch ladies and their personal effects cleared out of here by the afternoon bell.

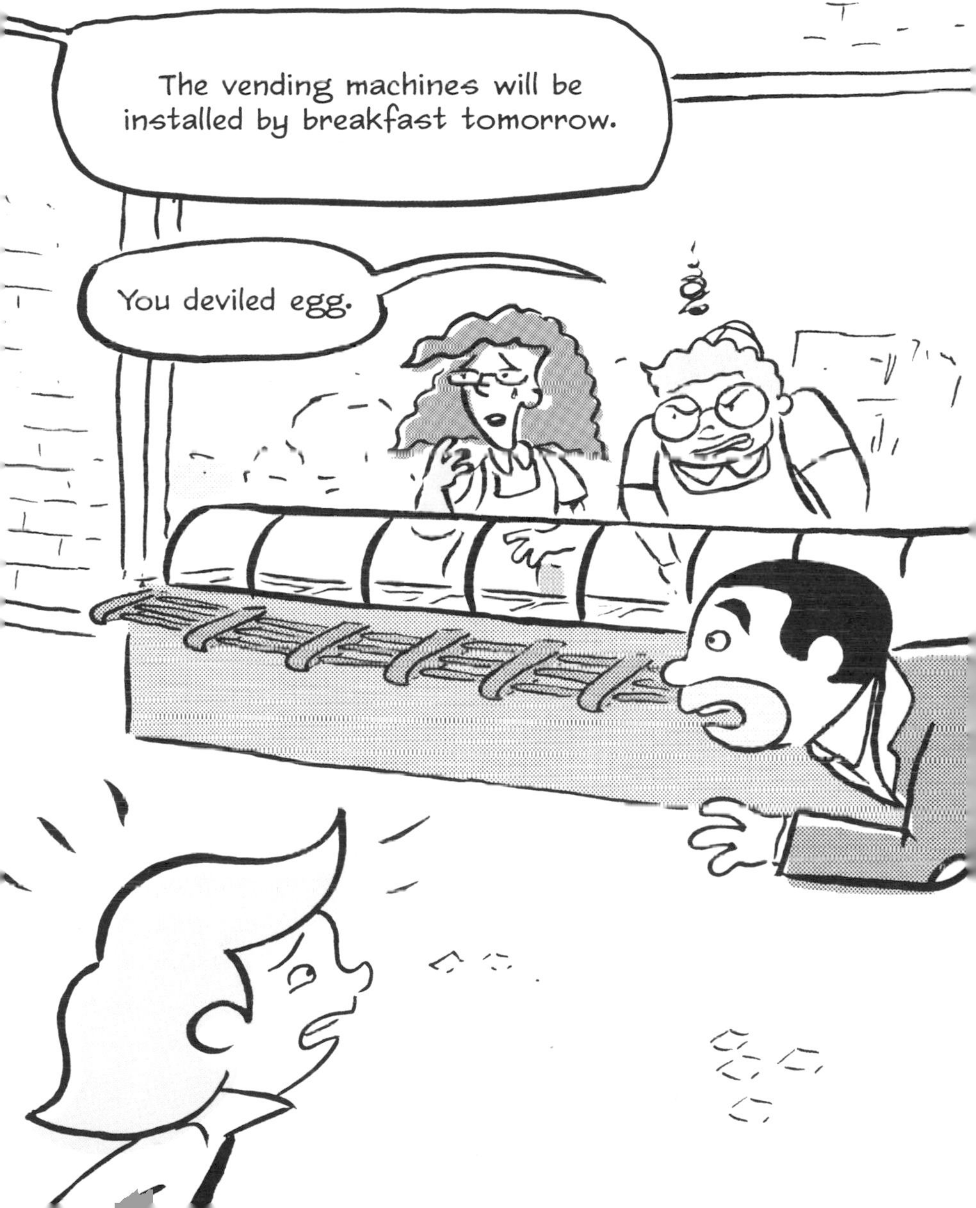
The vending machines will be installed by breakfast tomorrow.
You deviled egg.

FOR MY LICORICE-WHIP-SMART EDITOR, MICHELLE FREY

The author would like to acknowledge the color work in this book by Joey Weiser and Michele Chidester.

THIS IS A BORZOI BOOK PUBLISHED BY ALFRED A. KNOPF

Visit us on the Web! randomhouse.com/kids

Educators and librarians, for a variety of teaching tools, visit us at RHTeachersLibrarians.com

Library of Congress Cataloging-in-Publication Data
Krosoczka, Jarrett.
Lunch Lady and the video game villain / Jarrett J. Krosoczka. — 1st edition.
p. cm.
Summary: "Tech gadgets are disappearing left and right at school, and Lunch Lady must get to the bottom of it!" — Provided by publisher.
ISBN 978-0-307-98079-3 (trade) — ISBN 978-0-307-98080-9 (lib. bdg.) —
ISBN 978-0-307-98173-8 (ebook)
1. Graphic novels. [1. Graphic novels. 2. Video games—Fiction.
3. Schools—Fiction. 4. Mystery and detective stories.] I. Title.
PZ7.7.K76Lv 2013 741.5'31—dc23 2012025893

The text of this book is set in Hedge Backwards.
The illustrations were created using ink on paper and digital coloring.

MANUFACTURED IN MALAYSIA
April 2013
10 9 8 7 6 5 4 3 2

First Edition

Random House Children's Books supports the First Amendment and celebrates the right to read.